Contents

1. Vegas

My wife's cell phone buzzed and rang multiple times to announce the arrival of several text messages as soon as she turned the phone on after the pilot announced it was okay to do so.

"So Saroj." I said icily, "I guess those are all text messages from Jack?"

Saroj ignored me and her fingers worked the keyboard furiously as she replied to the text messages.

"Only two of them." Saroj said once she got done. "The third was from my sister saying Rohan is doing fine."

"And what did Jack want? Some recipe perhaps?"

Jack was our neighbour and "friend" back in New Jersey. He was divorced and lived next door, and lived with his son who was the same age as Rohan our son who is 6. I had started off liking Jack when we moved into his neighbourhood a year back. He was friendly, his son and Rohan got along very well, and he seemed genuinely helpful. Which he still was.

What had started bugging me was that he and Saroj seemed to have become a little too friendly. Saroj was a stay-at-home mom, having quit her job in banking as soon as we had Rohan. And Jack had a catering business which he managed from his house, and even when he had to be away, it was usually for dinner services at nights or on weekends. So, when I was at work and Saroj was home, usually, so was Jack. And Saroj often told me that he came over or invited her over to talk about recipes and food, a topic Saroj had gotten really interested in of late.

"No, Pankaj. He just texted the address of a restaurant he recommends. And wished us both safe travel and a great vacation." Saroj replied.

"You know what'll make my vacation great? No texts from Jack." I said as I pulled our handbag from the overhead compartment.

"Pankaj please. Don't start." Saroj shook her head and slid out from her seat.

After this mini-tiff of sorts, both Saroj and I were silent as we made our way off the plane, got our luggage from baggage claim and took a taxi to the Venetian - a posh casino-resort. I waited for her to break the ice, convinced that I was right in being suspicious of Jack. I was convinced that he had the hots for my wife, and was working slowly but surely to get her into bed. If, that is, he hadn't already.

Over the past few months, I had noticed a change in Saroj's appearance and demeanour. Usually her attire was pretty standard - jeans or trousers, with modest t-shirts or blouses, and frumpy sweaters. After Rohan's birth, Saroj had gone from a very fashion-savvy and spiffily dressed young woman to the archetypal suburban mom. But recently, I noticed she was wearing skirts more often, with tank tops or blouses with a low neckline. She was back to dressing the way she used to 7 years ago when we met and started dating in Mumbai. And I wondered if this sudden change had anything to do with her friendship with Jack. Although I was glad of the occasional throwback to our initial days together.

Ah, our initial days together. I had been smitten with Saroj the day she walked into the conference room on her first day of work in our bank. She was one of the new trainees, fresh out of business college. I was there in my capacity as my division's

Vice President, to address the newbies about our operations. She was dressed in a figure-hugging knee-length black skirt, a formal blouse with one button open, and a matching black blazer. She was tall and not just by Indian standards - 5 ft 10. Her skirt showed that she had an awesome butt and shapely legs. And even the formal blouse and the blazer could not hide the fact that she was exceedingly buxom - 34DD as I later found out.

I found myself staring at her a little longer than appropriate. She obviously noticed, looked right into my eyes, and flashed me a dazzling smile. And that was all it took to get me hooked.

I waited a few weeks before doing anything though. After all. Saroj, a fresh MBA 24 years of age, was 15 years my junior. I was touching 40, and although I worked out regularly to keep my body in shape, the grey was beginning to show at the edges of my hairline. I was still unmarried, thanks to a long relationship that ended abruptly 5 years ago. I still dated casually, and got plenty of action - a good looking, tall, well-built successful banking executives in his late 30s does not find dating difficult in a city like Mumbai. But most of the women I had dated had been my contemporaries. I had never even thought about going after someone in her mid-20s. Until Saroj walked in that door.

Although she got assigned to my division, I kept things strictly professional. I could see that she was getting a lot of attention from guys her own age, something she seemed glad and adept about handling. But I did get some fairly strong signals from her of her interest in me. She would complement me on my looks, ask me about my taste in music, movies, and books. And try to spend a lot of time talking about things other than work. And she kept talking about how she wanted to "settle down" but all the guys she met were too "immature".

After a few weeks, I convinced myself that I wasn't just some deluded old horn dog reading signals where there were none. Saroj was definitely indicating her interest in me. So, I asked her out. She readily agreed. And from there, things moved rather rapidly.

We had sex for the first time after our second date, and I was glad to see that Saroj knew how to use her body well. In a couple of weeks, she had all but moved in with me, spending about 5 nights a week at my apartment. In a month, we informed HR about our relationship, and Saroj was moved to another division as per company rules.

In six months, I was convinced she was the love of my life, and proposed. She accepted readily. Her parents were a little displeased that she was marrying someone so much older than her. But I charmed their pants off, and all was well. We were married, and soon Saroj was pregnant. After Rohan was born, Saroj told me she had no interest in going back to work. She had never really been too career-minded, she said, and was simply living out the dreams of her modern and demanding father who believed her intelligence was too rare to waste.

Soon, we settled into a happily married lifestyle, raising our son together. Saroj had a lot of close friends in Mumbai, many of them male. And her close friendship with them did rankle me a little bit. In other words, it made me insecure. Initially I stayed mum. But after I turned forty, my body began catching up with me. My stamina for sex was diminishing by the year. When we started dating, we had sex at least twice every night. Around the time Rohan turned two, it was down to twice a week. And of late, it was down to barely once a week.

The decline of my prowess did play a role in my insecurities growing. There were a couple of her male friends, young, good-looking, handsome, that I particularly felt insecure about. They were married too, but it still bothered me that they were so friendly with Saroj. We started having arguments about it. Saroj always dismissed my concerns saying I was being paranoid. But I knew my wife was hot enough to make anyone sin. I also knew she had a fairly colourful past, sexually speaking. So, I knew that she knew she had options. And that drove my insecurity and caused more arguments. These arguments became the norm for the next few years.

One day, a head-hunter called me up out of the blue, saying I would be perfect for a position that a Wall Street bank was looking to fill. It had always been my dream to work on Wall Street, and I had no hesitation applying. I got the job quite easily, and soon, we moved to New York.

The move was a source of some tension between Saroj and me. She was not so sure she wanted to move to a new place, leaving her friends and family behind. She wanted to "discuss" it. But I was in no mood to listen. Surely, she should understand what a rare opportunity this was for me. I wasn't getting any younger, and who knew when...rather if, such a chance would come by again. Eventually Saroj agreed, and we moved to America.

We got a big house in suburban New Jersey, in a good college district. Saroj's initial apprehensions gave way to enthusiasm about living in the greater NYC area. Rohan certainly loved it, especially the tradition of Halloween trick--or-treating which he could not believe existed. And soon we were a happy family again. Saroj did complain occasionally about feeling lonely. To be honest, I was relieved that all her male "friends" were thousands of miles away. But then Jack had slid into the picture.

Jack was roughly the same age as Saroj. Very handsome. I worked out to keep my body in shape. He clearly worked out to give his body shape. He had well-toned abs, arms and a chest, which he loved displaying in the summer months. His striking good looks, coupled with his charming personality, convinced me that he was a threat to be mindful of. But when I raised the concern, Saroj again accused me of being too controlling and insecure and jealous.

One summer day when I came home from work, I saw a scene that made me lose my cool. Nothing scandalous, mind you. The two boys were playing in the backyard. A few feet away from them, sat Saroj and Jack on lawn chair, drinking beer. Jack was only wearing a pair of cut-off denim shorts, the sweat glistening on his chest. Saroj was wearing a short skirt and a tank top. And they were laughing and talking.

Like I said, nothing scandalous. But watching Jack, all muscled and toned and sweaty, joking with my relatively scantily clad wife pissed me off. Saroj had put on a few pounds since Rohan was born, but the extra weight had been distributed evenly.

She still had a fantastic figure which had gone from tall-and-curvy-but-slender to simply tall-and-voluptuous - 36DD-28-38. She looked like a million bucks sitting in the lawn chair. But I was more pissed off at Jack's overtly hunky appearance than I was attracted to Saroj's knock-out looks at that moment. I yelled at Rohan, asking him to come inside. The tone of my voice was enough for Jack to take a hint, and he took his son and went home. And Saroj walked in, looking confused.

That night after Rohan went to bed, we had one of the most acrimonious fights we'd had. I accused Saroj of leading Jack on. She told me my paranoia was reaching historic levels. We argued back and forth, until she said,

"Pankaj, don't take this the wrong way, but don't you see your insecurity is stemming from your.....troubles in bed? I keep telling you to see the doctor. There are drugs..."

"So you're saying I should take Viagra or you'll fuck him? Is that it?" I exploded. I had been having troubles down there, but I knew it was more because of stress than anything. I certainly had no desire to walk into a doctor's office and tell him I was having trouble getting it up.

"What?" Saroj said, confused.

"Or have you fucked him already?"

Saroj slapped me in anger. I pushed her to the bed and stormed out of the room. I went to a nearby bar and had a couple of drinks. When I came back, Saroj was already asleep.

Over the next few days, we both calmed down. I apologized to Saroj saying I had been out of line. Saroj said she understood my concerns and would tone down her rapport with Jack, if it bothered me so much. And a few days later, I surprised her with my plans for us to spend a long weekend in Las Vegas. Just the two of us. Saroj's sister who lived in Philadelphia had agreed to take care of Rohan while we were away.

Now back to Vegas.

After we reached the Venetian, I finally broke my silence and mentioned how pretty the casino looked. Saroj also looked impressed and pointed out a few beautiful decorations in the lobby. We checked and went to our room.

This was my first time in Vegas and I was really looking forward to hitting the blackjack tables. So as Saroj went to the bathroom for a quick shower, I changed into some smart casual wear to hit the casino floor. I got dressed, turned the TV on and waited for Saroj. She walked out, her hair wet, clad in a bathrobe.

"Get dressed quickly." I said. "Let's go to the casino floor."

Saroj slowly walked towards me and sat down on the bed. She put her head on my shoulder and ran her hand over my cheek. I could feel heat radiating from her just-showered body. I turned and kissed her, slipping my hand into her robe, fondling her massive breasts. I felt her wet hair touch my ear. Saroj slowly pulled me down to the bed, and I was on top of her. I opened her robe and started kissing her boobs and fingering her clit. She started moaning and squirming as I continued playing with her. A minute or so later, she started unbuttoning my shirt.

That's when I got up off the bed. Saroj looked at me, with a quizzical look on her face.

"We should..." I said, buttoning up my shirt, "we should go check out the casino."

And I ran to the bathroom. In there, I unzipped and tried to coax life into my dick. The only reason I had interrupted that very hot session was that despite my best mental efforts, an erection refused to form. I sat on the edge of the bathtub and started jacking off my dick. But to no avail. A few minutes later, I gave up, flushed the toilet to make it seem like I had gone to pee and walked out of the bathroom. She was right. I did need to see a doctor. I decided to make an appointment as soon as I got back.

Saroj had gotten dressed when I was in there. She was wearing an elegant knee-length wrap-around skirt and blouse with sequins. She flashed me a bright smile, but I could see the disappointment in her eyes. I thought of saying something about the performance issue, but instead she said,

"So you'll have to explain to me exactly how blackjack works."

"Oh, it's easy. It's all about getting as close to 21 as possible..." I was glad for the change in topic and spent time explaining the game's rules to her.

On the casino floor, we had a lot of fun. We first spent some time at the blackjack tables. I made 4 grand while Saroj lost roughly the same amount, leaving us even. We then watched the action on some of the poker tables, a game I liked but was not confident enough to gamble in. We then hit the slots. By dinner time, we had made a small profit. We had dinner at a swanky Italian place on the strip. Our spirits were high. This really was turning into the vacation we wanted. We called up Saroj's sister and spoke to Rohan before deciding to take a walk on the strip.

As the evening wore on, I could not help but notice how smashingly sexy my wife looked. Tall, voluptuous, and with a beautiful face, she drew second and third glances from most men on the street. By the time we got back to the Venetian, I was feeling a stirring in my loins. We got into the elevator, and as soon as the door closed, I pulled Saroj into my embrace and kissed her. She kissed me back hungrily as I pawed her spectacular butt. An erection began forming and she could obviously feel it on her thigh.

"Ooooh Pankaj! In the elevator? Naughty!" she said between our kisses.

"I can't help it. You're just so...." I breathlessly started but was interrupted.

beepbeep

Saroj froze for a second, but continued kissing me.

"Check who it's from." I said.

"It can wait." she said and tried to pull me back into a kiss. That's when the elevator reached our floor and the doors opened.

"I said, check who it is from." I was feeling rage build up again.

Saroj took her cell phone out of her purse and looked at it.

"Is it Jack?" I asked.

"Yes, but Pankaj, he's just..." Saroj started saying. But I stormed out of the elevator.

I opened our room, turned the TV on and sat on the bed, looking very pissed off.

"He's doing it just to ruin our vacation." I said in an angry voice.

"No Pankaj."

"Saroj, I want you to text back in caps - NEVER TEXT OR CALL ME AGAIN"

"Come on Pankaj. Don't be silly."

"Saroj, DO IT!!!" I yelled.

She looked at me with tears in her eyes and a confused look on her face.

"Are you going to do it or not?"

"Pankaj, please. It's so unnecessary. And rude."

"Fine. I am going to sleep." I said, and started changing.

The next morning, neither of us made any reference to the fight last night. It hadn't been much of a fight. I changed into my night shorts, took a couple of Night Tylenol pills and was soon asleep. Saroj had been sobbing most of the time that I was awake. We had breakfast at a small diner and then decided to ride the tiny gondola in the hotel. We then went back to the strip, and checked out the other casinos - Bellagio, Caesar's, MGM Grand etc. Our conversations were mostly pleasant and cordial. Both of us were waiting for the other person to apologize.

We decided to have lunch at the Venetian's poolside restaurant. Saroj said she'd like to go upstairs and change. I asked what she wanted to change into, and her response was, a swimsuit. Despite the coolness between us, I smiled. I had not seen Saroj in a swimwear in several years. It would be a visual treat for sure. The swimsuit actually turned out to be a yellow bikini that went fantastically with Saroj's white complexion. It wasn't too skimpy or anything. But any bikini would have trouble containing her massive boobs. And her voluptuous perfectly shaped round butt looked great in the yellow bikini bottoms. She looked positively fuckable and if I had not been carrying the grudge from the previous night, I'd have jumped her right away. But for now, I just changed into swimming trunks, and wore a t-shirt.

Saroj tied a matching yellow sarong around her waist and we went to the poolside restaurant. We got a table right by the pool, and I could see that Saroj was getting a lot of admiring glances again, from men and women alike. I was particularly amused by an old bald white man who was swimming laps gradually, and whenever he was close to us, would slow down and check Saroj out blatantly. I don't think she noticed though.

I was only halfway into my main course when Saroj announced she was full, and wanted to get in the pool. I simply nodded and continued eating. Since she had just eaten, she couldn't really swim too much, so she just did a couple of different strokes at the end of the pool close to me. As she did the backstroke, I could not help but feel a surge in my pants at the way her huge tits struggled to break free from the bikini.

As I looked away from her, I noticed that the old bald white man was splayed on a pool chair on the other side, again blatantly staring at my wife. I also noted with a chuckle that he was wearing a speedo - not something suited for his old paunchy body. He noticed me looking at him and smiled at me. I looked away and back towards Saroj who had now waded to the other side of the pool.

The old man got up from his chair and walked towards the edge of the pool. Standing up, he looked even more ridiculous in his speedo, with his paunch flabbing over it. I did however notice momentarily, before looking away, that the crotch of his speedo was massive, as if hiding a football. Must be an enlarged prostate, I thought myself. The old man dove into the water with a clumsy splash and started swimming.

I watched curiously as he swam towards Saroj. And he said something to her. She responded with a polite smile and said something.

They were about 30 feet away from me so I couldn't hear what was being said. But the expressions on his face were very lecherous. I found the idea hilarious that such an ugly old man was actually even thinking of chatting up someone as gorgeous as my wife. She was used to the attention of hunks like Jack, after all. I was sure she'd slip away from him politely very soon.

"Sir, would you like to take a look at our dessert cart?" I heard the waiter say and I looked away from the pool. The dessert cart looked interesting. It had a chocolate souffle which I knew Saroj liked. So, I ordered it for her and a cheesecake for myself. The waiter made some small talk with me and put the dessert on the table and left.

I looked back and was surprised to see that the old man was still chatting up Saroj. She seemed to have an amused expression on her face and was saying short sentences herself. The conversation seemed to go on and on. Now she would occasionally giggle! I decided to put an end to the pathetic old man's desperate flirting attempts, so got up and walked towards the side of the pool they were at.

"Saroj!" I called out over the din of kids playing nearby. She was about 10 feet away from the edge. She looked at me. "The dessert is here. I ordered you souffle."

Saroj nodded and glided through the water towards me. I noted with annoyance that the old man swam after her.

"What did you say?" Saroj put her elbows on the edge and asked me.

"The dessert. I ordered you..."

"And who might you be? Her father?" the old man came to a stop in the water right next to Saroj and interrupted me.

"Hehe..I told you he's my husband!" Saroj giggled. "Pankaj, meet Alex."

"Pleased to meet you." Alex reached out his wrinkly hand towards me and I bent down in the waist to shake it.

Alex grabbed my hand firmly, and without letting go, said,

"So you're the lucky son of a bitch who gets to take this gorgeous little pixie home every night huh?"

Gorgeous little pixie? This old geezer was at least a couple of inches shorter than her. I snorted a little and tried to free my hand. But Alex's grip was surprisingly strong, and I found myself standing there crouching at his mercy.

"Why did a spicy bombshell like you settle for an old fart like him, huh?" Alex said and started cackling. Still grabbing my hand. My ears went red with rage and embarrassment. I looked at Saroj who actually had an amused expression on her face.

"Hehe...I don't remember actually." she said and started giggling.

Finally Alex released the vice-like grip on my hand. It relieved me, but only temporarily, because he put that arm around Saroj's shoulder and pressed it gently, and started cackling loudly.

I noticed him put his arm around her but Saroj either didn't notice or ignored it on purpose. She was still giggling. I was on the verge of jumping in the water and kicking this old man's ass. How dare he touch her in front of me? They had just met! But I resisted my instinct.

"Saroj, the dessert." I said in an annoyed voice.

She nodded and Alex finally took his arm off her shoulder. Saroj put her palms on the side of the pool and pooled herself out of the water. As she got out, I saw Alex staring at her butt rather shamelessly and with a smile on his face. I walked back with Saroj to our table. She took her seat and so did I. And, a few second later, much to my consternation, so did Alex!

"Yeah, their souffle is the best." he said, moving his chair right next to Saroj's. "I have eaten at the most expensive restaurants in this country. And the souffle here is the best."

"Is that so?" I sarcastically asked. I found it hard to believe that this uncouth old geezer was an expert in fine dining.

"Oh yeah, I'm loaded. Got a dozen real estate companies all over the country."

"Really?" Saroj asked in what sounded like an awe-struck voice. And that annoyed me even more. The old man was clearly trying to impress her with talk of his wealth and she was buying into it!

"Yup! Ole Alex's got a lot of cash in case you ever wanna leave this old fart." Alex said and winked at Saroj who started giggling again.

This was the second time he had called me an old fart and it was beginning to piss me off. I might have been close to 50, but this geezer was close to 70, if not older. Where did he get off calling me an old fart? And why the fuck was my wife laughing at his boorish comments?

"Yeah, ole Alex knows all about livin' it up in Vegas. In fact, why don't I take you to dinner to a real fancy place tonight? And then some fine cocktails?" Alex said looking at Saroj, and then without looking at me said, "Paankaaj, you can come too."

I was sure he had mispronounced my name on purpose. But before Saroj could say anything, I said,

"Sorry, but we're busy tonight. We have a lot of plans. Right, Saroj?"

I expected Saroj to concur with me. But instead, she was silent, and was looking at Alex with an odd expression on her face. That caused an awkward silence.

"Right, Saroj?" I said a little louder.

'Oh..umm...what's our plan for tonight?" she asked.

"You mean you ain't got plans?" Alex said, turning around to finally look at me. "It's settled then. I'll see you two in the lobby at 8!"

I glared at Saroj, expecting her to turn him down. Instead, she said,

"Okay, 8 it is."

"Splendid." Alex said stroking Saroj's bare shoulder. "See you then, little pixie. Bye Paankaaj."

"It's Pankaj." I said in a brusque voice.

But he acted like he hadn't heard me. Instead, he slowly got up, and while he slid away from the chair, his crotch moved just inches away from Saroj's face. I noticed Saroj's head turn at once as she looked at the enormous bulge in his speedos for a split second and then looked away. I thought I heard Alex chuckle as he walked away.

I was fuming silently until we got back to the room. Once we entered the room, I let loose,

"What a slimy pathetic old geezer! Why the fuck did you accept his invitation?"

"You could've said no." Saroj said calmly, unwrapping her sarong.

"I did. But you gave him a chance to put his foot in the door." I yelled.

"Come on, Pankaj. He's just a silly old man. What harm can it do?" Saroj said, walking towards the bathroom. I thought I detected a hesitant tone in her voice.

I started saying something in return, but I heard the bathroom door slam shut. A few moments later, I could hear the shower being turned on. So, I turned the TV on and sat on the bed watching it. It was over twenty minutes when Saroj finally stepped out of the bathroom wearing a bathrobe.

"Pankaj, did you notice Alex's.... you know.... swimming costume?" she asked in mischievous tone.

"Huh?" I feigned ignorance although I knew exactly what she was referring to.

"You know, the size of it? You probably didn't notice. It was huge!" she said with a curious look on her face.

That pissed me off even more. I have always considered myself reasonably well-endowed at 6 inches. But whenever I read about men with really big dicks, I wonder if women care about it. Saroj had never before mentioned any other man's size. So, this unexpected comment got me a little upset. But not wanting to seem insecure, I said,

"Well, it's probably an enlarged prostate or something." And went back to watching TV. Saroj shrugged and started getting dressed.

I would have argued with Saroj about her behaviour with Alex more, but we had a web conference planned. With our son. So as soon as Saroj got dressed, I took my laptop out, logged into skype and called Saroj's sister. Rohan was eagerly waiting for us, and we had a long conversation with him. he filled us in on every little detail of his two days with his aunt, from everything he had eaten, to the games he had played to what he'd seen on TV. It was almost two hours by the time we got done with the call.

At 8 pm when we walked down to the lobby, Alex was already there.

"Wow, you look absolutely ravishing." he said, staring at her up and down. He completely ignored my presence.

Saroj did look quite ravishing. She was wearing a pleated skirt that stopped an inch above her knees. And a sleeveless top with a bold neckline that showed about an inch of her ample cleavage. I had thought of making a sarcastic comment about how she was getting all dolled up, but had decided against it. The end result was, she looked fabulous, something that pleased me but also bothered me.

Alex's full attire further made me doubt his claims of being wealthy. His pants looked fairly worn-out and his blazer seemed like one of those cheap tawdry ones you get for 50 dollars at Walmart. He was also wearing a really horrible cologne, which he had clearly sprayed a lot of. This tawdrily dressed paunchy puny bald old geezer, was a stark contrast next to my wife who with her high heels, easily stood a head above him. But it didn't seem to bother him.

He led us to the restaurant which was on the same block. It did seem very swanky. When the waiter led us to our table, he pulled out a chair for Saroj. As soon as she sat down, Alex swooped in, taking the chair next to her, compel me to sit across from them. We started with small talk. Well, Alex and Saroj started with small talk. I was being ignored once again.

Suddenly, the sound of music filled the air. I noticed that the band was positioned quite close to us and they had started playing. As the music started, I could barely hear anything Saroj and Alex were saying. Alex had his elbow on the table and was sitting almost facing Saroj completely.

At one point of time, I noticed that he put his hand on her bare knee, and looked at Saroj with my eyebrows raised. She stared back with a slight shrug, as if saying, it was my job to stop him.

I did consider stopping him. But this old geezer was acting in such a lewd and disgusting manner, that I decided to let Saroj extricate herself from the situation. It's not like it was Jack touching her there. Even at this stage, with all the bravado Alex had shown, I did not consider him an actual threat, but an inconvenience. So, if his raspy wrinkly hands were bothering my wife, well, my wife should tell him to stop.

The drinks arrived. Saroj and I had both ordered a beer, and Alex had ordered a double scotch on the rocks. He said something to her, which obviously I couldn't catch because of the music. She nodded. Then I almost fell off my chair as Alex picked up his glass of scotch and put it to her lips. She took a small sip and coughed. Saroj hated scotch. She'd tasted it once many years back, and decided it was too potent a taste for her. As she coughed, Alex laughed and put the glass to her lips again. This time she took a sip without coughing.

Alex's hand had now come off her knee. But it was instead around her shoulder. Again, Saroj and I played the who-blinks-first game. I threw her a dirty look which she returned. The right thing to do would have been to rescue her from his leery grip by putting an end to this all. But this had now turned into an ego tussle. She was the one who should push him away, I decided.

Soon the waiter came to take our orders. I noticed that Saroj didn't say anything to the waiter, which meant the old fart had ordered for her. This bugged me even more. Saroj is very finicky about ordering food in a restaurant. Even when we go out in groups, she likes to order for herself. And here she was letting a practical stranger order food for her? I seethed in silence throughout dinner. Saroj and Alex kept talking, his hand rubbing her shoulder when it wasn't rubbing his knees or thighs. By the end of the meal, his hand had pushed her skirt a couple of inches higher, and much more of her thigh was on display then at the beginning.

I had refused to blink, but was feeling very disgusted. I fought my disgust by switching from beer to scotch as well. And downing a few of them in haste as dinner progressed. Maybe it was the booze having its effect on her, but I thought that Saroj didn't look as uncomfortable as before. She had gone from being a little squeamish of his touch and having a hesitant look of alarm on her face to now wearing a blissful smile. She was barely touching her food although Alex was wolfing his dinner down.

Finally dinner got done. I thought this was it, but instead, Alex got up and said to me,

"We're gonna dance a little."

I looked at Saroj, but she was avoiding my gaze. Instead, she got up from her chair and followed Alex to the bar area of the restaurant where a handful of couples were dancing. From our table, I could only see part of the dance floor. Alex and Saroj first started dancing in that area, with a foot of distance between them.

The contrast between them was stark. Saroj - beautiful, voluptuous, elegantly dressed, and tall. Alex - half a foot shorter than her, dressed in cheap threads, bald, ugly, puny but with a paunch that stuck out from his blazer. Saroj moved gracefully, Alex plonked around like a frog. But even with this mismatch, what bothered me was that the two kept their gazes locked into each other's. And Saroj, far from looking bothered, wore a happy smile as they danced.

Songs started and finished but they kept dancing for a good twenty minutes or so. Meanwhile the waiter had come and placed the check on the table and had made a few meaningful visits to look at it. Finally, I put my credit card in the check folder and the waiter took it away. I was about to get up, interrupt the dancing and take Saroj home, when the song changed to a romantic ballad. An ideal slow dancing song.

I watched in horror as Alex pulled my wife into a clumsy embrace and the two of them started gently swaying to the music. Alex started off placing his hands on the small of her back, but then gradually slid them downwards. Until both his hands were on her shapely butt. He then started gentle kneading her butt, without any resistance from her. I looked around and saw a few people around them snickering and pointing. Even in Vegas, watching such a clumsily dressed old codger feeling up an exquisite beauty like my wife wasn't a common scene.

I watched with disgust, but also with a sense of vindication. This dirty old man was skilfully putting the moves on my wife. Right in front of me. And she was doing nothing to stop him. Obviously, I had been correct in my suspicions about Jack and the other guys. If she let this old sack of dough go this far, who knows what she had done with Jack when I was away? I felt my ears burn in anger as I watched them. Finally, the dance came to an end. And the two of them started walking back to the table.

When Saroj took her seat, she looked into my eyes with a defiant expression. I was doing nothing to hide my rage. But it didn't seem to bother her. She looked away. I then looked at Alex. As he sat down, I almost spat out my drink in shock. There was a huge tent in his pants. He was sporting a rather substantial erection. And, it dawned on me, this beast of an erection had obviously been rubbing against my wife when they slow danced. Or maybe it was a result of their slow dance.

The three of us sat wordlessly sipping at what remained of the last of our drinks. The waiter came back with the credit card slip and I signed it. Alex looked at me and smirked, as if to say - "I was going to take you two to dinner, and instead you're paying while I rubbed my dick against your wife." I looked away from him towards Saroj who now wore a look that was all too familiar to me. After many a night on town, when we got home, she would sport this look - that of being drunk as well as being horny. Alex's monster erection rubbing against her had clearly had an effect.

Alex must have noticed it too, because I sensed a movement of his hand. And when I followed it, I saw it was headed towards his thigh again. Except this time, he didn't stop at just rubbing her thigh. It disappeared under her skirt. I looked up at Saroj who had now closed her eyes and had tilted her head back a little. Slowly her lips parted and I saw another familiar look. And alarm bells started going off in my head.

I realized that just a couple of feet away from me, Alex was fingering my wife. Was he doing it over her panties? Or had he slipped his finger inside? There was no way for me to know. What I did know was, I was at a crossroads. Either I get up, throw a fit, and kick this old man's ass. Or I continue to be what I had been until then. A silent accomplice.

I don't what made me opt for the second option. Maybe I was getting turned on by this ugly old man handling my wife like putty. But at that moment, I rationalized my non-action by telling myself, it's up to her to stop him. If she wants to prove me wrong and show me as a jealous paranoid husband, she should do something. I didn't realize though that Saroj was probably too drunk to think straight.

Alex noticed that I had noticed, and flashed me a triumphant smile. He then poked her thigh with his other hand, and she parted her legs even more, providing him better access to her cunt. Saroj's face now wore an overtly sexual look. her eyes were now half open, but she didn't seem to be looking at anything in particular. Her nipples were obviously erect because they were poking through even her bra and top. Her face had gone all red. And she seemed to be breathing heavily.

This scene lasted five minutes or so, until the band stopped playing and there was a minute of silence. Alex took his hand out from under Saroj's skirt. Saroj let out an audible moan of disappointment. Her eyes opened completely and met mine. She looked away in shame. I wondered if she would end it now. But it wasn't in her hands.

Alex got up. His erection seemed to have subsided by now. He said to me very matter-of-factly,

"I am taking her to my suite back at the Venetian. You can come along too if you want."

I tried to search for words, but couldn't come up with any. Alex held out his hand for Saroj. I expected her to take it. But instead, she was looking at me.

"Pankaj." she said in a breathless voice.

"Hmm?" I said.

"What should I do?" there was a plaintive tone of genuine conflict in her voice. Looking back, I now know that was the last chance I had to put an end to the depravity. I just stared at her.

"What should I do, Pankaj?" she asked, once more in that gut-wrenching voice.

A dozen different sentences sprung up in my head. "Don't go." "Let's go back to our room." "Leave this old fart here." "Stop the madness."

I didn't say any of them. I just shrugged. Saroj exhaled loudly. Alex was still holding his hand out for her. She took it and got up. Alex put his hand around my wife's waist and led her away. I got up and followed them, as if in a slumber.

I walked behind Alex and Saroj as we left the restaurant and went back to the Venetian. I followed them into the elevator. Alex slid his key and pushed the button for the top floor. once the elevator door closed, he stood there, again kneading her butt. The elevator reached his floor and we walked to the suite.

Alex led us to the "living room" of the suite and turned on just one small lamp. The room was mostly dark, with just the one lamp illuminating it. Alex headed to the minibar and poured three scotches, without ice. He handed one to Saroj and another to me. Saroj took her drink and sat down on the small couch. She took a sip and then looked at me, with a petrified expression. Again, she seemed to be weeping out for help.

For me to rescue her. But I felt helpless. I sat down on a chair across from her. Alex took his glass and sat down next to her.

Alex then reached for the remote and turned the TV on. He turned it to one of the movie channels, and sat there, with his hands around Saroj, who seemed like she would run out of the room at any moment. We all sat there staring at the TV. Even Alex, for the first time ever, seemed a bit nervous.

About ten minutes later, I noticed some movement. I saw Alex pick up Saroj's hand and put it on his crotch which now had that massive bulge again. I looked away towards the TV. A few moments later when I looked back at them, there it was. Alex's dick. I am not sure how big it exactly was, but it was a hell of a lot bigger than mine. And thicker. It was standing up from his open pants like a flagpole. And wrapped around it were my wife's elegant fingers. She was gradually stroking his dick, from the base to where the thick bulbous head protruded.

I looked at Saroj's face. She was staring at the TV, as was Alex.

But her stroking of his dick was getting faster and faster. This went on for a few minutes and then Saroj stopped. She took her hand off the dick and stared stretching her fingers. Her hand was probably tired. So, Alex took her other hand and put it on his dick, and she resumed stroking it. By now the monster cock was moist with all the precum that had oozed out. I could see even Saroj's fingers glistening. And I realized I too now had an erection in my pants that needed some relieving.

When Saroj took another break to change hands, Alex took the opportunity to take her top off. She offered no resistance and was now sitting there in a black bra struggling to contain her massive tits. As Saroj, now without her blouse, started jacking him off again, Alex started playing with her tits. He put one finger inside the bra cup and moved it all around. Then he scooped the boobs out of her bra. I stared in shock at how trashy Saroj looked at that moment, her boobs spilling out of her bra as she gave some dirty old man a hand job.

"Enough with the hands." Alex brusquely said and slapped her hand away. He reached for her hair and pulled her head down into his lap. Saroj resisted a little. Only a little. I suspected it was for my benefit. But within a few seconds, I could see her wide-open mouth descending on Alex's upright dick. She could take in less than half of it in her mouth before she let out a gagging noise.

"Not used to the size, eh?" Alex said and chuckled. "I can see why. from that tiny tent in his pants."

Saroj took his dick out of her mouth and looked at me. Her eyes fell on my erection, and I think I saw a hint of a smile on her lips. But Alex was getting impatient now. He roughly grabbed her hair and put his dick back in her mouth. Saroj now started sucking his dick enthusiastically. A little too enthusiastically. She made gagging and slurping sounds as she went to work on his dick. And I could not help but be aroused at the sight of this massive shaft going in and out of my wife's mouth.

"You've taught her well. I'll give you that much. She sucks dick better than any Indian chick I've been with." Alex said as he nonchalantly unhooked her bra. Saroj slid the bra off and threw it on the floor. Now as she was hunched over on Alex's lap sucking his dick furiously, her boobs swayed and touched his balls.

Alex noticed, like I did, that Saroj slowly moved from being in a sitting position to putting her knees on the couch. She was now bent over with his shapely butt in the air. he reached for her ass and pulled the skirt up until it was bunched around her waist. Half an ass cheek each peeked out from the side of her panties. Alex started fondling her fleshy ass as she continued to suck his dick.

"Take it all the way in, slut." Alex said and spanked her on the ass really hard.

Saroj tried, pushing her mouth down, but could not take more than three fourths the length in.

"All the way in, you curry-munching cunt." another loud slap on her ass. And then he pushed her head down. I started hearing gagging and spitting sounds as Saroj's head turned upside down. It seemed like his dick was now going down (or up) her throat. Saroj was in the most incredible position I had ever seen her in. Completely topless, skirt up to her waist, panties on display, and head upturned over a dick.

Finally Alex let go and Saroj's head sprang up off his dick. She inhaled loudly and started coughing.

"You liked that, didn't you?" Alex asked.

Saroj shook her head.

"Not you. This dickwad sitting here. You liked watching your wife take my whole dick down her throat like a sword swallower, didn't you?"

I stayed silent. What could I say?

"Well, then you're gonna love what I do to her next."

Alex got up and pulled Saroj by the hair towards the side of the couch. She dragged her knees sideways on the couch to keep pace with his hair pulling.

"What you have here, my friend, is a slut. And I will show you how a slut is to be handled." Alex said and pulled Saroj's head over the side of the couch armrest. Her stomach was resting on the armrest and her torso was hanging upside down over the side. From where I was sitting, I could see her hair had fallen over, and her massive tits were hanging next to her chin. She put both her palms on the floor for support. On the other side of the couch was Saroj's upraised butt and her knees which were still on the couch cushion.

"You know why she is a slut?" Alex said as he roughly pulled her panties down in one motion. Even as she was being man-handled, Saroj co-operated by lifting her knees so Alex could take the panties off. Saroj's perfectly shaped big butt was now completely naked and on view. It was hoisted in the air like a shapely white hill. And her wet pussy was visible from between her legs.

"Because only a slut...."

Alex continued and loudly spanked her right ass cheek. Saroj let out a yelp.

"..lets an old geezer like me...."

SMACK! SMACK! One on each ass cheek. Two more yelps.

"....play with her cooch..."

SMACK! SMACK!

"...in front of her husband."

Alex's hand formed red prints on Saroj's ass which was now shivering with the onslaught. I could not see her face, but if she was in distress, she certainly didn't say anything apart from her yelps.

"I will now show you how a whore like this is to be fucked." Alex said and stepped out of his pants. His huge dick was now fully erect and throbbing and I got a good look at his thick bush which was completely white. He put one knee on the couch next to Saroj's leg, and his other leg was on the floor.

He took one step forward and with one hand lifted Saroj's left knee which was closer to me. He roughly pushed it ahead and upwards so it was propped on the armrest. Her ass cheeks opened up in this position and her cunt and asshole were both visible. Saroj moved her hands on the floor a little to balance herself in this new position. She looked incredibly hot, naked except for her skirt, thrown over the couch rest like a rag doll. Her long shapely legs splayed and open as this puny paunchy old man prepared to enter her.

Alex took a step forward until his dick was touching her labia. He rubbed the head of his dick up and down her labia, her clit and even through her ass cheek. Saroj's cunt and ass were now almost pulsating with desire, and the way she moved was a clear invitation if not an appeal for Alex to take her. But Alex was taking his time.

"Look at how dripping wet she is." Alex said pointing to a big wet spot on the couch's armrest.

Finally he stopped moving his dick up and down and placed it at the entrance of her cunt. I was sceptical of her ability to take it in. It was obscenely thick, and Saroj would feel filled even when my dick entered her. So, it was no surprise that the first couple of inches took some time going in. Saroj inhaled loudly and moaned as he pushed the behemoth in, her cunt lips wrapping around it.

"Oh sluts like these will pretend they can't handle it. But what they want is a big dick. I don't care if you're Indian, Chinese or

German. All women want a big dick to pump them." Alex looked at me and said, and slid more of his dick inside. Now more than half of it was in Saroj who was grunting every time he pushed it in.

Alex seemed to have decided that was as far as he wanted to push it in. He withdrew it a little and then started fucking her. The whole sight looked so perverse, it almost made me cum. My tall voluptuous wife, thrown over the couch with her hands on the floor, her boobs slapping against her chin with every stroke. And fucking her, a puny fat bald white man. His hairy ass rocked back and forth as he pummelled her. The wrinkly skin on his scrawny legs a stark contrast to her smooth milky legs. His hairy and flabby paunch rubbing against the curvature of her ample buttocks as they fucked made a small but audible scratching noise. It was heard only intermittently however, through the thuds of their thighs together.

Alex then put both his hands on her shapely waist, moved forward and started banging her really hard and fast. He started grunting as he did that, and Saroj joined in with obscene sounding grunts of her own. Her boobs, hanging upside down, where now slapping against his chin really hard. And I noticed her nipples were more erect than I had ever seen them. Alex moved his hands to her hips and held on tight as he started pounding my wife even harder. From her shrieks, she seemed to be enjoying every moment of it.

That was when I finally and fully came to terms with what was happening. My wife was being fucked like I had never been able to fuck her before. Saroj was a gorgeous woman who deserved the best kind of sex, which I hadn't been able to provide her. And my jealousy and paranoia in the past had been nothing but an oblique admission of my inability. her being loyal to me would have been a waste of her god given looks and body. Maybe that's why I had not stopped these proceedings. Somewhere deep within, I knew that she needed this. She deserved this.

After what seemed like an eternity of fucking her like that, Alex pulled his dick out. I thought he had cum, but that was far from the case. He stepped off the couch, his massive dick glistening with her pussy juices. He spanked her ass hard and said,

"Get up you dirty little slut!" Even in my state of shock and arousal I could not help but smile at the irony of this puny old codger calling her 'little'.

Saroj obediently took her palms off the floor and pulled herself into a standing position. Her skirt fell into place covering her pussy, and she stood there breathing hard staring at me. The look on her face was one I had never seen before - that of a wild animal in heat. Her eyes were burning with desire. There was drool all over her face. And her massive boobs were flushed and heaving with her breathing. She was staring in my direction but I don't know if she even registered my presence.

"Bedroom!" Alex said and reached up to grab her hair. He pulled her behind him as he headed towards the suite's bedroom. As I said, she was a good half a foot taller than him so his pulling her by the hair made her bend down a little. Plus she was still wearing her heels. In threw steps, she stumbled and fell on all fours. But Alex was in no mood to wait for her to get on her feet. He continued to drag her to the bedroom. Saroj followed the best she could, being dragged on her hand and feet. And I gazed in marvel at my wife's jiggling butt as she was led away, like the bitch in heat that she was, to the bedroom.

I got up and walked to the doorway of the bedroom. Alex, in another surprising display of strength, had flung Saroj on to the bed. Alex then got on the bed and almost ripped off her skirt and threw it to the floor. He then took her heels off and threw them to the floor as well.

Saroj's tall, shapely naked body was curled up on her side on the bed. Her hair looked dishevelled. Her huge tits were heaving, taking her erect nipples with them. She had a glazed look on her face as she stared into nothingness. Alex meanwhile took off his own shirt and shoes and got completely naked. All this while he was talking to me.

"You Indian men were blessed by God with such incredibly hot women. But you keep them subdued, compel them to suppress their sexuality. What that does it turns them into sexual volcanoes ready to erupt any time they get some attention. Turns them into sluts waiting to be set free. That's what this little pixie is, isn't she? A slut. A volcanic slut."

Alex got on the bed and spanked her ass really hard for the umpteenth time that night. Then he pushed her so she was on her back and lifted her legs by the knees so they were in the air. Her dripping pussy was on display as he held her long legs up like some logs of wood. Holding her legs like that, he continued with his monologue.

"This slut...or should I say whore...is slutty even by the standards of regular sluts. In my 65 years, I have never bedded a woman so easily. That too in front of her husband. What does that tell you, Pankaj? Your wife has so willingly opened her legs for an ugly old fart like me. With you around. Can you imagine what she must be up to when you're not around?"

I looked at Saroj. But she seemed to be ignoring whatever he was saying. I watched in amazement at her hands which were between them, trying to reach for his erect dick which was inches away from her cunt.

"Haha, look at that. She is reaching for my dick. She hasn't had enough. When was the last time you fucked her, Pankaj? And I mean REALLY TRULY fucked her like the whore she is? You should fuck her regularly or any guy who is willing to put in a few hours to chat her up and make her feel like a woman, will take her to bed"

I did not respond to Alex's description of my wife, and neither did she. This night had convinced me that Saroj had indeed been screwing around behind my back. Alex was right. My wife was a cock hungry slut, and I should not have expected her to be anything but.

Alex smirked and pushed his hips forward to penetrate her as he placed her calves on his shoulder. Saroj moved her hips to accommodate him enthusiastically. He pushed his dick inside and started playing with her huge tits as they fucked. Another intensely perverted but erotic sight - my tall gorgeous wife laid out on her back, her long shapely legs on the wrinkly shoulder of this bald ugly geezer as he fucked her.

After a few minutes, he leaned forward, making Saroj's body bent in the waist almost to forty-five degrees, and kept fucking her. I had by now grown immune to the animalistic grunts and moans both of them were letting out. They were engaged in the most primal form of coitus - fucking for the sake of fucking. Not once, I noted, had Alex kissed Saroj's full beautiful lips. He was obviously interested in a different set of lips that he was now assaulting with his behemoth dick.

--- As Alex's fucking picked up tempo, Saroj responded with louder grunts. The bed was shaking with the intensity of their raw fucking. Saroj moved her legs off Alex's shoulder and wrapped them around his waist. I watched aghast as she locked her legs around and pulled him deeper into her. I realized that my wife had now taken all of Alex's monster cock inside her. Will I ever be able to satisfy her in bed after this, I wondered.

Alex responded to Saroj's legwork by ramming her cunt even harder. Minutes ticked by and I realized that it had been almost half an hour that this fucking had lasted. Was this man ever going to cum? He kept going and going. Their grunts kept getting deeper as well as louder. With each thrust, Alex seemed to be planting his flag deeper and deeper into what was my territory.

Finally after what seemed like an eternity, Alex flinched and let out a loud grunt as he increased the pace with which he battered my wife's cunt. Then his butt cheeks clenched, and so did Saroj's. It suddenly hit me - he was riding her bareback! No condom! And Saroj wasn't on the pill. He was shooting his seed into her - and judging by the amount of time he kept pumping, it must have been a lot of semen.

Alex finished pumping his seed into her with a final hoarse grunt, and then collapsed on top of her. I could see his white chest hair mashing into my wife's delicious boobs. She kept her legs wrapped around his waist and hugged him in a tight embrace. The two of them lay there writhing and moaning for a couple of minutes, until they caught their breath. Alex then, for the first time that night, kissed my wife on her lips. It was a wet sloppy kiss - I could hear them drooling and salivating. The kissing went on for a few minutes.

Then Alex tried to free himself from the grip of Saroj's legs which were still wrapped around him.

"No...please..." Saroj said in a pleading voice as she begged her new lover to stay with her.

"Yeah, in a minute, slut." Alex said and freed himself. Saroj lay there with her legs open as Alex stepped off the bed. I could see a river of cum oozing out of her cunt.

Alex walked towards me, completely naked. His dick was semi-erect, but was still big enough to slap against his thighs as he walked. He walked past me and beckoned me to follow him. I mutely did. He poured two drinks and handed me one. He took his own and downed it in one big gulp. He put the glass down on the table with a thud and walked back towards the bedroom. I noticed how wrinkly and flabby his old man butt was.

Alex stepped inside the suite bedroom and said to me,

"Finish the fucking drink and let yourself out."

With that he slammed the door shut. I sat down on the couch

where he had first fucked my wife and started drinking.

As I sipped my drink, I could hear muffled sounds of conversation and laughter through the door. That lasted for about ten minutes. After that conversation stopped. And a few minutes later, I could hear the faint sounds of my wife's moans. I finished my drink, and let myself out of the suite. I returned to our room, jacked off a couple of times and fell asleep.

I was woken by the sound of the door closing shut. I opened my eyes and saw Saroj walk in, fully dressed, with her purse. She put it on the table and laid down next to me silently. I thought of something to say but words failed me. After fifteen minutes of silence, I got up.

"I'm going to get ready and go to the casino floor." I said.

"Okay." Saroj calmly said. "I am going to take a nap."

The next two days I saw little of Saroj. I spent my time in the casinos playing blackjack, and won about 20,000 dollars. She spent the day sleeping and spent nights and evenings with Alex. Our last night in Vegas, I ran into them in the elevator and Alex magnanimously invited me to the suite to watch, "as long as I didn't get in the way". In the room, I watched incredulously as Alex threw my wife over the couch armrest like the first time, but buggered her in the ass this time. From the ease with which her asshole accommodated his giant dong, I surmised it wasn't the first time he had fucked her there.

Neither of referred to what had happened on the flight back to New Jersey, nor when we got back home. We got back to our normal life as if nothing had happened. I came to terms with my being a willing cuckold and stopped pestering her about Jack. Although I never caught them in action and never asked Saroj to confirm it, I was sure they were having sex now. That is, if they weren't before.

What did change was sex life between us. I found my stamina

and desire return and Saroj and I were now back to having sex almost every night. She was insatiable and I often wondered if I was able to fulfil her desires. But I didn't really care. My sex drive was back on track and that's all that mattered.

A month or so later, I came home to a surprising sight. Alex was sitting on our living room couch playing with Rohan. He greeted me like an old friend and complimented me on my beautiful house. Saroj came out of the kitchen, saying Alex would stay for dinner.

Over dinner, with Rohan around, the conversation stayed polite and mundane. But it did lead to an interesting revelation. It turned out that Alex's boasts about being a rich old geezer were bullshit.

He was a fucking greeter at a Walmart in Maryland, barely making ends meet! He could only afford to stay in that suite in the Venetian in Vegas because he had won some contest on the radio. His income was probably less than what we spent on gas. All his life, he had held a string of minor clerical jobs, was divorced, and had no kids. I tried to gauge Saroj's reaction to that information, but she didn't seem surprised or bothered.

After dinner while Saroj put Rohan to bed, Alex and I sat in the living room sipping on brandy. I could not think of anything say, although I was dying to ask him - WHAT THE FUCK ARE YOU DOING IN MY HOUSE???

Saroj came back to the room. Alex and I were sitting on different couches, and Saroj seemed to think for a few seconds before sitting down next to me. Then she dropped the bombshell. She was pregnant. I was a little astonished, although I guess I should have expected it after watching Alex fuck her bareback and deposit his wad inside her fertile womb.

"Is it mine or his?" I asked. After our Vegas tripped, she and I had often fucked bareback.

"I don't know." Saroj shrugged. Alex had a smug smile on his face.

"Or is it Jack's?" I asked tartly. Alex let out a chuckle.

"I can get a paternity test done. That's why I invited Alex over. To talk about....what to do."

And the three of us talked it over. Alex said he didn't care. He was sure he had bastard kid all over the country, and one more didn't make a difference to him. I said I didn't care whose it was either. I would consider it my own kid. We spoke about it for a while and thrashed out the details. With that matter settled, I expected Alex to leave, but instead, Saroj led him to our guest room. She then joined me in our bedroom and slept snuggled next to me. But when I woke up in the middle of the night to go to the bathroom, her side of the bed was empty.

That was the last time Alex visited our house. Saroj would drive over to Maryland once every few weeks and spend the weekend with him, until her third trimester, when driving became impossible. I wanted desperately to know what she had been up to. But I didn't ask, and she didn't offer any information.

The baby came two weeks three weeks after schedule. When Alex came to the hospital to see it, he joked that the baby had to be his - he was known for never coming too early. But the baby was definitely his. The brown hair, the blue eyes, the odd shape of the forehead - I knew I would be bringing up Alex's son as my own.

2. Occasional Cheating

I am a married woman of 35 years but have a nice body shape. No one can say at first glance that I am 35 years because I have got very nice and attractive features and a figure from heaven. I am tall. My height is more than 5' 6" with a slim body as I take very good care of my body. I have a great, praiseworthy, and an attractive figure. My waist is still 34" while my breasts and hips are 36" though I am a mother of three children and my first child is nearly 14 years old. And all of them have my complexion which is white reddish. My lips are thin with small-mouthed and my eyes are wide big black coloured and have long black hairs. I am living with my family and my husband very happily. I think my husband loves me more than any other husbands love their wives. My marital life was nice.

Since we are not newly married, we don't have a continuous sexual relationship but we follow a routine twice or thrice a month. May be this is enough for all woman but I don't think why I think that this is not enough for me, but I have never thought about it seriously. I loved my husband and this is fact that I had only given myself to my husband but as I got older, I sometimes wondered what another man would be like. I had no thoughts of finding out but it was interesting to think about it.

My husband has a friend named Rahul from his childhood who lived near our house. We have very good relation with his family. We use to go to each other houses without any hesitation on every occasion. Rahul's wife Deepika and I have very good friendship as our hubbies had. Rahul is very nice and well-mannered man. He keeps track of all our small needs. He has a very charming personality. I must admit that he was very attractive. But I never think about him in this point of view, I mean sex with him not that he has told me that he sees me in that way. We always meet like sister and brother. Although we have met so many times in solitude. My husband had never objected whenever I met him nor he objected met his wife with my husband. We were like one family and we don't care that we have no blood relation.

Once it was noon and my husband was out of station while children were sleeping and I have nothing to do so I went to Rahul home to meet his wife as usual we meet once or twice in a week. When I entered the home Rahul's wife Deepika was not at neither home nor the kids were there. I called so many times to Deepika but there was not any response. I kept wondering what the problem was and why nobody's responding me. I stood there for a while and after few seconds Rahul shouted from the bathroom that he is coming out. "Bhabhi please wait a minute for me. And after few minutes he came out from the bathroom. His hair was wet as he recently took the bath. He became very pleased to see me and asked me to sit. I asked Rahul about Deepika, I mean bhabhi and kids. He told me that they have left just an hour for her native city as her mother is ill and that she called her in hurry so she couldn't meet me. He asked me if I wanted a drink or tea. I laughed and said that now you will make tea for me? Then he told me, if you don't want me to make it then you should make it, as I need it. So, I went to the kitchen and that was not unknown place for me. I don't know but I was too nervous today as I was alone with him. It was not the first time I was alone with him for me. When I fumbled around in the kitchen, I was thinking about an excuse to leave, but couldn't. So, I prepared the tea both for us. He was in lounge when I brought the tea and I sat with him in one sofa and put the tray on the table near the sofa. We started talking and I inquired that why he is at home at this time, he said that he was not feeling well. I asked him about his sickness but he didn't tell anything. I offered to take him to a doctor but he refused. He said that he has already taking medicine. We were talking on every topic. He was looking at me strangely and all I could think of is why is this strange. I was thinking about what is new and soon I realized that I felt something and it was the lust in his eyes.

He started talking about what I was wearing and I looking very nice today. He added that it gave extra charm to my personality which was already extra graceful. I was wearing the red colour salwar kameez as I usually wear. I felt shy for a while and then said thanks to him. Then he said how my husband is lucky that he has found so nice, beautiful, gorgeous and so sexy wife. I found myself once again in an embarrassing position and told him.

"Rahul what are you talking today, you have never talked like this before."

Then he said you mean that I should have talked it before.

"No, I don't mean like this but I consider you as my brother and Rahul you have a nice and beautiful wife."

"But not like you" he replied.

Then he turned his conversation towards his martial life and told me that his martial life is not so satisfied and that his wife doesn't care about his desires. I was surprised that how Rahul is talking today? He continued his conversation and told me that he wants to talked with me on this topic from long but he did not get a chance.

I was now fully confused and wanted to leave. So, told him that I should go now as the children were expected to awake but he requested me not to leave him alone and I stayed there I don't know why? He started talking about his sexual life and I started to feel nervous as Rahul was talking about sex and I was feeling lightheaded. I felt for the first time that something might happen that day. Suddenly he moved near to me as we were seated on one sofa and I became astonished when he grabbed me from my waist and put his mouth on mine. My whole body tensed as Rahul warm lips touched mine. I followed my marital life and was going to get out of there. As I started to turn around, Rahul grabbed me in a powerful embrace. I was trying to escape from his grip but truly not from my heart. His body was tight against mine and I couldn't help but be turned on by how well my breasts fit under his massive chest. He was kissing my lips passionately and his hands were on my breast rubbing them gently. I was really in double mind at that time, that what should I do? I was feeling this rush of sexual tension like I never felt in my life but at the same time I knew it was wrong. At first, I resisted but it was surprisingly feeling good. I tried to pull back but the empowering embrace made it impossible and Rahul's warm lips was not more ignorable for me, As Rahul lips were pressed tight against mine, I started to feel a hot sensation deep within.

Our lips melted together as if they were becoming one. I responded to him unintentionally. Then he parted his lips and wanted to slide his tongue against my mouth. First, I resisted but then I parted my lips and allowed his tongue deep inside me. His warm tongue slowly entered my mouth. We were motionless. He warmly licked my mouth as I was fighting for some sort of control. I didn't kiss back but I was not stopping him either. He was passionately sucking and licking inside my mouth as I was losing control. I always liked Rahul and maybe there was this passion. I was feeling nice so I raised my tongue. When our tongues met it sent a shock wave shivering through my body. I was beginning to lose control of my inner sexual power. I passionately licked his tongue back as we started to deeply kiss each other and I forgot all about my husband or anything else as I was so turned on by this incredible sensation. Nothing else was on my mind but this powerful kiss. As he pulled his tongue from my lips and started to lick my neck, forehead, nose and neck. I was too excited at this time but I muttered to him that we are married and shouldn't do this. But he was not hearing me. I wanted to stop him but couldn't and he re-entered his tongue into my mouth as we started to kiss wildly again. After sometime he again made his way down my neck. I again told Rahul to stop. Rahul magically licked my neck and ears and the warmth of his mouth on my erogenous zone did not allow me to notice his hands on my breast this time. His hands were now on my impressively inviting breast and he was rubbing and massaging them. Now this was out of my control.

I again tried to pull myself from this carnal spell but by this time he had moved his hand in my neck as it was too low cut, I asked him once again that Rahul this is sufficient and we should stop it. He was very expert and well known about the woman psychology. Within flash he released me from my kameez and left only in my bra. He unhooked it releasing my tight tits. My ripe breasts were beautiful and inviting. He knelt down and took one of my erected nipples into his mouth. His warm tongue licked across my swollen nipples and was sucking my tits like they were his lifeline, which was sending me into a sexual confusion my body was so filled with passion that I became weak. Rahul lifted me off the ground and held me as he continued to suck my tits. Rahul licked my tits up and down. He laid me on couch. I felt like this was a chance to stop this erotic heat. I laid there half naked wanting him on me. I thought about how I secretly wanted another man at least once in my life. I wanted him now really, as I probably couldn't have found my husband as hot as Rahul. He was now trying to take my salwar off. I whispered once again not to do like this. But I was wondering how it would feel to have another man taste my love and that thought sent my mind in a naughty fit of desire. He took off my salwar which slid from my legs. As Rahul took off my salwar, the exotic feeling of being totally nude in front of another man sent a shiver up my spine as instinctively my legs spread open. He leaned and put his mouth on my pussy lips and kissed, licked it.

I could not believe I was letting Rahul to suck my pussy. I was powerless to stop his oral attack, I again whispered out in a frantic but orgasmic way that I couldn't do this I am married. He told me married can do this very easily, don't worry you will feel well.

"But I will never forgive myself for this entire my life" I replied.

"How can you say your husband so loyal to you? Doesn't he go to other women?" He said to me.

"But I don't care what he does but I couldn't". Without me replying he took my swollen cunt lips against his mouth and let his tongue in to probe. Rahul sucked and licked inside of me. Rahul licked me deeply as my pussy was on fire. It was too incredible and pleasurable, which I had never felt like this before in all my sexual life. Now it was not in my control and my tight little cunt and whole body was burning and I grabbed Rahul head and was burying his face into my wet cave and I started moaning and bucking wildly. Rahul was licking my clit as I moaned like an animal. Sweat was pouring from my body as I was yearning to be entered. Would I let another man's rock-hard cock enter my cunt where I have never imagined letting any other man cock? But Rahul was sending my body into a sexual frenzy as his face was buried into my drenched pussy. Rahul was relentless and experienced, as he knew exactly what a woman wanted. He had really aroused me and I felt his cock on my cunt. I felt nervous and excited as I knew exactly where this was leading and I realized I was losing the battle.......

After a long time, Rahul whispered that he desired that I should take his cock my innocent married mouth. First, I refused that I have never done it and that I don't know how one can take this in one mouth. But he insisted. As the passion filled my body to the point of thrusting, explosion I argued within myself. If I were to suck Rahul's cock, I might be able to quench my thirst and satisfy this stud without allowing him to put his cock into my cunt as I wanted still to stay true to my husband. I wanted him to be the only man who I tasted. Rahul was fully erected and he had the biggest dick I could ever imagine. It was a good eight inches long and thick twice then my husband. After some argument, I leaned in and put my mouth on his cock. I kissed and licked his cock for a while and then I opened my mouth as far as I could and took in his head. The swollen head of this prick needed more space. I opened my mouth as far as I could and took in his head. Rahul moaned in delight as I was fulfilling his desire. I bobbed my head back and forth trying to mouth fuck this man. I hadn't had much experience in this area. As I continued to slide his huge cock in and out of my mouth Rahul continued to tell me to suck his dick. I was sucking his dick which was now so excited and pleasurable experience for me and my hand went to my cunt which stuck up my cunt. It was gushing with juice and was begging for more. I knew now the obvious, I was going to get fucked by Rahul it was really totally a new experience for me as I have never sucked my husband's cock as he never asked for it.

My husband had not given me what Rahul is giving me now and if my husband were here, I would tell him this is real sex. I needed to be fucked now and Rahul sensed my urgency and pulled his monstrous crank from my mouth. He had really the big one, twice than in thickens and long from my unaware husband. Who never think that his loyal wife will suck his best friend cock and she was going to take his friend's dick in her lovely pot. The thought of this huge cock inside of me sent my body into a shiver. But I my inner core was begging for his dick to ram me. By this time, I couldn't control the passion.

And I fell back and eagerly spread my legs. He was rubbing his over powering cock against my pussy lips. I knew what he was doing. He was not giving it to me unless I begged. He was rubbing it to my clitoris and I had a fire inside my cunt that only a long, hard cock could extinguish. He knew that well. So, I started to beg and cry for his cock. I took his cock and put it on my pussy hole saying stop it and insert this in me. I was so swollen and wet. So, Rahul had very easily had his cock head inserted in my cunt as it was too wet but due to his bigger cock, I felt little pain.

Aaaaa aahhhh! ..big and loud noises poured out of my lips but as no one was at home, it was safe. Rahul then grabbed my legs and held them up as he slid his dick further in my cunt. He had to pull back and push forward a couple of times to stretch my tight cunt. He had really big cock, which made my pussy hole resized more than my husband's custom fit hole. I was screaming with ecstasy as Rahul vibrating eight inches cock easily deeper into my love hole. My legs were straight up in the air and my fingernails dug into Rahul's hips. As he pumping all of his 8 inches rock hard into my cunt hole. He was slowly pulling his dick back and forth. He was fucking me in very sophisticated manner, which I appreciated very much, and I wanted him to fuck me in this way forever

Rahul was giving me what I was mercifully begging for. He was fucking me strongly, and I was feeling his hard rock cock in my depth of my cunt flesh. I also started having pleasure and started jumping under him to accompany his moves. His testis starts making noises with every hit to my buttocks. I was not in this world but I felt I was going in and out of conscience as he fucked me. I was numb to the world as I was being fucked like a wild animal. Rahul opened my cunt with his rock solid wide eight-inch cock. He pumped me fast and hard. Rahul fucked for a long time and was now looking tired, so he could not control my legs anymore. As we were doing all this in the couch so my feet were planted on the ground and I was bucking like a bronco. Rahul was ripping me in half with his huge package and couldn't get enough. I was now in full control of him so he asked me to ride on him now. And this was the last desire of mine that I want ride on him. He pulled out his cock from my pussy and lay on his back, and I climbed on top of him. By now my shyness and loyalty to my husband was gone. I caught his 8" cock in my hand and guided it on my pussy hole. My proud pussy took in his eight-inch pole in one stroke. His long cock went in my pussy like a fish in water cave as I needed it so bad. I bounced and bucked so hard; I thought this thick prick was going to tear me in half. I was jumping on him; I took him in even farther than when he was on top on me. I couldn't keep up anymore, the massive size of his cock was getting the best of me and I was slowing down. Rahul put his hands on my butt and started to pull me down deep onto his dick. That was very nice and I was crying for deep and hard fuck from Rahul. My breasts were jumping up and down which he caught by his hand and squeezed them.

That was my thrust for fuck as I have been not fuck like this from long, and I was wonder how a conservative woman like me begged to be fucked like this. I needed to get fucked and begged Rahul to finish me off. Then he asked me to turn I wonder that what he wanted but without any question I turned and he came just behind me and put his dick in my wet pussy he inserted his cock in my pussy from my ass side. Now he was fucking me from behind with his full power and I was bearing his all-powerful stroke very happily as he was really giving me the nicest pleasure of my life. And I gave him all I had. Now we both were too exhausted and I asked him to finish it. And he increased his rhythm of stroking. After few minutes he and I both came together. He filled my pussy with his heavy load, while this was my third cum. I came so hard I felt like someone let the air out of me, we lay there for a while and were kissing each other. This time I was kissing him with lot of love, because he gave me lot of pleasure, the pleasure that my husband had nerved give me in my whole martial life.

We talked and I told him that he compiled an innocent married woman, beg you to fuck.

He laughed and said your fucking was my dream from the beginning.

But you have never showed it to me. I replied.

He said I know that you were not that type of woman who can do this so easily.

After some I asked for his leave now and he helped me to dress, as I was hardly able to move due to hard fuck.

When I was leaving him, he hugged me tight and kissed me, he asked me that when we meet next. I told to him that I can't promise anything right now but if I get any chance, I will definitely inform you. He started insisting me for more after that encounter of ours. It was hard for me to say no again and again to him all the time. So, whenever I got any chance, I call him and allow him to make love to me. I never take risks. I call him only when I fill its really safe. I never ignored my husband's or my children's needs till now. I know I will never do that in future too. Yes, I cheat my husband sometimes but this occasional cheating and hot sex with Rahul helps me to stay happy and fulfilled. You won't believe that after I started fooling my husband, I have started to love him more intensely. Now I can't tolerate a simplest problem of my innocent husband and became very attentive to him. I try to fulfil my innocent husband's every needs. I must admit that he also started responding very well to my changed behaviour. Now I can openly say that he is madly in love with me also.

3. Shy Lady

When I got transferred to Mumbai, I told my friend to search for a house. As I'm new to the place, I found it difficult to get a good house and finally he took me to his friend who was staying in a two-bed room flat. His name was Pankaj and he was staying with his wife. He wants to share his flat with a known person, so that he can save some money. I also agreed to stay with him and shifted my things to his flat. Pankaj said that his wife has gone to her mother's place, a remote village, for delivery and she will be coming next week. He will be using one bedroom and I will be using one. Kitchen & bathroom will be shared by both of us.

Days went on and I got used to the new place. I also like that flat, as many chicks and aunties are staying nearby. One day, Pankaj said that his wife is coming that evening and he has to pick her from the railway station. But unfortunately, as he has some very urgent office meeting, he requested me to go and pick her up. He had given me the train details and left to office.

I left for the railway station by 7:00 pm to pick her. She got down from the train with her kid. I got stunned to see her. She was such a beauty. She should be around 30 years of age. Very fair, big eyes, sharp nose & small red lips. She got a nice structure with little extra flesh. Her breasts were very big, round shaped and slightly hanging because she didn't wear bra. I guessed that, she didn't wear it so she can easily give milk to her child. I went near to her and introduced myself.

"Hi, I'm Kris. Your husband's friend. He asked me to pick you up."

"Yes. He told me. I'm Saroj. It's nice to you to come here to pick me."

"It's my pleasure. Can I carry the child?"

"Sure. Why not?"

When I tried to pull the child from her hands, it hugged the mother's neck. My left hand got struck up between the child and her right breast.

OOOOH my how soft were her breast? I also came to know that it is really very big. My hand also became wet suddenly. I slowly removed my hand outside. OOOOOPS. My hand became wet because of milk oozing from her breast. I sniffed and enjoyed the tasty milk smell. She hung down her head with shyness. I took my kerchief and wiped my hand.

"Ok. Saroj, shall we go?"

"Yes Kris."

I allowed her to go first and watched her backside beauty. Her buttocks are also big and round shaped. It was slowly moving left and right when she walked. Suddenly I had a lust to lift her saree, and see her beautiful buttocks. I controlled myself, sighing heavily with lust, followed her and we reached the auto stand.

While returning in the auto, she has not spoken much. She was born and brought up in a village. so, she was shy. I thought that it will be easy for me to seduce her as she was not much educated. We reached home and found that Pankaj has not returned. As the kid started crying, she went to her room in a hurry. I understood that she will feed milk to her child. I went to my room and changed my clothes. I watched TV for some time and surprised to see that she has not come out of the room. With curiosity I went in her room. There she was lying in bed with her left breast exposed. Both she and the kid were sleeping. I clearly understood the situation. She was feeding her baby lying in bed. Due to train journey tiredness, she slept immediately.

I went near to her like a cat and watched her breast closely. OH MY, she had a beautiful, big, round breast. As it was not exposed in sun, the breast was rose in colour. Nipple was big and brown colour and the circle was black in colour. On the nipple tip, a milk drop was glistening. I bent forward to lick the drop. Suddenly, door bell rung. Oh God, Pankaj has returned. I immediately rushed back to my room and waited. Again, door bell rung and Saroj rushed from her room and went to open the door. I also went out acting like I just heard the sound of the bell. Pankaj thanked me for my help and both of them went to their room.
I returned back to my room, thinking my fate. Just missed.... I was longing for that milk drop in her nipple. I took the hanky, which was wet with her milk. I took it in one hand, sniffed the milk smell and started masturbating by keeping my hand inside the underwear. That night I took the oath to drink the tasty milk from her beautiful, big breasts. Thinking about how to achieve that, I really didn't know when I slept.

Next day morning, I woke up and found that my underwear was fully wet due to the sperm leaking. I was thinking about Saroj the whole night and leaked a lot. I took bath and got ready to go to office. That time Saroj was cooking in the kitchen. She was wearing a saree, which was lifted up to her knee. Her legs were very sexy and strong like a pillar. baby hair spread below her knee which tempted me. I felt my cock was raising inside. She smiled at me and gave breakfast. I finished breakfast and left to office.

For past one month, I was talking to her nicely, got her to be my friend. Now I gained her confidence in me and talked to me freely. My lucky days came soon. Next day morning, Pankaj said that he is going to Delhi for an office job and will return after 1 week. I was very much delighted to heard this. That evening I returned home with rasgullas. That night me and Saroj were eating rasgullas.

Saroj: "Kris, you are so nice to me. The sweets are really good."

Kris: "Saroj, you are more sweeter than these rasgullas."

Saroj face became red because of shyness. She said "Please Kris. don't praise me like this".

I told "Saroj, If I would have been your husband, I would never leave you like Pankaj. I would take leave from office and sit with you".

Saroj laughed and told "Thank you Kris. I'm glad that you have so much affection for me".

She said that she has to sleep now. So, I told good night to her and came back to my bedroom. I was thinking for long time about drinking her milk and finally got a superb idea. Decided to implement my plan next day, I slept well that night happily.

Next day Saroj woke me up and said "Good morning Kris".

Without opening my mouth, I simply wished her by lifting my hand. I also showed pain in my face. Saroj sat near me and asked, "what happened Kris. why you are not talking to me".

I took a paper and wrote like this "Saroj, my throat is paining very much. I was not able to say anything. I will consult a doctor and come back."

Immediately she said, "Kris, better go to ayurvedic doctor. Natural medicine is better. I don't trust allopathy medicines at all. Please listen to me and consult an ayurvedic doctor."

Being a village born girl, she was very much confident in ayurvedic treatment. I spoke to her with difficulty, "Saroj, for you only I'm going to consult a ayurvedic doctor." This made her happy that I'm listening to her.

I went out, roamed for two hours, went to an ayurvedic drug store and bought some oil and returned to flat. Saroj welcomed me and asked, "Kris what happened. What did the doctor say?"

I told her, "Saroj, as you said I consulted a very old ayurvedic doctor. He is the best in this state. He gave this oil to apply on my throat for one day. If still it was not cured, he said that it can be cured only by a natural medicine" …. I stopped there and looked at Saroj's face.

She asked eagerly, "what is that medicine Kris."

I asked, "Do you really believe in ayurvedic treatment Saroj?"

She said, "Of course. in our village we take only natural medicines. we won't use allopathy at all.

Now tell what medicine you have to take, if it is not cured by today?"

I hesitated for some time and said, "Don't get me wrong Saroj. He asked me to drink breast milk continuously for three days. He told that only the natural medicine in the breast milk will cure my throat pain."

Saroj's face became red because of shyness and kept quiet keeping her head down. Then she said, "I'll pray to God that you will get cured by today itself." Without letting me talk, she went to her bedroom.

She was afraid that I may ask her milk, that's why she left immediately. I smiled inside and went back to my room. I simply apply the ayurvedic oil at my throat and slept. By afternoon, Saroj woke me up for lunch.

She asked me, "How is the pain, Kris."

I pretended that I was not able to speak and showed in sign that it was paining very much. I also told her I can't take lunch because of pain. Then again, I went to sleep. By evening, Saroj woke me up again. She was carrying a glass with full of milk.

She told me, "Kris. You are good friend of mine. I don't want to see you suffering from pain. So, as the doctor said, I poured my breast milk in this glass for you. Please drink this."

I told her slowly, showing pain in my face. "Saroj, you are very nice. But doctor said that I should drink directly from breast. Then only the medicine will work. It's ok Saroj. I think it will be ok by tonight."

Saroj's face again became red with shyness and without saying a word, she returned back to her bedroom. That night, I acted that I was so tired and showed pain in my face. Saroj was very much worried about me and she really felt sorry for me. At night 10 pm. Saroj was watching a TV serial in her room. I changed myself only to a lungi, removed my underwear. I took the tomato ketchup bottle and slowly went to bathroom. I poured lot of tomato ketchup in the bathroom floor and again kept back the ketchup bottle in the kitchen. Again, I went to bathroom and made loud sound like vomiting. The sound was too much that, Saroj ran from her bedroom to the bathroom.

She got shocked to see that I was vomiting and floor was full of blood. Saroj cried, "Oh my god. Kris, what happened? I think your throat problem has become worst."

I pretend that I was in half conscious. So, Saroj held me tightly, so that I won't fall. She also poured water in the floor to clean the blood. I acted like I lost my consciousness and rest my head in her right breast.

Oooooooooooooh. How soft it is... Like a pillow. I also slowly untie my lungi, without seen by Saroj. Saroj took me back to my bedroom slowly. On the way itself, my lungi fell down and my cock was jumping half raised. Saroj saw my cock and her eyes popped out. She was thinking how big and beautiful it was. She slowly laid me in the bed and sat near me. She got confused what to do next and was thinking for some time. After that she slowly lift my head and kept in her thigh. She removed her last two buttons of the blowse and took out her big, beautiful right breast.

I was watching this by my half-closed eyes. Her breast looked heavy and nipple was also very big and also long. I understood that it was full of tasty milk. She slowly opened my mouth and pushed her big brown nipple inside my mouth. I started sucking it. Yummy, the milk was very tasty. It started pouring like a waterfall inside my mouth. I also licked the nipple slowly and also the circle. I also slightly bite it with pleasure.
Saroj murmured, "AAAAAAAHHHHHHHH. Kris, please don't bite. it hurts me. Drink the milk fast, so that your throat will be cured".

I smiled to myself, took my hand and pressed the breast, so that more milk will come out. I drank happily by making the sound "slurp.. slurp... slurp". With my other hand, I touched her hip and felt the softness. I also tried to take the whole breast inside my mouth. But I was able to swallow only the half of it, as it was too big for my mouth. I was drinking, drinking and the milk was also pouring continuously. I emptied the right breast and simply sucking the nipple for more milk. Now Saroj understood that I need more milk, she lifted my head and kept it on her left breast side and pushed her left side nipple into my mouth. Pretending that I'm half conscious, I took her left hand, and kept it on my huge cock. She got shocked first and saw my face. I acted that I'm sleeping. She thought I have done it without knowingly. While I'm drinking the milk, she got asleep in the same position. I slowly kept my penis inside her left hand and started masturbating with her hand. I was drinking milk with sound "slurp... slurp.. slurp" and at the same time she was moving the cock within her hand with sound "chuk... chuk.. chuk". After some time, I emptied her left breast also and started licking her nipple and around circle. I also licked slowly the entire breast inch by inch. It was very soft like cotton or silk. I also slowly removed her saree and looked at navel. WOW, it was very deep and looked like a small vagina to me. I slowly put my tongue inside her navel and slowly rotated it. I licked it with lust. Suddenly, I lost control and my cock shot out the liquid. I purposely jerked my cock towards her face. My liquid drops shot out at her face and some drops entered into her mouth also. She woke up in a shock due to this. I immediately acted that I'm getting conscious now. Seeing the situation, she thought that she only played with my cock in her sleepiness. She immediately removed her hand from my penis and kept my head above a pillow. She also cover my lower body with my lungi and left the room in a hurry.

Next day morning, Saroj wake up with a cup of coffee. I smiled at her after receiving the coffee cup. She also smiled at me and asked "How's your throat Kris?".

I said "It's better now dear. Thanks for your sweet milk".

She said "Don't talk about it Kris. I feel shy" and she left the room. In the afternoon, I went to her room.

"Saroj, again my throat is paining now. I think I need your milk again."

"But Kris, I feel guilty about this. Is this right Kris?"

"Saroj, we are good friends. And the friend in need is friend indeed. I think I'm close enough to drink your breast milk."

"Ok Kris, I want your throat to be cured first. C'mon drink my milk."

I lay down in her lap and she opened her blouse and bra and took out the big right breast. I stared at it and slowly touched it and said" It's really beautiful Saroj. I'm a lucky guy to suck it."

She smiled at me and said "I'm happy that you like me very much. Please drink as much as you like Kris."

I sucked the nipple and started pressing the breast so that milk can flow into my mouth. She moaned softly "UMMMAAAHHH-HHH". I also opened her bra fully and start pressing the left side breast. Saroj not knowing what to do and also aroused by my act start lamenting

"Kris please please don't make my horny. This is sin. You are making me sin". I immediately took her left hand and put it inside my underwear. She gasped on touching my big rod and tried to remove her hand. But I firmly pressed her hand against my rod and started squeezing it. Now she got fully aroused and closed her eyes. She started to feel my rod by moving her hand from top to bottom. I immediately understood that this is the time for fucking move. I got up from her lap and lifted her up. I hugged her tightly. She also hugged my tightly. Then I looked at her eyes closely. She also looked at me. I got the signal from her eyes and took her to bed.

She lay down in the bed and welcomed me with both her hands. I lay down above her and we started kissing. I kissed her slowly in her forehead then neck breast and came down to her black forest. I removed her saree and also untied her petticoat. Her thighs are like pillars and very soft. I kissed her thighs gently and slowly spread them wide. OOOOOHHHHHHHHHHH MYYYYYY-YYYY, rosy lips were smiling at me and it was slightly covered with black hair. I bent my head and started licking her vagina.

Saroj lost control and started shouting "Yes Kris Yes. Lick it. Lick it. Bite it hard. Cmon. Bite it"

I slowly bit it and made her cry with joy. Now she removed my lungi and underwear. My big penis started jumping as soon as it got released from underwear. It was erected fully.

Saroj gasped on seeing my rod, "How big it is. I love it, Kris. I love it". I moved towards her face and ask her, "Want to taste the cone ice cream dear".

She said "No Kris. I won't do that".

I said "Cmon dear. Don't hesitate. We won't get a chance like this. Let's enjoy".

But again, she said, "No Kris. I don't like the smell". Then I thought for some seconds and went to the kitchen and came back with honey bottle. I pour the honey in my penis and applied all around it.

I said "Saroj, just lick now. If it tastes good, then you continue. Otherwise leave it."

Saroj slowly licked the touch of penis and the honey was sweet to her tongue.

She happily smiled at me and said, "I will take it fully into my mouth Kris. C'mon push it to my mouth".

I slowly push it half the way to her mouth. She started sucking it hungrily. I felt heaven there. She slowly sucked it like a cone ice cream. I also moved my hip front and back like fucking her mouth. Having completed sucked it, her attention went to my balls. She first licked it in circle and took it fully into her mouth and started munching it with her tongue. She licked, sucked, munched my penis for 5 minutes.

I started shouting "Saroj, you bitch. You are an expert now. I want to fuck you dear. I want to fuck you in all your holes".

Then I asked her to bend and lay like a dog. She also did like that. I opened her vagina from backside and slowly inserted my penis inside the hole and pushed it. It went inside happily as lots of juice already flowing inside her vagina.

She cried in joy "AAAAAAAAAHHHHHHHH YESSSSSSSSS MMM-MMMMM". I pushed my penis inside her vagina fully and started pumping.

I moved my buttocks slowly front and back and rammed my dick forcefully. On each thrust she shouted "AAAAAAHHHHHHHH" which made me mad.

I cupped her both breasts and started squeezing it also. She also moved her buttocks back and front and cooperated me. I fucked her like a dog for 5 minutes. Then I explored suddenly filling her vagina with my sperm. We both lied in the same pose for some time and departed.

Now Saroj lost her shyness and she was really happy. She hugged me tightly and kissed my cheeks. "Kris this is my day. I have not enjoyed like this in my lifetime. Thank you".

I also kissed her and smiled at her. "Saroj, as I said I want to fuck all your holes. Now I want to enjoy your ass hole."

Saroj got frightened and said "But Kris my asshole is very small. How can your penis enter it? I'm afraid that it will hurt me".

I said "Dear don't be afraid. I will see to that you enjoy it."

I again went to kitchen and came back with castor oil bottle. I asked Saroj to bent down and took some oil in my middle finger. I slowly inserted it inside her ass hole and started rotating it so that castor oil will be applied inside her ass hole.

"Saroj, suck my cock dear. Make it ready for the ass fuck."

Saroj took my penis again into her mouth and started playing with her tongue. She took it inside her mouth deeply and started moving her mouth front and back. AAAAAAAAAHHH-HHHHHH it was really wonderful. Within 5 minutes my penis was erect again and was standing up happily for fucking. I asked Saroj to bend and asked her not to be afraid. I applied castor oil all over my penis. First, I put one finger inside her ass and started moving it in and out. Saroj started moaning "UUUUMM-MMM OOOOOHHHHHHHH". I made her enjoy this by doing for 2 minutes or so and made her ass hole ready to take my BIG FIN-GER now.

"OK Saroj, be ready now. I'm going to insert my penis. Take a deep breath and welcome my penis inside your tight asshole."

I kept my penis in her ass hole mouth and rotate it slowly. This will increase her ass hole sensation and it will be ready to open freely. I slowly insert my penis. OH GOD, it was soooooo tight and I'm able to insert only a tip of my penis.

Saroj started shouting "Kris please stop it. It's hurting".

I said "Don't worry dear. It will be ok now". I took a deep breath and pushed it slightly deep. It went inside one more inch and Saroj was full of tears now.

"AAAAAAAAAAAAAAAAAAAAAAAAAAHHHHHHH. Kris it's hurting very much. Take it out please".

Without hearing a word, I again pushed it hard deeply. Now it went slowly inside due to the castor oil lubrication. "SAROJ, yes we did it. I'm inside your asshole now".

Now I slowly took it out one inch and again pushed it inside. Though it is paining Saroj also started enjoying it.

"Kris, I love you, Kris. I love you. Fuck me, Kris. Fuck my ass hole and tear me into two parts. C'mon fuck it".

Being encouraged by her words I started fucking aggressively. The sound "Chuck chuck chuck chuck" came from each movement of my penis. I made my movement fast and start fucking her fast with deep thrusts every time. I fucked her asshole like this for 5 minutes and flushed her ass with my cum. We lied down in the bed for half an hour motionless. After that we kissed each other hungrily and slept down.

After this incident we started living like husband and wife. Whenever chance came, we started enjoying it every second. After one year I got transferred to Kolkata, so I had to leave her. Though we have separated now, many times I use to cherish myself by thinking about my lovely sex experience with that shy lady Saroj.

4. NYC

After I left the shores of India and on landing in the land of opportunity United States. I am originally from Mumbai and had my share of sexual experiences from college and work. I got married to an IT software engineer and since he had to leave back immediately, I stayed back for three months to get the visa etc. The marriage was arranged as my parents had got fed up with me for always coming late and having boyfriends they did not like. I also got married since I had a breakup and wanted to leave the place and go to USA. I was disappointed after marriage as my husband did not have sex with me nor fondled me. However, I thought maybe it was due to him having only 1 week vacation after marriage and not much privacy available at his house. After the breakup for the last five months, I was longing for sex from my husband but did not get any after marriage. Three months passed and I was desperate to have sex.

I boarded the Air India flight to NYC and as I was struggling to keep my cabin bag in the compartment above. A handsome 5'10" tall guy standing behind me offered to help me. I noticed he was very well built and wearing a tight blue t shirt and track pants. As I sat down at the window seat, he smiled and sat next to me and introduced as Veer.

Let me tell you about myself, I am 5'6" tall with a fair complexion, shoulder length hair and have a well-maintained body with a 36-29-35 figure. On that day I was wearing a long 3/4th length black skirt and a loose green top. As I looked at Veer I remembered my husband, a 5'8" tall...thin guy and got excited with the feeling that I will share the next 20 hrs with someone like Veer so close. Soon an old lady came and occupied the third seat. I guess she and the other air-hostesses took us to be husband and wife. Soon the flight took off and Veer with his talks made me laugh. He would occasionally come near me and whisper in my ear and that sent some current in my body. We talked about our relationships and learnt that he had divorced his wife 4 months back and had come to India to settle a few things. I felt sorry and wondered why would any wife leave someone like Veer. He also commented me on my looks and said how much lucky my husband is to have me.

Soon we had our dinner. Veer again came close to me and said, "Today is our first night, are you excited".

I was taken aback but somehow, I smiled back at which he said, "good, you too are excited, let's hope the lights go off early".

I said, "No, I am not excited. And anyways the flight is crowded."

Veer said, "Don't worry, I will take care of that. When you go to the toilet, just remove your bra and panty and I will get the message whether you are excited or not."

Saying that he asked the old lady to excuse and said "Come on. Let's go."

I got up and followed Veer. He opens one of the toilets and asked me to go. As I was about to go in, as some privacy was available in between the two rows of toilets, he kept his hands on my waist and came near me and said, "I promise, you will enjoy" and blinked his eyes as he moved his hand from the waist slowly to my thighs and around over my ass. I went in and closed the toilet. As I stood there, I smiled to myself in the mirror and was very excited with the whole thing. After getting a bit fresh, I unhooked my bra and took it off and also dropped the panties and kept them in the purse. I felt good that I had shaved my pussy in the morning. I came out and Veer was waiting for me outside. I did not look up at him and walked to the seats. He followed with his hand on my waist and as we waited for the lady to get up, he pressed his cock on my ass and also lowered his hands and had a feel of my ass again. He also removed his blanket from his cabin luggage and gave it to me. The blanket was big enough for both of us and also thick. As we settled beneath the blanket, he also removed the hand rest in between and kept his left hand over my shoulder. I rested my head on his arms and looked at him and smiled. He tried to come forward and kiss me but I moved away my face. I was scared since the lights where still on. He asked me what all I like doing while having sex. He touched my boobs gave a slight squeeze and said, "You do have good shaped boobs, I would love to suck them shortly". Soon the lights went off. He now moved my face towards him as he came close and gave a slight kiss on my lips. It was very sensual and I immediately rested my head on his arms and closed my eyes and smiled. He again kissed me but this time our lips parted. We kissed for some time making sure that we don't make a noise. He soon moved his position and was now sleeping on one side facing me. With his well-built body I was now completely hidden from everyone as I moved closer to him. We again kissed each other and his right hand now massaged my boobs. His hand now moved down and went beneath my t-shirt as he roamed his hands over my stomach and navel for some time. he talked sensually with me and kissed me in between. He then moved his hands up as he circled my bare boobs and pinched my erect nipples. With his thumb he started playing with my nipple making it more erect. He also squeezed the boobs and his kisses became wilder. He then moved his hands on to my thighs and tried lifting the skirt. He did not succeed in doing that so told me to lift myself a bit so that he could push the skirt up. I did as he told and he made sure my back side of the skirt was up near my buttocks. He now had his right hand on my right knee as he slowly moved up pressing my thighs and moving his hands between my legs. I had kept my legs close to each other but as his hands moves over my bare thighs, I got excited and parted them a bit. He got the message as he moved his hands up near my pussy. I sighed as his hands touched my pussy and made me pushed my legs wider. He now had his whole palm rubbing my pussy and at the same time kissing me on my lips. He soon had his finger exploring the other portion on my vagina and he slowly inserted his finger into my pussy. I moaned slightly and took an edge of the blanket and kept in my mouth. He by now had 3 of his fingers inside my pussy and gently moving it up and down. I was very excited and rubbed his penis over his track pants. I felt it to be very long and thick and slowly moved my hands inside his pants and began stroking his penis. He had shaven his hair and that excited me even more. We continued our session for about 10 minutes as he continued finger fucking me and I kept stroking his penis. I soon was wet and had juices coming out from my pussy. He then moved his hands back to my boobs and started squeezing them. He pushed a portion of the blanket down and my right boob was exposed. He squeezed it and slowly moved his lips over it. He kissed my nipples and made circular motion with his tongue around my exposed nipple. He then started sucking it as he continued squeezing my left boob. He then moved his right hand down to my pussy and inserted his fingers inside while he continued sucking my right boob. I felt awesome, I looked around and saw that my co-passengers where fast sleep and that made me feel safe and more excited.

After some time he told me to change position and have my back touching him. I did as he told and we were now sitting on our sides with me pressed against his body. He had also removed his penis by pushing his track pants down a bit. I moved my hand behind to again check the size of his penis. It covered my whole palm and was quite long as I moved my palm over it up and down for some time. He tried to press his penis over my ass but the skirt was coming in between. He then unhooked the skirt and pushed it below as it drops below my knees. His long erect penis was now touching my bare ass as he pressed it a few times. His left hand was now underneath me and covering my left boob while he moved his right hand over my right boob and started squeezing both of them. Slowly he then moved his right hand below and rubbed my pussy and pushed his fingers in and out for some time. I lifted my right leg a bit as he pushed his penis in between my legs. I felt his tip touching my pussy as he slowly directed it inside my pussy with his hands. I could now feel at least about 4 inches of his huge cock inside me as he slowly started moving it up and down. I was controlling my moaning with the blanket as he continued doing it for some time. It was feeling wonderful and I helped him by also moving my ass up and down slowly so that he could manage to get more of his penis inside me. We both where soon sweating in the AC and after ramming me slowly for around 15 mins he increased his speed and soon discharged his cum inside my pussy as we both felt exhausted. It was one of the best sex I ever had. As we returned to our normal sitting position, I bent down below and lifted my skirt back up and adjusted my T-shirt. We both went to sleep soon after.

In the morning when I got up, the lights where already on and Veer was awake. He greeted me "Good Morning" and came near me and asked "How was your night?". I smiled and gave him a kiss on his lips. I excused myself to go the toilet. I got fresh and put the bra and panty back and came back and sat on the seat. Veer said "I wish I would get a chance to lick my pussy" I in my mind said "yes. And I wish I could get my mouth over your cock" We soon had breakfast and then it was announced that the flight will reach London and those travelling to USA can stay in the flight if they wish to as it is only one and half hour's halt. Veer said "Wow, we should plan on doing something, you want to get licked. right?" The flight landed in London and most of the people got out from the plane. We had only about 4 people stay-ing back in our section and they were about 5 rows behind. Soon one cleaner came and was cleaning the toilets in the first-class area in the front. As soon as he was done, Veer told me to get up and we went to the toilet.

He asked me to get in and followed and closed the toilet behind. he immediately hugged me and started kissing me on my lips. Not worried about the noise now our tongues tangled as we had a long wild smooch. He pressed me against the basin and also started rubbing and squeezing my boobs with both his hands. He then removed my t-shirt in a flash and unhooked my bra and took it off. He now started sucking my boobs wildly and biting the nipples in between. I was very excited; I kept my left leg on the toilet seat. he pressed his penis on me and also lifted my skirt and pressed my thighs. I had my hands on the back of his head as he was sucking and licking his tongue all over my boobs. He opened the hook of my skirt as I allowed it to drop on the floor. He pushed my panties down with one hand and I was now completely naked in front of him. he lifted me and made me sit on the basin as he opened my legs with both his hands. He bent down as he started kissing my legs and thighs and slowly reached the pussy. I lifted my legs over his shoulder as his face was now completely in between my legs. He first kissed me over my vagina and then with his tongue started kissing my upper and lower lips. I spread my legs a bit wider as he with his hands opened my vagina and started licking it and inserting his tongue inside. He kept licking for some time and as I was getting another terrific orgasm, I moved my hands trying to get hold of something. I managed to hold onto a bar with one hand and the other hand kept it over his head as I wanted him to continue. Soon I was almost exhausted and he stood back, I got down from the basin and pushed him against the wall and gave him some wild kisses and even biting his lips. I lifted his T-shirt and pushed his pants down. I knelt down and I was in front of his huge bulge over his underpants. I opened my mouth wide and bit it slightly. I then removed his underwear and his huge 8"-inch penis was in front of my mouth. It was very thick as I held the base of it on my right hand and opened my wide mouth and covered the tip of it. I then moved my mouth down. I tried to push as much of his huge cock as I could inside my mouth and after having almost 6", I took it out. I repeated the action for few times and also kissed his balls in between. I roamed my hands all over his length, licking the full stretch and the big perfect head. He kept hold of my hair and guided me to continue sucking his huge cock. After about 5 minutes he again lifted me kept me on the of the basin, spread my legs wide apart and directed his penis straight into my pussy. He pushed it deep inside as I cried in pain and excitement at the same time. He continued pushing his huge penis in and out as we kissed and his hands squeezing both my boobs. I went through multiple orgasms as his cock went deep inside. He lifted me from the basin with his cock inside me and pushed me against the wall as I bent my legs around him. He rammed me continuously deep for some time and then released his cum inside. As I stood on my feet, he again gave me a kiss and praised me for the wonderful sex. We soon put on our clothes back and came out of the toilet. It must have been for about 25 minutes and was lucky that no one disturbed us.

We came back and sat on our seats as the flight soon started back for the USA. We exchanged our email ids as he was going to catch a connecting flight to California and promised to meet me whenever he visits NYC. We landed in NYC and after collecting our baggage and completing the immigration, we hugged each other as we kissed passionately for a long time. I said bye and came out of the airport still remembering the wonderful flight I had. I was so much in my thoughts that I even failed to recognize my husband waving at me.

5. Taxi Ride

It was a cool, rainy night. A strong breeze was blowing and the moment was captivating. Saroj felt a tingle in her skin; a tingle that suggested she should have been touched, loved before she came here. She ought not to have held herself back from him; her body ached now and complained of the tender spots at which she wanted to be touched, stroked and held.

And now she was several thousand miles away from him, in the midst of friends. A group of very close, very intimate friends, including Deepak, but that didn't mean the same thing as a special one who she could let touch the most sensitive and deep of her body zones. She squeezed her thighs together to try arrest the growing sense of warmth between her legs but only succeeded in arousing herself some more.

"Come on, get into the car!" Rani called out to her. Four guys and Rani and she were out on the town, the seminar for which they had come to Mangaluru having ended earlier in the evening. All of them had a few drinks, and Saroj, who normally could hold her drinks rather well, was already feeling a little heady.

She could not decide whether it was the weather, the close encounter she had had with him or just the dizzying proximity to her old friend Deepak. Whichever it was, she felt vulnerable. She had inkling that if anyone propositioned her tonight, she would be his. That scared her, and she was extra alert to make sure that she stayed within limits. But the very fact that she was extra conscious meant that things she would have normally taken in her stride were appearing to her to have overtones...

Like the fact that six of them were to cram into a taxi cab that was to seat four passengers. Five would be a squeeze, but six was really overdoing it. None of them however wanted to make it a split into two vehicles; it would just take away the fun of being one big gang. Two of the guys squeezed into the single seat next to the driver. Rani, Saroj, Deepak and the other guy got into the back.

Even though Saroj and Deepak were married to other people, the tacit understanding in the group was if there was any activity, Saroj and Deepak would be paired. Just a natural couple with a great relationship. There were no sexual overtones. Deepak had more than once told Saroj that he would have loved to marry her had he met her in time. And Saroj had routinely laughed at him, eyes sparkling, and her manner hovering between a flirtatious woman and the demure shy housewife that she was.

Today was no exception and subtly but surely, it was worked out in such a way Saroj and Deepak were going to be next to each other. Four of them in the back of the car meant some squeezing and sitting at angles. Rani and Ricki sat quite comfortably; Ricki at the window and Rani in the middle. Next was Saroj and Deepak was at the other window. The only difference was that while Ricki and Rani sat next to each other, Saroj had her leg slightly resting on top of Deepak. The formal relationship between Ricki and Rani meant they would sit square next to each other. And the intimate equation between Saroj and Deepak meant that if Saroj was half on Deepak's lap that would be fine. In fact, Saroj was expected to do that so that Rani would be comfortable sitting next to Ricki.

Rani squeezed Saroj's shoulder; a gesture that could have meant anything from thanks for making it comfortable for me, to I know what that closeness to Deepak means to you.

The taxi jolted off to a start. There were jokes and laughter, but also complaints and exclamations as the taxi bounced and bumped along.

"This is just too much!" exclaimed Rani as the cab threw her against Ricki and she clutched at the seat in front of her to steady herself. Her breasts were pressing against his arm and she was embarrassed.

"Let me make more space for you," said Saroj, getting half onto Deepak's lap. She was now sitting on one leg with her legs on either side of that leg of his. This made substantial space for Rani who spread out now with a loud "Whew!"

The road surface wasn't getting any better but fortunately, the cabbie had brought them to their first stop; a hilltop from where they could see the rough sea stretching to the distance. It was dark and they could see distant lights. They stood at the railing as the guys reached for matchboxes and cigarettes. Saroj and Deepak wandered off a bit. Deepak didn't smoke; another one of those things she secretly admired in him. They stood there watching the silhouette of palms swaying wildly. To Saroj it seemed those palm trees were representative of the wild swings on her inside.

Their hands touched briefly when they stood at the railings. She didn't move her hand. He was surprised but he didn't show it. Very gently, subtly, he moved his hand away. He gasped in surprise as the woman of his dreams allowed her own hand to catch up with his. This time he did not move off, rather he allowed himself to feel the soft warmth of her hands. Perhaps for the first time in all these years he could actually feel how she felt.

Saroj just needed the warmth and the touch. Tonight, she felt the need for so much loving. She just craved touch and warmth and her Deepak was here tonight; the same Deepak who for years had hovered around her, needs unstated but obvious.

"Come on, guys!" someone called out to them. We don't want to be late at dinner. It broke the reverie. Saroj's hand felt alone as Deepak was quick to pull his hand back and move away. "Come let's go," he said to her in a voice that was barely a whisper.

This time when they climbed into the car, Saroj seated herself on Deepak's lap, her legs straddling his one leg. As the car lurched and jumped, she allowed her body to sag onto his. At one point she felt the need to spread her legs and brace herself for a big jolt. And in that movement, her pussy ground against the thigh between her legs. It was not intentional and it caught both of them by surprise. But the warmth that he felt on his thigh was unmistakable. Equally unmistakable for Saroj was the tremble of passion she felt in the grinding.

She gasped and leaned back a bit. Her hair was in his face and she rubbed the back of her head against his face, hoping the darkness in the cab would allow her this small liberty. He shuddered involuntarily and his cock shot to attention all at one go. The grinding pussy against his thigh was bad enough but the tingling sensations triggered by the hair and her head were maddening.

He let his hand rest on her hip. And just stay there. Saroj let her body rub against him more and more as the journey wore on. The dampness on his thigh was now unmistakable. Deepak did not dare make a move of his own as this woman was someone, he had worshipped from a distance but never considered the possibility of touching her. She was married. And she was so much a family woman he could not have imagined anything of the sort.

She could not say for sure what made her do it, but at some point, she felt she move more squarely onto his lap. She regretted it almost instantly, because her ass felt the outline of a raging erection in his lap. Deepak gripped the handle on the door of the car with his left hand. This was getting to be crazy. He shut his eyes and hoped the erection would die. But the car had other ideas. As it swayed and lurched, her ass and her pussy ground onto him mercilessly.

Deepak wanted to control her movements. His hand slid up from where it was on her hip, but under her blouse and Saroj felt a rush of heat surging up to her face when she felt his hands on her torso. He tried to hold her steady but merely ended up gripping her hard. His hand was now just below her breast and he was extremely conscious of the curve and the sumptuous flesh further up. She caught his hand through the blouse. She didn't push it down or away. She seemed to be limiting where it wandered. A jostle of the cab jerked her hand and she ended up guiding his hand onto her breast. The motion rubbed his hand on the lace and he distinctly felt her nipple.

Deepak's other hand went to her thigh and he rubbed her thigh. His other hand cupped her breast. Saroj froze. This was her Deepak, doing to her what she desperately needed and wanted to avoid tonight. She felt so vulnerable. She didn't want to fuck or even let anyone other than her husband Pankaj touch her. She had never fantasized about anyone other than that other mysterious him. And here she was with Deepak.

Deepak was maddened with lust and Saroj's passive response to where his hands had ended gave him a sense that he had a chance which he could well afford to take. He pulled up her skirt on the side which was towards the door. His hands felt the warmth soft flesh of her legs. It wandered to the inside of her thigh. Saroj felt her legs involuntarily open. She now shifted herself to face slightly away from the side Rani was facing. Deepak could see her profile and her mouth was so clearly hanging open with lust.

Deepak's hand moved to the inside of her thigh and felt the heat source. She was wet and hot as hell. He palmed her crotch. She shifted uncomfortably, and all she succeeded in doing was press down hard on his impossibly hard cock.

Saroj fucked down on the protrusion between her asscheeks and thought to herself that this was ridiculous and she needed to stop it. But the driver was driving so recklessly and the road was so bad that she was just being forced to dry fuck Deepak. She wanted to control this before her own lust got out of hand or before Deepak lost his composure. She had kept him at bay for so long and it would be a pity now to allow years of restraint to be unleashed thus.

She figured she needed to get off his lap. She held onto the seat in front of her and raised her body to start to move off him. She held herself up poised and looked down to Rani and asked her to make space for her.

In that instant, Deepak had unzipped his pants and gave his cock a well needed massage.

He let out the pillar of hot flesh as it had got snagged in his jocks and needed reorientation. But Rani was taking too long to make the space Saroj needed and Saroj's arm was beginning to ache. Saroj let herself down and she was shocked to feel the penis under her. Under her skirt. Deepak had his hands pulling her panties aside. It dug into her soft pussy flesh. Saroj raised herself a bit and shifted and Deepak made the most of the moment to try pull her panties down. They were now just above her knees allowing him access but not allowing her to spread enough.

But this was not what Saroj had in mind. This time she propped herself up determined to move onto Rani's lap if necessary. But the car had a mind of its own. The pothole into which it went with a bang had Saroj lose her grip and Deepak had his hands in the right places. He caught the momentum of Saroj's falling hips and impaled her on his cock.

She squealed and fortunately that squeal was drowned in the chorus of protests and groans from all other passengers. Now she had another man's cock in her. She stayed put. Enjoying the jostling and the jiggling from the ride. She ground around once on the cock in her and then raised herself off to try and move away. Just when his cockhead was nearing the outer lips, his hands on her hips prevented her from rising.

She held on to the seat and kept her body up, poised to avoid the fucking. But every light bump was a prod downward onto the waiting cockhead. She gasped and bit her lips to control the noises which seemed to her to be a full giveaway. And then when her hand ached, she just had to sink back.

Oh! That feeling was so good. She sat back and luxuriated in the warmth of the pillar embedded in her. Her hand dropped to his hip as she held him. Then her fingers felt the body under her. Of a friend, and yet of a stranger. She tried to raise herself again. But this time her own spiralling lust forced her to fall back with a sigh. Deepak's hands were now on both her breasts clutching hard as she rode him.

Rani looked the other way; it seemed as if she knew and wanted to ignore what was happening. Saroj timed her fucking now with the lurches and bumps of the car. She joined in the chorus of "ooohs" and "aahs" as the car jerked about. She fucked Deepak hard and furiously. She felt his cock swell as the hope of a mutual orgasm became the new goal. She held on to the seat ahead and propped herself up. Deepak fucked upward. The car took a long climb to the hotel on the top of a hill. They would be there very soon. Saroj started to bounce with a sense of urgency. She adjusted her angle so that the sensations from the upper front of her cunt could be maximized.

Just then the car reached the portico of the hotel. "We are here!" chorused the rest of the team as they spilled out of the car.

"You guys go, Deepak and I will join you," called out Saroj, her unbridled lust allowing her to be bold in her suggestion. She patted the driver on the shoulder and asked him to take the car to the car park.

She now reached forward and gripped the passenger handle on

the top of the passenger seat in the front of the car. The cock was just out of her cunt and she could not take the vacuum even for a moment. She searched desperately for a second anchor that would allow her to fuck this cock mindlessly till both of them achieved release from the build-up of desire.

She could only grab the driver's shoulder. He turned to look if he was being called and noticed the hands under her blouse kneading her breasts frantically.

"Listen," she managed a gasp. "Just drive!"

And she bounced up and down. Moans escaped her lips as she cared not, now also that the driver knew exactly what was happening.

"Aaaaaaaaah, Deepak my darling!" she cried out. Her hands provided her with the leverage she needed to fuck the cock and twist and turn. She felt the head nosing probing and filling her.

"Take this and this and this and this!" she mumbled. The driver was stunned as he drove quickly to the darkest corner of the parking lot. Her finger nails dug into his shoulder as she felt the cock rake her pussy lips.

Deepak was going crazy with the way the cunt was pushing back his skin. With each thrust downward his cockhead was unsheathed a bit more and got a little more swollen. He pinched and twisted Saroj's nipples wanting to give her at least some of the pleasure he was getting.

But she was wild and driven that night. She fucked in a way that pleasured every layer of the labial lips. And she smothered her Deepak's cock with her juices and her love sheath.

"Oh yes! Yes! Yes! Yes! Yes!" she screamed as Deepak's cock surged with cum and signalled the end for him.

His hands slid down to her hips and she held her from there and pulled her down onto his cock. His hands guided the intensity of her thrusting and he felt his seed boil over.

"Take this my darling, my love," he hissed as he shot upwards into her.

"Oh! That is such a lot!" she moaned as she took it all in. Her pussy clenched and snapped at his cock. She felt a surge of juices flow down from her cunt, soaking his pubic hair and his cock.

In the throes of his orgasm his hands flew around and clutched at her breasts and her thighs. His finger nails dug into her soft body as he pounded every ounce of his cum into her.

Her own nails dug into the shoulder of the driver who watched transfixed as the couple fucked each other wildly.

Saroj turned around and her wet open lips planted a full kiss on Deepak. She sucked in this tongue and kissed him with an animal vigour as the quakes subsided slowly. She let her body down. The pussy was snug against the base of his cock. She ground herself and squeezed out every ounce of pleasure that either of them was going to get in those moments.

Then she did something she could not relate to the Saroj she knew. She wiggled her hips and he shuddered and wailed a low animal moan as the last vestiges of fluid remains were squeezed from him and pooled between his legs with her own juices.

She lifted herself off only when the penis was now just a jut of over-sensitive flesh, quite useless to her.

In one jiffy she was out of the car. She pulled back the panties up in a race to catch the juices running down her legs. She ran at a trot into the brightness of the hotel, wondering how she was going to face either Deepak or the taxi driver on the way back.

6. Lonely

We live in Mumbai. We've been married for about fifteen years now. My wife is a knockout; at least I think so. She's dusky with really lovely, fine, regular features -- a slender nose, superb cheekbones and an exquisitely sculpted line to her chin and jaw. Her eyes are dark and large and she lines them with eye-black. Her mouth is really sexy with a full lower lip and the upper one bowed over it, and her teeth are very white and even. Her hair is dark and thick, down to the small of her back. She has a lovely long, graceful neck which leads to a pair of truly gorgeous breasts: sloping and high and full, tipped with long nipples that harden very, very readily, and set in really sex aureoles. I love the way they pucker and her breasts get swollen and heavy when she's aroused. Her waist is small and her belly is nice and firm and flat -- no love-handles, no sagging pouches, just the slightest, but firm, curve. Overall, she's a near-perfect 38-26-34. Sometimes I wonder how I got so lucky!

Saroj is hopelessly and delightfully addicted to sex. She's not a nympho or anything, but nothing gives her as much pleasure as good, hard, demanding fucking. I won't go into the full story of how we started on the cuckold-scene except to say that we've been doing it, with great satisfaction, for nearly ten years now and it was entirely mutual: I shared with her my desire to see her being fucked, and fucked hard, by another man, a bull of a man and, at once, Saroj accepted. Her excitement was evident and I was filled with a mixture of joy and arousal and a terrible dread.

Anyway, it started and that first incident was sado masochistically mesmerising and utterly irresistible. Our chosen bull was a hired gigolo. We'd decided it would be best to start with someone skilled and also relatively anonymous. The man was very, very good. Good looking, well-built, exceedingly well-hung and something of an artist when it came to sex. Nothing rushed about his technique and his stamina was truly awesome. He took his time and it was more in the nature of a seduction. They were together for a long time that evening. And I watched with a pounding in my head and heart, my eyes burning, my ears echoing with her cries of lust and passion as he fucked her again and again and again like I have never been able to do. She loved every minute of it, panting and moaning and writhing ecstatically with him, letting herself be taken repeatedly and her love calls were obscene and erotic. I can still remember the sight of her on her forearms and knees on the living room carpet, rocking back and forth, her swollen breasts swinging and jiggling, her face turned up and over a shoulder and radiant with passion while he took her from behind straddling her hips. I watched his big cock grinding in and out of her cunt and saw how he fucked her first for her pleasure and then for his. He topped it off by fucking her mouth and creaming in her face. It was the first time I'd seen her do that -- with me, she'd always refused, but this time she seemed unable to say no to anything, she acted like a wanton sex slave. I moaned as I watched his cum spurt into her open mouth and splash on her face and breasts and saw her smiling lasciviously as he finished.

It took us two days to recover and then, when I was fucking her, I kept thinking of the guy and I knew she was, too. It added to our pleasure, each knowing the other knew but not saying. Our orgasms were terrific. That night I asked if she'd like to do it again and she said yes, of course, as often as possible. And that's how it began.

Now in India social norms are very different from what they are in Europe and America. It's a far less egalitarian society and most (practically all) households have live-in full-time servants and domestic staff. The wages aren't high so this isn't as impressive as it sounds. Besides, one needs the staff because the other basic infrastructure really isn't that optimised for people to manage on their own. Anyway, the servants (men and women) are always economically less well off than their employers and significantly so. Most of them don't even have a basic education. They often come from villages seeking work in the cities and take jobs in houses and as errand boys in offices or chauffeurs and such. Indian society has always regarded them (unfortunately in my view) as 'socially' less privileged (no one uses the word inferior any more, but that's what they mean). Contact with servants is required, by social mores, to be distant and aloof. No familiarity. They do not dine at table, for example. Nowadays things are changing and the new generation of servants is better dressed and considerably more modernised. The women, for example, now use make up, simple though it is and only on special occasions, more often and dress better.

The point is that any kind of overtly familiar relations with servants are very much still a scandal. Forget about sex with them. That's completely out. So, imagine the thrill when our next bull was one of our house servants, a sturdily built young man in his early twenties, lean and hard-bodied, and rough in his manner. We arranged it between ourselves without telling him. The rest of the staff was given the day off. He stayed. And then Saroj went about seducing him and in no time at all they were fucking in the bedroom while I watched, hidden, my pulse racing and with a huge hard-on. The guy was terribly excited at the chance of being able to fuck his mistress and it showed. She had to control the pace to prolong it. He fucked her hard and called her all kinds of names (whore and slut and so on) and took her two or three times in different positions but this time, unlike with the gigolo, she was in control. I can still see her riding his cock, squatting over his lap, her face flung back, her mouth open, gasping and calling out loudly, her buttocks bouncing off his thighs, her cunt sliding up and down on the long thickness of his dark cock. He kept watching her, transfixed, and squeezing her big breasts.

After that, there was no turning back and we went on steadily. Saroj took more servants, other gigolos and then we moved on to acquaintances and then close friends.

***

THREE OR FOUR YEARS after we entered the scene, for the first time, Saroj had two bulls together. That was her idea, entirely. She claimed that the only thing better than one bull was two. I was thrilled. The very thought was erotic. It was one of my most ardent fantasies and I couldn't believe that she had suggested it. I knew this was another beginning, in a way. Soon, I hoped, I'd be able to take her to living out my next level of fantasies -- full-fledged orgies with several guys fucking her, having her to a live sex show for a select audience and even whoring herself to complete strangers. I'll tell you later how much of that we've been able to get to; actually, it's quite a lot of it.

Anyway, this was then a special occasion for us and we arranged it carefully. Two years earlier, I'd bought a lovely beach property about two hours' drive south and had the existing house completely redone. Saroj worked on it, with an unerring touch and gave it a truly wonderful, warm feel. I'd put in a pool, too. It has two floors, with three bedrooms on the floor above with a wide terrace or balcony that runs along the front so that each room opens out onto the upper deck. The floor below is at garden level. I have a study that looks out on the garden and pool and the sea beyond. The living room actually opens out fully so that it almost feels as if the garden has climbed the patio and come right in. There's a little dining alcove on one side with a table that can seat 8 comfortably, another breakfast nook on the patio, a large, airy kitchen with a big pantry and larder. The two-car garage is just beyond. We've entertained here often and I have vivid memories of the innumerable times I've watched my wife with other men here -- in the house, in the garden, in the pool, on the white sands with the sea curving around their writhing bodies.

Saroj chose her lovers for the evening. Some distance from the house there is a small village. The young men come out in the mornings and evenings and, living so close to the sea, many are adept swimmers. Ever since we got the place and started work on it, Saroj had been eyeing the young men hungrily. One or two of them are exceptionally sexy. The best of them all is a tall, superbly built youth in his mid-twenties.

Ram is dark and very good-looking. His body is truly stunning, sculpted like a classical statue. He's tall and has the broad shoulders, wide chest and high, narrow hips of a strong swimmer, and a swimmer's long, smooth, sinewy muscles. His belly is rock-hard and cobbled with a prominent six-pack. About a year earlier, we called him over to the house ostensibly to help with harvesting the fruit of several coconut trees that grow in our orchard. He agreed and I could see Saroj's mounting excitement as she watched him climb the tree effortlessly using just his bare feet and the palms of his hands, his muscles rippling like snakes under his taut, dark skin.

When he was done, an hour later, she rewarded him suitably. We were both thrilled to find that his endowments matched his physique and, better still, that he was evidently a skilled, caring yet demanding lover. He now tends the garden, cleans the pool and general looks after the place for us when we're not there.

Ram was her first choice for the special evening. After a lot of thought and discussion -- we considered a friend, one of her favoured gigolos, others -- we finally decided that it should be her favourite servant-bull. And so, it was.

We left the city late Friday night, the three of us, Saroj, I and the servant. I took the minivan which I used for moving heavy stuff from our city apartment to the beach place. Behind the driver's cab in front was a low door that led to the back of the van.

Since I'd only used it for moving, the small windows at the back were boarded up and I'd taken out all but one jump seat. The servant, Hera, sat there.

As we drove down the expressway, I could see that Saroj was getting hot. She'd opened her blouse and was slowly caressing her breasts. Her skirt was riding high on her thighs and when I saw her move a hand between her legs, I asked her if she wanted to go back with Hera. She almost groaned in relief and before I knew it she was out of her seatbelt and into the back. Pretty soon I could hear him grunting loudly and calling her to suck his cock harder. I grinned to myself.

Soon I could hear the two of them fucking in the back. We left the expressway and got onto the country road and I pulled over and killed the lights and went back to watch. He was fucking her on her back on a rug on the floor of the van, thrusting into her hard and she clung to him, her body rocking with his thrusts, kissing him feverishly, her hips bucking under his. The van was rocking with their movements. It turned me on. I sat on the jump seat and watched. My presence didn't stop them. I saw the servant kissing my wife, pushing his tongue into her mouth as his big cock slid in and out of her cunt. He was a lean, dark young man, quite good looking and one of her favourites. After a while, they stopped and he slid out of her and she immediately rolled over and got on her forearms and knees so that he could mount her from behind doggie style. Her face was only inches from my knees. I was tempted to push my cock into her face, but I resisted and decided to save that for later. Instead, I contented myself with watching. The servant knelt behind her and quickly ran his cock deep into her cunt and began fucking her hard and she gasped and cried out, going _Yes! Yes! Yes! _ and moaning and begging him to fuck her harder. Her body rocked back and forth as he pounded in and out of her really hard. I could see how much she was enjoying it. Her face glowed and her breasts swung heavy and swollen with excitement and her nipples were hard as pebbles. Her sexy gold necklace bounced against her chin as he moved faster. I could actually hear the slap-slap-slap of his thighs against her buttocks. He gripped her waist and kept pistoning in and out of her body grunting and gasping, calling her a whore and a bitch, goading her to take his cock. I knew she loved the obscene love-talk and I heard her respond in the same words, egging him on to keep fucking her.

I was thrilled with the performance and wanted to see it through but we were running late now so I moved back to the driver's cab and pulled out onto the road again, letting them finish off in the back.

We got to the beach place late and went straight up to bed, leaving Hera to unload the luggage -- not that we had that much. I told Saroj not to wash. The smell of him on her turned me on. She smiled and threw herself into a deep chair and split her legs open for me.

"He came inside me," she said, with a sly, knowing smile. She pulled open her cunt lips and I saw the remains of my servant's stickiness in her slit. She dragged one slender finger through her cunt and sexily licked her fingertip and, with her other hand, squeezed her breast. "Come here, you," she said throatily. "First lick me. Then you can fuck me."

It wasn't the first time I'd done or that she'd asked me to, and I loved it. I flung myself to my knees before her and drove my face into her crotch. Within seconds she was murmuring in pleasure, her hips writhing and jerking under my face. I could taste her juices mingling with the servant's cum -- it made my head swim with excitement. She grew hotter and hotter and her cries rose and now she began to goading and taunting me, knowing it would only fuel my arousal.

"Yes, come on! Lick my pussy, lover!" she said. "Lick me clean! Yes! Come on! Lick up Hera's cum from my cunt!"

Mad with lust now, I jumped to my feet and pulled her off the chair to her knees in front of me and pushed my cock into her mouth. She took it deep into her mouth with a loud groan and began sucking me off feverishly. I cried out my pleasure for her mouth was incredible -- warm and wet and she used her tongue with a wizard's cunning.

I wanted her and I wanted her brutally, in the same way that I had seen the servant take her. I pushed her head away and made her turn around on all fours and I got behind her and thrust hard into her which made her cry out sharply. It was music to my ears. I began fucking her hard, feeling her cunt going into lust filled spasms on my cock which was now slippery with that wild cock-tail of her juices, my cum and the servant's. She spurred me on, calling to me, comparing me with other men.

"Come on! Fuck me! Fuck me like the other guys do, baby! Like your servants fuck me! Come on! Do it!"

"You like them, slut? You really like fucking them, don't you?" I cried.

"Yes!" she went. "God, yes, I love it when they fuck me! All of them! Come on! Take me! Oh yes! Yes!"

And right through, with her rocking and jerking under me and my cock thrusting in and out of her cunt and my hands under her groping and squeezing her bouncing breasts, I kept thinking of her, just like this, and in a hundred other ways, with another man, and I knew with a dreadful certainty that she, too, was thinking of one of her lovers. It was irresistibly erotic.

***

SATURDAY MORNING. I woke to find that Saroj had already started her weekend with a bang -- literally. She was there, right there in the bed beside me, fucking the servant again. How long they'd been at it I had no idea. They were taking their time, going slowly, murmuring very softly. She was smiling radiantly up at him, kissing and caressing him tenderly, her hands stroking his smooth, strong, dark back. I propped myself up on my elbow to watch, grinning and instantly aroused.

"Good morning," she smiled, turning her face to me and I thought to myself how lucky I was to be married to such a beautiful, sexy, slutty woman. "Slept well?"

"Very well. You?"

"Like a log. Then he," she nodded to the servant, "came and woke me up." She giggled. "Something like an alarm cock."

I guffawed. The servant grinned, not understanding our words in English but knowing that it must be something ribald. He was bent over her on his knees between her legs, his strong arms stretched out, his knuckles on the bed. His hips were moving rhythmically up and down and in tight circles over her crotch. She was moving in a tempo to match him and now she pulled her legs up so he could go in deeper and squeezed his buttocks, pulling him deeper into her.

"Mm, that feels good, baby," she said in the vernacular. "Oh god yes, I love your cock in my pussy! It feels so good, baby!"

The youth grinned and bending his head began to suck and lick her stiff nipples. I left them and swung out of bed.

An hour later, I was on the terrace deck with a cup of coffee when she came out, freshly showered and smelling of some subtle lemony fragrance that was really nice. Her hair was tied up in a tail behind her head. She wore jeans and a completely transparent white shirt. It was unbuttoned and the ends were brought tightly together and knotted under her breasts so that a lot of cleavage and midriff showed and, through the transparent cloth, even her nipples.

"Nice?" she said pirouetting for me.

"Very nice."

"Will they want me?"

"They'd want you if you wore a parka, babe," I snorted. "You know that."

She smiled. "I'm so excited. I can't wait! When do you want to start?"

I looked at my watch. "Love, you've had enough since last night. Take it easy. It might get really ... demanding. I think we'll start off in the evening, what do you think?"

"So long to wait!" she pouted. "Can't we start earlier? Please?"

"No," I said earlier. "We can't. And you can't have a snack either."

She stuck her tongue out at me. "Spoilsport! Not even a little tickle?"

"Not even the littlest tickle."

She groaned in mock despair and I laughed and pulled her to me and kissed her, feeling her breasts press heavily against my chest.

"Let me at least suck your cock," she said softly into my mouth.

I slapped her bottom and pushed her away with a chuckle. "Stop, woman! There's going to be a lot of action later. Save your energy for that. Go on, read some sexy stuff, watch a movie or something. I've got work to do."

***

THAT WASN'T UNTRUE. There was a lot of work to be done around the house. The roof needed work and we had a problem with a section of one wall and the pool needed cleaning. We set about, the three of us, Hera, Ram and I, stripped to our waists.

We took the pool first, drained it, cleaned it, let it dry and set it to fill again. We were almost done by lunch. I left the guys at it and went in. Saroj had fixed us -- her and me -- a light lunch of soup and salad and some cheese. We ate in the breakfast alcove and Hera came in to say that the pool was done. I thanked him, not missing the longing, lustful look that he got from my wife and told him to take a break, get something to eat and we'd start on the roof.

Through the afternoon the three of us worked till, finally, at about five, as the sun began to slide down into the sea, I called a stop. We'd found we needed some gear still and, now acting on our plan, I told Hera to come with me to the nearest store, a good 15 minutes' drive away, to get it so we could finish working to-morrow. I phoned ahead and told them to keep the stuff ready.

I'd heard splashing by the pool and knew that Saroj was there, very likely in that ridiculous micro-bikini she loved, with cups that were barely the size of band-aids and panties that were hardly more than a thin thong -- they just about covered her cunt lips and, behind, left her buttocks totally exposed with the rear strand going between her butt-cheeks. I told Ram to go find out if she needed anything.

Meanwhile the servant and I went off. We took the pick-up I kept at the place. Driving down, I looked at him out of the corner of my eye and understood why he turned on my wife so. He had good, strong, aquiline features, a square jaw and his body was rugged and hard. The wind blew in his dark, thick hair. His arms were muscular, the forearms broad and sinewy. I shifted into overdrive and settled back.

"So, Hera. You really enjoying fucking my wife, don't you?"

His head whipped around, startled. We generally didn't talk like this outside of the actual act. Then he grinned.

"Yes, boss," he said. "She is very hot."

"One of your favourites, eh?"

"Yes sir. She is my absolute favourite."

"What do you like doing best with her?"

He grinned. "Everything sir. She's fantastic! I mean, the way she gives a blow job, boss, it's really something else! And man, she's so hot and so tight when I shove my cock into her!" He made a pumping action with his clenched fist, grinning. "Oh man," he went on, now mimicking a fucking action, hands spread as if holding her waist. "I'm going to fuck her tonight, real hard! Just wait and watch, boss! You're going to love seeing us!"

"Yeah," I said. "Lucky me."

"No, lucky me boss!" He was positively crowing now. "I'm the guy gets to hump your wife, remember?"

Boy, have you a surprise coming, I thought to myself, but said nothing.

The store had my stuff ready and I paid, we turned back. On the way, I stopped briefly at the village (the same one where Ram came from) and kept Hera waiting for a few minutes in the car.

Back home, I slotted the pickup into the carport and told Hera to unload the stuff and then come to the pool. I went ahead, tossing off my t-shirt. He nodded, grinning.

That grin died a few minutes later.

Hera came out to the pool, dressed in only his pants, bare-chested, and rocked to a complete stop. I expected his reaction and was right by him. I loved the look on his face: his eyes popped, his jaw dropped and a strangled cry erupted from his throat.

By the edge of the pool, Ram stood stark naked, legs apart, his magnificently sexy body glistening wet. His hands were low by his hips, on my wife's head as she knelt before him, clad only in her ridiculous bikini, giving him a long, loving blow job. Ram's hips jerked back and forth. Her head moved to and fro. Her fingers were curled around his thick cock, pumping it. Her cheeks billowed when she took him in deep. It was obvious that she loved every minute of it.

"Yeh! Come on! Suck my cock, slut! Suck it hard!" Ram grunted.

Beside me, Hera started forward, shouting, "You bastard! I'll kill you! She's mine!"

I grabbed him by the shoulders and held him back. "Easy, stud, easy. Just watch. There's a kick in that too. Trust me."

"But ... but boss! She's ... he's ... I mean ..."

"I know." And then I snapped. "So fucking what, hero? You think she loves you? You think you're the only guy she fucks? You know you're not, so what the fuck are you getting antsy about?"

"I ..."

"Yeah, right, so shut up. Just shut up and watch. You can fuck her later."

He moaned but obeyed and I noticed that his anger was quickly turning into excitement. I loved this. The bull as a cuckold, I thought to myself. It was a delicious twist.

By the pool, Saroj's cock sucking was getting more frenzied. Now she slipped her bikini bra off and started fondling her breasts in arousal. Ram pushed her head back finally and she groaned, moving onto her back, kicking off her micro panties and spreading her legs for him, reaching for him.

"Come on, fuck me, Ram!" we heard her say loudly. "Fuck me hard!"

The youth got between her legs and we saw her body arch and heard her loud cry of joy when he squeezed his cock into her slit. Her feet rose behind his knees. Bent over her, he began fucking her with long, slow thrusts, moving his cock slowly in and out of her cunt. She moaned loudly and now her face turned to where I stood with the servant.

"Oh god," she said to us. "He's so good! His cock feels so good inside me!" Her body writhed ecstatically under his.

I grinned to myself. This was really sexy.

"Come closer," she said. "Come here and watch. I want you two closer!"

I nudged Hera forward. I could see his cock was bulging in his trousers. We got up close, right by her and, lying on her back, she stretched her arm up Hera's leg and squeezed his cock.

"You want me, too, don't you, Hera?"

The servant nodded.

"Soon," she murmured sexily, wantonly. "Very soon. Let me enjoy this for now."

She turned her attention back to Ram who grinned up at us. She'd obviously let him in on the plan. Good. He began moving faster and deeper and she cried out, now arching and tossing and writhing under him, her hips bucking up and down under his, her breasts jumping and jiggling with his thrusts.

"Take off your pants!" she gasped to Hera. "Quickly!"

The servant shed his trousers at once and her hand closed on his cock. "Oh god, oh god," she moaned and I could see her intense excitement at having one cock in her cunt and another in her hand.

Suddenly she let go and looked at me. "I want you to prepare him for me."

I stared. "What?"

"Prepare him. Suck his cock. Let me see you suck his cock. I want to see you sucking his cock!"

I looked at her stunned. I'd never done anything of the kind before. Saroj's eyes blazed. "Do it!" she snapped. "You're the cuckold, remember! That's what you do!"

I looked at her, thrashing like a whore under the young man who was fucking her and grinning at me, contempt and derision in his eyes. The young man whose bloated cock was sawing in and out of my wife's cunt, who was kissing her and sucking on her swollen tits, banging her harder and harder. And I looked at the servant standing next to me, lean and dark and sexy, his erection monstrous, his expression a mixture of arousal and desire and impotent frustration. And my own cock hardened further.

I turned to the servant. "She wants me to suck your cock, Hera," I said softly. "Don't come in my mouth. Keep that for her."

I moved slightly behind him and curled an arm around his body and ran my hands down his torso. My god, but it felt sexy! I felt his body stiffen in surprise and momentary resistance, but I persisted and slowly caressed him, moving my hands down to his crotch. My fingers closed around his cock. I'd never held another man's cock before and the first touch was electric. It felt incredible, hot and throbbing and burning in my fingers. He jerked away, spinning around.

"Easy," I murmured, moving with him, facing him now, once again taking his cock in my hands. It was impossible to resist. His mouth opened and his breath came sharply. I felt a quiver of excitement rippling through me. I wasn't prepared to kiss him. But I knew, with sudden certainty, that I did want to suck his cock. I had to know what it felt like, tasted like. I moved closer. He turned his head away, needlessly as it happened, because I was already going down to my knees before him.

"Easy boy. Relax. Enjoy it." I murmured.

Again I took his cock in my hand, marvelling at how good it felt, the thickness and hardness and weight of it. I cupped his balls and slowly inched my face closer. I pressed my mouth to his hard, flat belly. His cock was against my neck. I moved my lips lower, moved his cock over my face. It filled my sight. I couldn't resist. I groaned and opened my mouth and slipped my lips around it.

God, that first touch of a cock in my mouth! It was the purest heaven. It was heavy and hot and big and smelled and tasted wonderfully musky. I ran my tongue around his cock-head, then pulled him in deeper and began sucking him. Behind me, I heard my wife's long, shuddering moan of excitement and the cackle of the guy fucking her and the shouted groan of the servant whose cock was now in my mouth. I sucked harder and I felt his hands on my head and his hips began moving back and forth. His early cum spurted into my mouth and I swallowed it and suddenly I knew I wanted to finish this, wanted to feel a man creaming in my face. I kept sucking.

Beside us, on the tiles, Saroj and Ram were fucking like demons now, watching me suck off the servant. I sucked harder. Saroj whimpered, her hands mauling her breasts in frenzied excitement.

"Stop!" she called suddenly and nobody knew who she meant. "Stop! Now! All of you, stop!"

She eased Ram off her and got to her knees and her face joined mine in Hera's groin. The servant cried out as our tongues battled over his cock.

"Go, go suck Ram now," she said to me. "I want Hera to fuck me."

And there we were, husband and wife, me sucking one guy, she the other. Fuck, but it felt sexy! Ram's cock was even bigger and stiffer and already slippery with his gunk and her juices, a totally different taste and experience. I closed my eyes and let myself drown in the pleasure.

A sharp cry made me look around and I grinned. Hera was on his back on the ground, his knees at the edge of the pool, his feet in the water and she was in a deep squat over his cock, slowly impaling her cunt on it, her fingers tight around its base.

"Oh baby yes!" she cried, throwing her head back. "Oh fuck yes!"

"Come on, whore! Take my cock!" he shouted.

Saroj moaned and began moving slowly up and down on the servant's cock, leaning forward, her arms outstretched, her hands on the ground beside his hips. I watched her as I kept blowing Ram and she watched me and I could see the incredible arousal and excitement on her face. She had really surprised me and I couldn't believe how sexy it felt. My balls were aching. I longed to thrust my cock into a mouth or a cunt. But that wasn't on the menu. Not yet anyway.

Her movements grew more erotic as she arched her body back, moving her hands behind her and began rotating her hips with every downward thrust so that she was sort of corkscrewing her cunt on his cock.

Under her, the guy grunted, his hips heaving and bucking, his hands under her thighs. She cried out softly, tossing her head back, her breasts bouncing.

"Come on, Ram!" she gasped. "Let me suck your cock now!"

And there it was, finally. My wife with two guys. Ram pulled away at once and went to her as she turned her face to him and I saw him pushing his cock into her face. I groaned and fell back, sitting with my legs stretched out, frigging slowly, desperately wanting a fuck for myself but helpless and totally, totally blown with arousal. Inches away, the two guys were fucking my wife in her mouth and cunt together.

They broke apart and she turned around and got on her fours between them, now sucking Hera while Ram began to raid her from behind. Their grunts and moans and cries rang in my ears. I couldn't take my eyes of her sexy body lurching and jerking back and forth and to and fro between theirs, one guy's cock drilling her cunt, his cock appearing and disappearing between her butt cheeks while the other guy's cock filled her face. Their hands were all over her body, squeezing her tits, stroking her head and back and she was in seventh heaven.

And then I had my revenge. A crowd of six swept in, the four guys and two girls from the village I'd stopped at from my way back from the store. Saroj didn't know that I had arranged this secretly well in advance. I'd known that Ram had bragged about his affair with Saroj to his friends, but he didn't know I knew or that I'd been in touch with them long before -- or that I'd actually even fucked the two girls some months earlier.

They were all young, in their late teens and early twenties with the supple, strong bodies of young people who spend a lot of time outdoors. The guys were all dark, muscular and well-shaped physiques like Ram and the girls were absolutely irresistible. One, Ritu, was a complete knock out with the loveliest face -- dark almond eyes, a slim nose, a long neck and breasts to die for in a superbly curved body and the other, Pammi, a year or two older, was like a cauldron of molten sexuality, earth and sensuous with large breasts and a wide mouth and a stunningly curved body. Both were dressed in long, loose skirts and button-down blouses cut close to their curves. Both wore gold necklaces.

I was already on my feet when the trio on the floor cried out in shock and alarm and stumbled apart. They lurched to their feet and I laughed at their expressions.

"Hey look! They started without us! No fair!" One of the guys cried, grinning and starting to undo his pants, moving towards Saroj, his eyes flashing hungrily.

I flung my arms around the two girls, my hands on their breasts, flipping open the buttons of their blouses. They were naked underneath. They giggled and one of them kissed me hard.

"You've been sucking cock?" she said in surprise.

I nodded. "Yeah. First time. Now I know why you girls enjoy it so much!"

"Oh god, that's so sexy!" the other said and I wondered what the fuck it was with these women?

I looked at Saroj and Ram and Hera and laughed. "Surprised? Good! You want more than one guy, right, Saroj? Well guess what. I got you a whole lot more! Come on, let's see if you can take them all! You ready for that?"

But the four guys had already joined Ram and Hera and formed a ring around her. I saw clothes being shed, heard cackles and laughter, so them looking down. I sauntered over with the girls for a closer look.

And there she was, the hub of arousal in a circle of lust, with six mighty spokes pointing at her in offering and she was going mad, fisting two, sucking one, moving on, whimpering and groaning in wild arousal.

I entered the circle and she saw me and I knew at once from the look in her eyes what she wanted of me, and at that moment, I was thrilled and overwhelmed with excitement and arousal. The guys were all terrifically sexy bulls, with dark bodies, hairless torsos, smooth skins, and very well-muscled -- I ran my eye over their wide, cleaved chests and hard bellies and down to their rampant penises and knew I just had to taste them all.

"Suck them," Saroj said. "I want to see you suck them all!"

The guys laughed and jeered as I stepped forward, uncaring and unmindful of their taunts -- right then, music to my ears. I dropped to my knees before the first guy, running my hands lovingly down his body to his crotch. I ran my tongue over his bulging cock-head. He grunted and held my head and pulled it forward and I let him in, taking him deep into my mouth and sucking eagerly, working his cock-head with my tongue. Next to me, Saroj moaned, staving off the hungry men, masturbating shamelessly in front of them all. I looked the other way and saw the two girls getting hot too, their blouses off, their hands working their swollen breasts, their faces bright with excitement.

A few minutes later, I moved on to the next guy and, as I took him between my lips, I heard a loud gasp beside me and saw that the first guy was already with Saroj. She leaned back on her elbows; her legs spread. He kissed her deeply, with lots of tongue play, then moved lower, to her breasts and then lower still, to her cunt. I heard her gasp again, louder, and saw her flinging her head back and then sinking down onto her back as the guy began licking her slit in earnest. She moaned loudly, her head turned to one side, her hands in his hair, her legs split wide. I knew just how much she loved this and now he was finding out, too. She hissed her pleasure, her tongue sliding out of her tongue and arching sexily over her upper lip. Her hands slid slowly up her body to her breasts. Her hips writhed and undulated heavily under the guy's face.

"Oh! Oh yes! Oh god yes!" she moaned, her body jerking slowly now as if under a man's thrusts.

The second guy pushed my head away from his cock. Immediately I turned to the third. His predecessor laughed down at me.

"Fucking wimp!" I heard him say.

He dropped to his knees before Saroj's face and she turned her head and her mouth opened and drew him in almost gratefully. The guy licking her slit stopped and moved up between her legs, pulling them apart, kneeling between them on his haunches. Saroj paused her cock-sucking briefly and, looking at the guy with a naked hunger glittering in her eyes, arching her face, pulled her cunt-lips open for him.

"Come on, fuck me!" she cried. "Take me, lover! Give me your cock!"

The others laughed, including the guy fucking my face who pushed my head back and said, "Hear that, wimp-boy? See how we can make your slut beg for it?"

"Yeah, for a real man!" said another.

The guy between her legs laughed and pressed his cock-head quickly into her cunt. Saroj fell back with a loud groan, arching her back steeply as he went deep into her and instantly her head spun around again to the guy who'd been in her mouth -- except that it was another guy this time, the third, who I'd just finished.

By the time I got to number four I was tiring of all that cock-sucking. My cock was raging, too. And now number one had yielded, without coming, to numbers two and three who were taking turns with her. Number four left me and joined them and she was riding one guy with two cocks bobbing at her face. And Hera and Ram were still waiting.

I got to my feet and turned back to the girls. "Come on. Let's hit the beach," I told the girls. "I'm not such a wimp, you know. I'll show you."

"We know, remember?" the younger one said slyly and took off with Pammi at a run, laughing, tossing their clothes as they went with me pounding behind them. We left Saroj to her lovers.

We swam naked, me and the two girls and they really knew how to show a guy a good time. Lots of kissing and fondling and breasts and tongue and then we headed up onto the beach where one of them began sucking me off, bending over my lap while the other sat beside me, kissing me, frigging herself. I fucked them one by one, Ritu on her back and Pammi from behind and then decided that I wanted to play sexy games in soft sheets and stopped and led them back to the house.

By then, Saroj and the guys were playing sex games. Pin the cock on the stud. She had a blindfold on and her job was to match the cock to the name. No peeking. Only touch. A real contact sport. We stopped to watch her, bending over a guy on his back, kissing him, moving down his body, taking his cock in her mouth suck-ing him hard. She couldn't guess and the guy flipped her on her back and began fucking her heavily.

"What happens if she can't guess?" I asked one of the local heroes.

He grinned. "No problem. She can keep going till she does, or she moves on to the next guy. Or she calls quits."

"Bet she hasn't done that yet."

"You said it, chief. Fuck, what a number you've got here! And oh yeah, we also make it tougher. Sometimes it's the same guy again."

"And if she gets it right?"

"The guy gets knocked out. Has to stop immediately. It's all technique."

"How's that?"

"You keep changing your fuck style, you see."

I didn't see, but who the fuck cared. Certainly, Saroj didn't. I saw that she didn't cut it with the current guy. She said later and called for another who immediately took the first guy's place, turned her over and entering her from behind. She cried out as he rammed into her and began fucking her hard, gripping her hips and slamming his thighs against her buttocks. She got his name right in seconds and he yelled in anger but kept the rules and slid out of her. Next guy.

"Come on," one of the girls said to me gently. "You can come back later. For now, just be with us." She was right. I knew I should leave before something contrary welled up inside me and asked me to turn my head and forget how much I was truly enjoying this.

We went up to the bedroom and the girls loved it with the smooth clean sheets and their squeals became moans when I lit up the room with candles and started tormenting them properly, not just fucking them, but going long and slow with lots of foreplay.

I pulled out a vibrator, too. They'd never seen one before and they went ape-shit over it. One began masturbating while she sucked me as I lay on my back. I drew the other one's hips over my face and slowly ate her pussy.

I'm not clear any longer on who was doing what to whom exactly but some things remain vividly in my memory. It seemed to go on for a long time and I can recall their cries and moans as I fucked them and the warm softness of their mouths and the tight heat of their cunts and the satiny smoothness of their dark skins and the turgid weight of their breasts and the stiffness of their nipples. I remember the way Ritu thrashed under me when I fucked her on her back, plunging greedily in and out of her cunt and the way Pammi whimpered when she mounted me. And the way they got into a lesbian act, too.

I was fucking Ritu again on her back, drilling her slowly, fighting to keep off an orgasm and she was rocking back and forth slowly under me with her face buried between Pammi's legs. I bent forward and began sucking on Pammi's tits. She hissed in pleasure and pulled my face up and kissed me like a wild animal, her mouth wide and her tongue electric in my mouth.

"She likes it in her ass, you know," a heavy voice drawled next to me. "Actually, they both do. You should try that."

I looked up and saw Hera and Ram watching me. I grinned at them.

"How come you're here?" I asked.

"Got knocked out of the game," Ram grinned.

"Still going on?"

"Yup. But we don't get any of that action now. No problem," he shrugged. "We can get that anytime. But we're hungry. Thought you might spare one of these two."

"Go ahead," I said generously. "Who d'you fancy? Or you want both?"

"No, you finish your thing with Ritu," Ram said.

He started moving to Pammi who was moaning with Ritu's tongue-fucking of her cunt and was on the verge of an orgasm anyway, her hands mauling her big brown tits, her face glowing with pleasure. As they came up she pulled away from Ritu and went to the two men, kissing Hera hard, writhing her body lustily against his, then turning to Ram. She groaned loudly and began sucking Ram, turning on her back and opening her legs for the Hera who spent some time sucking her big brown breasts before executing a perfect muff-dive. I got excited watching them and began fucking Ritu harder.

"In her ass, you said?" I asked Ram.

"Yup. Slow and deep. Use some lube. Or butter."

I thought to myself. I remembered we had some Vaseline in the drawer of the bedside table and that was just a stretch of an arm away. I got it, not stopping in my movements in and out of Ritu's cunt. I uncapped the jar and pulled slowly out of her.

"Come on, bitch, I'm going to fuck your ass now," I said to her.

Despite what they said, I expected her to resist. Instead, she moaned in excitement and bent more steeply forward with her shoulders on the bed, lifting her buttocks up and spreading them for me, showing me her dainty puckered flesh of asshole and, reaching between her legs, curled a finger up into her cunt.

"Take me!" she gasped. "Please! Do it!"

I salved my prick, then around her asshole and into it with my finger and then pressed my cock-head to her ass. She whimpered but her ass yielded at once. I'd not done this often but remembered it being incredible. I squeezed my cock-head into her ass and she gasped, her head jerking up, her face twisting and her fingers clawed at the sheets. I cried out as her ass convulsed on my prick and went in deeper and deeper and then began fucking her ass slowly and deeply. It was incredibly hot and tight and my cock glided smoothly in and out of her ass.

Next to us, Hera and Ram had begun fucking Pammi. She was on her back with her hips at the edge of the bed and Ram was between her legs, gripping her hips and pumping away hard while Hera knelt over her face and pushed his cock down into her mouth.

"Oh yes! Fuck me! Fuck me! Fuck me!" Ritu moaned, her body writhing and rocking to and fro on the bed. "Oh god yes! Oh yes!"

"Like it?" Hera asked me over his shoulder.

"Oh fuck yes!" I gasped. "She's incredible! Her ass is fantastic!"

Ram laughed. "Yeah. So's your wife boss. You should see that, you really should. Right up her ass. They're doing it now. And then they're going to do it in her ass and in her cunt and in her mouth. Three in one. Bet you've never seen her do that!"

I stared at him dumbfounded. I'd seen Saroj being sodomized before and knew she enjoyed it. But with three guys! Together! This was an incredible dream come true. I forgot where I was, what I was doing. All I knew is that I had to be there, where she was.

I stumbled out of the room, not caring about the girl I left behind, barely hearing the taunting cackle of laughter that followed me out. I hurried down the stairs to the hall.

They'd moved indoors. The four local guys and Saroj. I fell to my knees, awed and feverish, my heart pounding. This was just unbelievable. I hadn't planned on this. I wasn't even sure I had wanted this, so much, for so long, for her to be taken and used like this. And now there was no way I could stop it. And I knew I didn't even want to. I only wanted to watch and watch and watch and I didn't want to stop watching. I could see that, though she was tiring, my wife was still in the throes of ecstasy and enjoying being pleasured beyond my wildest imagination, or her.

So I watched it through. Saroj was still blindfolded and the guys were laughing and taunting her as she lurched around blindly. Visions and snapshots:

A guy on his back on the low glass-topped coffee table in the living area and Saroj straddling the table, standing and then bending deep forward, her hair cascading over his belly and sucking his big cock, taking it deep in her mouth.

Saroj on her back on the dining table, her legs forked wide, her body jerking and arching, her swollen breasts bouncing, a guy standing between her legs, holding them wide and high, slamming his hips back and forth, rocking his cock in and out of her cunt.

Saroj with another one of the locals, her back to him, slowly lowering herself onto his long, thick cock crying out, her face twisting and her hips rising and falling, rising and falling along the length of his cock-shaft, moving a good five or six inches. And then leaning back and turning her face to him and letting him put his tongue deep into her mouth and slam his hips up and down under her.

And oh yes, the sodomising of my wife. Oh yes. How can I forget that? They all did it, all the four of them, one by one. One guy from behind, bending her forward and easing himself into her, and her shrill cry echoing above their cheers. And the next guy doing the same but with her on her back, bending her legs up high and her face contorting as his dark cock tunnelled deeper and deeper into her ass, till his balls were pressed to her cunt-lips. And the last two, one taking her on her side, lying behind her, the other lying under her and making her sit her ass on it. All of them fucked her in the ass. All of them.

Even in pairs. Two together. Wasn't that what I wanted, after all? Somehow, I wasn't so sure anymore. But she was. That was certain.

I saw her upright on her feet, laughing brightly, coiling her dark hair above her head and then arching quickly forward over the armrest of the sofa to take into her mouth the upright cock of the guy who lay on his back on it, his arms folded under his head, his knees over the armrest, grinning up at her as her hair cascaded over his hard, flat belly. And another local, laughing, coming up behind her and her spreading her legs for him and his cock running swiftly into her cunt and her muffled moans and gasps as he began fucking her rapidly, holding her hips and rocking his own to and fro, back and forth, to and fro, slapping his thighs at her buttocks, making her body rock under his, her breasts bouncing and the guy under her squeezing and fondling them and both of them calling out obscenely to her.

Several minutes, an eternity, later, the guy behind began fucking her ass, sliding out of her cunt and gently pressing his cock to her ass. I saw her tense fractionally, then yield with a shuddering moan and he was through, going deeper and deeper into her ass. She groaned loudly, her head flung back, one hand gripping the backrest of the sofa, the other scrabbling behind her at his hips and at her buttocks, and then the guy on the sofa put his hand on her hand and pushed it down to his groin again. The guy behind her began sodomizing slowly and heavily and deeply and thoroughly, groaning in pleasure, moving his hips slowly to and fro, sending his cock drilling deep into her ass.

They paused after another eternity -- but only to swap places. The guy in her ass moved out, grinning and beating his meat. She moved up onto the sofa and now knelt on the seat, her face over the backrest. The guy who'd buggered her now stood in front of her face. The other guy got behind her. And they did it all over again. In her cunt and mouth first -- her mouth filled with the cock that had just been in her ass -- and then in her cunt and ass.

And then one of them pulled her over his lap and made her sit on his cock and then began slamming his hips up and down and jerking her body hard up and down on his cock. I heard her crying out and saw her body tossing wildly, her breasts bouncing furiously, her hair flying and her cries loud and high and shrieks of the purest pleasure. That's when he slowed and beckoned to two of the others. One came up, grinning, winked at me and, twisting his fingers in her hair, turned her face into his crotch and my wife moaned and began sucking him deeply.

Meanwhile the other slipped behind her and I saw her stiffen as he pressed his cock-head to her anus and then saw her head snap up and her mouth tear open and the room filled with her long, loud shriek of pain and pleasure as he entered her from behind, his cock separated from the other guy's by just a little bit of her flesh; and that one wasn't letting go either and pulled her mouth to his cock again.

They broke apart and the guys changed positions and they did it to her all over again, just like that, in all three orifices and now one guy was on his back and she moved over his lap, her back to him and slowly, gingerly, sank her ass on his cock, shuddering, moaning, wincing. Very slowly, her buttocks writhing and squirming on his lap, she leaned back, her hands behind her. He reached up and squeezed her turgid breasts and I watched as my wife turned her face over her shoulder and let our servant kiss her. He began moving gently under her and she groaned softly.

Moaning, Saroj obeyed like a sex slave. She cracked her legs further apart. The local youth who'd just fucked her now moved between her legs and bent over her. She turned and kissed him and I saw him press his cock to her cunt-lips. She tensed for a moment, then yielded, and he was through, running his cock slowly and deeply into her flesh, skewering her with his cock, her long neck arching stiffly, her mouth tearing open in a long, shuddering cry. And a third guy was there right away, his big cock sawing the air in front of her open mouth. His hand fell to her blindfolded face and twisted her head to one side and she groaned and took his cock, fresh from its recent invasion of her ass, deep into her mouth.

I watched and watched and watched the four bodies, rocking together, going on and on, till she gave in, finally and called their names and where they were fucking her, and the guys groaned in mock despair but finished anyway, one coming in her butt, another in her cunt and the third flooding her mouth.

She'd saved the best for last, and she called the last guy's name even before he got to her and tore off her blindfold and blinked and her eyes were hazy and glassy with lust and increasing exhaustion.

"Take me," she said, her words slurring. "Yes, come on, please, fuck me!"

Oh god, that guy was good. A huge guy, with big slabs of muscle on his chest and belly and thick bulging biceps and broad forearms and thighs like tree trunks, intensely handsome and with an enormous cock. With a cock that size he ought to have been the first one to go, she could hardly have mistaken him for any of the others but I knew she'd kept him for the last.

She sucked him for what seemed like ever, slowly finger-fucking herself kneeling before him and then he pushed her away and made her turn around and got behind her and started fucking her from behind and it was really hard. He went in quickly and she moaned and then he began moving, rocking his hips back and forth, slapping his thighs at her buttocks, making her cry out and call out with pleasure. Her breasts bounced and shook. She turned her face over her shoulder and he bent forward, squeezing her tits and kissed her deep, pushing his tongue into her mouth. He rose and now he was moving faster, like a madman and her cries were really high sharp broken. He bellowed and gripped her hips and slammed into her hard, jerking her body backwards onto his cock viciously. Again. Again. Again.

Jamming his crotch to her butt. Each lunge made her scream. Again and again and again. Then he rose up in a squat over her hips, knees deeply bent and went wild, bent over her, his finger steepled in her back, then under her body, then bent even further and on the floor and his hips were plummeting and rocketing up and down and her body was thrashing wildly under his.

Watching them, the other three began cheering and whistling and calling, clapping loudly, saying _come on! Fuck her! Fuck the bitch hard, man! Go! Go! Go! Fuck the whore_! Beneath him she was gasping and moaning and crying out, saying _Fuck me! Oh yes oh yes oh yes oh god yes! Fuck me!_

I saw her rearing up then falling forward and her hands flailing in a frenzy at the sofa armrest before her and I saw her screaming as she orgasmed and then seconds later the guy flung his head back and cried out and pulled out of her and dragged her trembling body to her knees and pushed his cock into her mouth and then he came and came and came, his hot white sticky cum spurting into her face and down her throat and settling all over her breasts and face, his seed mingling with the others'.

Saroj moaned softly and turned slowly onto her back on the floor. A slow, lascivious smile creased her features. She ran her fingers dreamily through the gobs of gunk spattered over her body. It was all over -- between her legs, between her breasts, on her breasts, her face, her belly, her thighs, her buttocks, everywhere. She licked a fingertip sexily.

"Mm, god, that was some good fucking, boys!" she giggled. "My cunt's really sore! And so's my ass! You guys really know how to fuck! I just loved your big cocks!"

The men laughed. One of them jerked his thumb towards me. "Your wimp's here, bitch. He's been watching."

"Hope he learned something!" another cackled.

"Doubt it. He doesn't have the equipment! Maybe we should have just creamed in his face!"

They laughed and Saroj smiled and I felt a rush of excitement.

"Come here, you," she said beckoning to me. "You know what to do!"

I did indeed. And I did it. It was the first time I'd done it in front of a bull before and it felt very, very sexy. I went to her and began cleaning her with my tongue, slowly lapping all the accumulated gunk and jizz of the other men off her body. The men were silent for a moment and then I heard them chuckling and then jeering and taunting me but I didn't care. It tasted wonderful and it was even better off Saroj's sweet, smooth, sexy body. In no time at all I had her whimpering softly, writhing in pleasure as I worked my way around her body from head to toe, reserving her cunt for the last. I rimmed her ass, sweeping up the gunk there and then finally moved to her cunt. It was flooded with their jizz and it took a while for me to get it all and, by then, she was in deep rut again, groaning and whimpering in pleasure.

She pushed me away and got to her feet and beckoned to her new lovers.

"Come on guys. I'll fix you something to eat," she said and, naked, led them to the kitchen. "There's beers in the fridge," I heard her say.

Suddenly I felt lost and very, very lonely.

7. *I began to cry uncontrollably.*

"**M**rs. Sharma, it is nice to meet you." It appeared as though my son Rohit's friend Hardik was at least a gentleman. Maybe some of his polite ways would rub off on Rohit, I thought.

"It's nice to meet you as well Hardik."

"I want to thank you for inviting me to dinner with you and Rohit. Hostel food is such a drag." He said.

"You are most welcome; I'm sure Rohit was happy to have someone to talk to besides me. He says that I tend to get a little preachy."

"Do you?" Hardik asked.

"Maybe just a little," I replied. I looked around before I spoke again. "If the waitress comes by, please have her bring me more wine. In the meantime, I'm going to the ladies' room."

If I had known what was being said while I was gone, I would have walked directly from the room and left them both to find their own way home.

"You really going to help me do this?" Hardik asked.

"Sure I am, she needs to come down to earth."

"This is pretty drastic," Hardik admitted. "I mean, she is your mom."

"Yeah, well she has it coming."

"I see you found more wine," I suggested as I sat down between them.

"Yes the waitress came by just after you left."

"I drank the wine in silence. It was a little more sweet than I remembered but it wasn't bad. Almost any wine was good on a cool evening. After several minutes of silence, I began to feel a little light headed. "I think I need fresh air." I suggested. It was a good thing that I had already paid the bill. I doubt that I could have managed to do it at that moment. I really was feeling confused.

When the three of us left the parking lot of the restaurant Rohit was driving. Hardik and I were in the back seat. I should have said something but I just slipped inside the open rear door of my own car.

It seemed that even before we left the parking lot Hardik was kissing me. The kisses were not those a young man should give the mother of his friend. At least not if he wants to keep his friend. At first, I resisted his attempt to slip his tongue inside my mouth. but eventually I gave in. I suppose it was pure instinct, at least that's my story as to why I opened my mouth to his tongue. It didn't take long for me to forget I was more than twice his age.

I felt his tongue in my mouth and I reacted without thinking at all. My breathing was shallow and fast while I sucked on his tongue.

"You like to kiss don't you mom?" Rohit asked from the front seat. He almost snapped me out of it, but not quite. I shook my head even though he couldn't see me. Hardik could see me, and I could feel him.

I felt his hand move under my sweater. I welcomed the feeling as he massaged my breast, while kissing me yet again. I could feel my body react, but my mind wasn't quite able to process what was happening. At least not in real time. I seemed to be a few seconds behind in my thinking somehow.

He had his hand under my skirt and my panties pushed aside long before I realized it. I felt something small and hard inside. It took me a second to realize that it was his finger. I realized that I was squirming only after my body was in motion.

I had his cock in my hand without any memory of how it got there. I was moving my hand up and down his shaft without thinking about what I was doing. I suppose that it was just instinct.

"I can tell you like his cock," Rohit said. "Don't you?"

"Yes," I mumbled. My voice wasn't recognizable even to me.

"Do you want to suck his cock mom?"

"No, I don't like to do that." I replied

"But I would like to see you do it. You will do it for me won't you mom?" Rohit asked.

"Yes," I replied after a second or two. I realized that the car had stopped moving when I heard doors open. I felt hands help me from the car. I went willingly.

"On your knees mom," Rohit's voice demanded.

I slipped to my knees and almost immediately felt a cock pressed against my lips. I opened my mouth and took it inside. I felt the heat of it and the smoothness as it moved inside my mouth. I would have lovingly sucked it, but all I could do was hold my mouth tight since Hardik was fucking my mouth as he would have a pussy.

He pushed in and out for what seemed like a long time. Then I felt him stiffen as he put his hands on my head and pulled me hard onto his cock. It slipped deep into my throat as he came. I choked as I tried to gasp for air. For a second, I was afraid that I would die with his cock blocking my airway. Finally, he removed it.

I must have passed out because the next thing I remember was waking up alone in my motel room. I tried to convince myself that it was a bad dream. I almost had myself believing it, until I found the pictures on the night stand. I was very recognizable on my knees with Hardik's cock in my mouth.

I began to cry uncontrollably.

8. You dumped my best friend

That was not a very good morning for me, I had broken up with my girlfriend last night, we were in a relationship for last 2 years, but last night suddenly she said, "I want to break up with you, as our relationship is not going anywhere, due to some reason; I don't know what, but just something is missing in our relationship. Our relation doesn't have that spark. We are together for 2 years but I can't feel anything for you. Don't take me wrong you are good looking, have a nice job, and also a good human being, but I can't see a soul mate in you."

I just thought that I'm the biggest fool in the world who wasted my precious 2 years with a girl who don't feel anything about me.

After 2 minutes of silence, she breaks the silence and said, "hey! Don't be sad yaar, life doesn't end with end of any relationship, we are still good friends."

Me: "hmmm, ok no problem, good night, I have to leave now."

My ex: ok, bye, goodnight. And came forward to hug me, but I'm not in mod to hug her and just forwarded my hand for a shake hand, and said good night again and put on my spectacles to hide the fact that I was about to cry and left her house.

That night, I couldn't sleep the whole night. I was living in the golden memories of last 2 years. How I proposed her, our first hug, our first kiss, our first meeting etc. At around 11:00 in the morning I was normal and thought of going out to watch some movie. Just at that time some time knocked the door of my flat. I thought it was the milkman who has come late. I was just in my shorts and try to find the shirt, but then the person knocked the door and started shouting. "What the fuck, why did she come here."

I opened the door and found my ex's best friend standing there, with an angry face a brass knuckle in one hand and baseball bat in other and some tie like thing tied on her head and tilak of lipstick on her forehead. I quickly shut the door in front of her, and she started shouting again, "You coward, you son of a bitch, open the door, you bastard".

Me: Go away, I am not going to open this door without my bullet proof dress, which is also water proof now. And I laughed on remembering how she dumb she is looking wearing that.

She: Laugh, how much you want, but remember one thing, this is the last day of your pathetic existence in this world.

She was like a devil in angel's body, always creates disasters for others, it was her hobby. But in some corner of my heart, I felt some strange feeling for her. I liked to argue and fight with her. When I can't see any escape, finally decided to open the door.

I opened the door slightly, and told her, "Surrender your entire weapons first, if you want to talk."

But she just punched my bare chest, with the brass knuckle.

Me: Hey! keep that away, that hurt.

She: You dumped my best friend, you Mother fucker.

She tried to hit me, with the baseball bat but she couldn't hurt me as I had only opened the door slightly.

Me: I did not dump your friend, you bitch. We both mutually made the decision to break up with each other.

She: Every man says that. Did you give her any option, when you told her that you want to break up with her? She tried to hit me with the baseball bat couple more times, but when she got that, she can't hurt me with the bat, she tried the knuckle again, but I was ready this time and close the door, and her punch landed on the door.

She suddenly starts weeping and shouting, "Oh Mother Fucker, you Rascal, you broke my hand".

I opened the door and start laughing while watching her with pain on her face.

She: You Rascal, you are laughing, after breaking my bones. All the weapons she had were dropped by her and she literally starts weeping. The doctor in me woke up and I got worried about her as I had never seen her weeping.

Me: Is it alright? Show me your hand. And I took her soft hand in mine carefully and took her inside. It always feels good to have a beautiful girl's hand, in yours.

She stared at my chest with surprise, with a shine in those eyes; I could feel she is impressed by my athletic body. I love working out hence I keep myself in shape.

After a couple of seconds

She: Are you so poor to have a shirt. Although she pretended to be angry, but what I saw was lust in her eyes for me. She continuously glaring at my bare hairy chest. I felt so awkward that I put my hands in front of my chest.

She started laughing and said, "Why are you behaving like a girl?"

Me: What else a boy can do, if a bandit queen like you stands in front of a boy and stares at him like she is going to fuck him.

She (looks at me in anger, and said): Am I supposed to laugh on this. Where is my bat? Did I come here to fuck you, bastard?

And searched for her baseball bat and found it near the door. She ran take the bat and start running to harm me.

Me: are you crazy? It can hurt. You already hurt yourself, is it not enough for today?

She took the bat like a sword in her hand and looked like Rani Lakshmi Bai come to harm a British soldier and I am the poor British soldier.

I ran to my bedroom, she followed me; I jumped on the bed and moved to other side of bed. She climbed on the bed and loses her balance and falls on her stomach. Her big bouncing ass came in view. I was mesmerized for a moment; she gathered herself and tried to, hit me by the bat, but I caught the bat and threw it away, she tried to punch me, but I caught her hands, then she kicked me, but I was quick to go back, and see lost her balance again, but I caught her through the waist and stopped her from falling down. And suddenly I found, her boobs covered in her loose top in front of my mouth. And I could see inside her loose top. There are 2 big melons waiting to be sucked. And just then, she shouts

She (shouting): cockroach

Then she jumped on me, binding her legs around me. And suddenly our lips locked with each other. I just got shocked, and felt 440 watts current was running through my body. And unknowingly my lips and hands start their work and I had started sucking her lips. And my hands started to travel all over her back and finally discovered their destiny, the big soft and round mountains. I started pressing them hard and pushed her closer to me. She also started responding and starts sucking and biting my upper lip and catches my hairs with one hand and starts pulling them. She started scratching my back with her nails of other hand. She was very wild during the kiss. We remained lip lock in same position for a couple of minute and then suddenly she left me and pushed me away. Both of us were heavily breathing.

I tried to catch her again but she pushed me away. Suddenly she starts shouting, "Shit – how can I do this with a monster like you, I came here with my weapons, you rascal, how dare you cheated my angel like friend, she is weeping because of you."

Me (shocked): She is weeping because of me????(I start shouting) and told her what happened last night in detail.

"It was me who got hurt, then why she is weeping?" I said.

She: But she looks upset.

Me; Of course, she will be upset, if even your pet dies you get sad for few days and our relation is more than it or at least I think so.

By remembering the memories of last night, I got upset again. Then she came near me and said, don't get upset, you are pretty handsome guy, you will get someone soon who really love you.

Me: It is lunch time do you want to eat something?

She: Do you know cooking?

Me: Yes, I live alone, so there is no choice. I have learnt to cooking but right now I'm not in a mood of cooking, we can order something to nearby restaurant, they give free home delivery. And I winked looking at her, she smiled.

"Do you want to have some beers too?" I asked.

She: Ok

I ordered the pizza and beer. And while she switched on the TV, even before I gave a warning, the porn movie I watched last night, started playing. Her eyes and mouth were wide opened as she looked at the TV and then me and then back to at the TV. I did not have any courage to look in her eyes. It took few seconds for her to get back to her senses and she switch off the TV. Silent remain in room for few seconds in room and then she said, I want to go back home and turned around but I caught her by her hand and pull her towards me and said, "Please don't go dear, I love you. And I had hugged her from behind, and placed my lips on her neck and started licking her neck from behind. At the same time inserted my fingers and starts moving them on her belly and slightly moving upwards, feel her big boobs by moving my hands on that big honey pots. I started squeezing them slightly, she closed her eyes and starts moaning in low voice. I moved from her neck to her ear and started licking her ear lobe. She starts trembling and moaning in louder voice. I stopped licking and pressed her boobs, she turned around and opened the eyes and looked me and said, "What is this?"

I didn't say anything, just took her top and pulled it up to her neck and started watching her beautiful boobs. I was unable to remove my eyes from the sight I had watched, her fair and smooth belly and 2 sweet big pots of honey, although they are covered with the black lacy bra, but it hardly covers 1/4th of the total boobs. I got mesmerized and when I had not taken any step further, she on her own removed her top and came near me and started moving her hand on my bare chest and held my one hand and pulled me towards the bed. When we were standing on the edge of bed, she pushed me on the bed. I felled on bed on my back, her beautiful curvy body hypnotized me and I was not in stage of thinking what to do next. She took charge and just climb on me, put her lips on my chest and started kissing my whole chest and finally settled on my nipple. She slightly bites on my nipples, by which I suddenly came back to my senses and started moaning. She continued sucking and biting my nipples.

I put my hands on her bare back and my hands are moving all over her back. And she now came on top and starts kissing my neck. I caught her big ass in my hands started pressing it with all my power, and moaning due to her advances she is very wild and bite at many places on my chest and neck, but it is even aroused me more. I had started moaning loudly, and said to her "yes baby, you r the best, you are very hot," and she just smiled and continue her bites and liking on my neck. I just removed my hands from her ass and started opening the hooks of her bra but they are too, tight, and in that aroused stat I was unable to open them, so I just pull the bra straps so hard that the hooks are broken, and then she quickly removes the bra from her body.

Then she stands up and removed her jeans, now she is standing in front of me in just a panty. She looked like an angel come directly from heaven into my bed, 36" 28" 38 figure, and milky fare colour of her body made me crazy. I just pulled her towards me and then push her on my side on the bed. Then I came over her and took her one boob in my mouth and other in my one hand. I started sucking her boobs one by one vigorously and she started moaning in loud voice, ummh, aahh yessss and shouted, "continue you asshole, suck them properly, don't bite them, you asshole."

My other hand went to her panty and I started removing her panty with my one hand, she pushed her hips upwards to help me. I left the boobs for a moment and remove her panty in one jerk. The gates of heaven were open to me.

She crossed her legs, to hide her love spot and for the first time in all this I have seen her turn shy. She looks even more beautiful while blushing, her cheeks turned red and dimples formed on them that looked very beautiful. I separated her legs and to take a clear view of her swollen pink lips of her pussy. It was thin was small and it looks like a virgin pussy, a lot of water flowed through her vagina. I quickly removed my shorts and underwear in one jerk; put my dick on her love hole, both of us moaned by feeling the contact of each other's love tools for first time. I started sucking her lips and said to her in low voice, "I love you darling, promise me you will never leave me like your friend."

She: I love you too, and I will never leave you, my darling.

We lip locked again, she inserted her tongue, in my mouth, and I inserted my dick in her wet pussy. Her pussy is very tight, and my dick had not entered inside her in the first push, then I properly set my dick and inserted it with a powerful jerk, she shouted but her voice didn't come out because I had locked her mouth with mine. We orgasm together within few minutes, I had cummed deep inside her, and we both started kissing each other.

9. Movie time

I had sex with my sister-in-law when she was just 18 years old. It was not a one side attraction but a mutual understanding. After that I have had sex many times but could never forget those great moments with my sweet sister-in-law. Saroj was a god damn virgin at the time when I tore her apart. Let me describe her first, she has a very pink complexion, height 5'7"(I love tall girls) with a great slim body with amazing hard and big boobs. I had never seen such a body before and possibly will never see. She had a great curve, with small but inviting breasts and a round well shaped ass.

My wife was in the hospital to give birth to another son of us. I am very horny and therefore I use to watch XXX movies in her absence and sometimes masturbate. One day when she was in my house with her parents, I felt that someone is peeping in my bedroom through the window opening in the back corridor or my house. Though the window was closed as it was damn hot outside and the air-conditioner was running on a high speed but the curtain was slightly opened from one side and through that gap my sweet sister-in-law managed to peep in. There was a dressing table with a big mirror, close to that window which made me able to see that she was watching the movie. She was not able to see me as it was a little bit darker inside given the curtains. That time I was damn horny and watching an anal fucking scene was my favourite.

My rock hard and naughty dick was in my hand and I was rubbing on it slowly. I slowly got up and turn on the light inside the bedroom. Immediately, she ran away towards the front side of the house. But I was sure that she will come again. Again, I started masturbating my nasty dick. After a while again I sensed that she is behind that window and this time she was able to see me masturbating. Now I was going to be mad as I knew that my pink sweet sister-in-law is watching me masturbating and I cummed immediately, I exploded my thick, hot and huge cum on my thighs. I could easily see an interesting look into her brown shining eyes. She seemed to be drowsy and I was sure that she got her pink pussy wet. When she saw that I finished my job and was about to get up she again ran away, scared. I could see her watching her BASTARD brother-in-law. But I have seen what she was doing behind the window.

I was attracted to her after that hide and seek. I had decided that I would have her if not now then later but I never wanted to use. I wanted to make her so horny that she falls into my lap by herself and therefore I started showing her xxx movies whenever she comes at my place, in the same manner that I just slid the curtain of my window to let someone peep into my bedroom. When she would come to my place, I would look at her with a smile and just give her a small gesture to come to my window. It was like a silent agreement between her and me which she understood. She saw the movies for several times.

After that Saroj had seen me peaking at her many times and always she used to give me that heart-melting smile. I thought that she was attracted to me but kept my thought myself. But one day in a birthday party I managed to talk to her I went to a corner where she was standing alone. At first, I talked to her on general topics and immediately I changed the topic and told her that I have seen her peeing into my bed room. She seemed embarrassed and wanted to leave but immediately I told her that I didn't mind that and also if she likes to watch those movies, I could arrange for her when she will come to my house again. She looked a bit relaxed but left immediately and mixed up with others. During that party she looked at me several times and smiled. Once she came closer to me and whispered that her summer vacations will start after two days and she will try to come to my house but she was scared of her parents. I consoled her and said you don't have to worry I'll arrange something. Whilst coming back to my home I asked my mother-in-law to leave Saroj at my home due to her summer vacation and she agreed. I had to spend two days, which were like two years to me. But when the day came, I still remember it was a Saturday, in the evening she came with her parents. She was looking gorgeous in a blue lawn print shalwar, Kameez. As she entered into my house, she gave me a look that I thought my breath would stop. Her parents left for their home after taking dinner and told me to help her to complete her "homework" which I promised happily. In the night, my wife asked her to sleep with her and that was a terrible moment but there was no other way but to wait for a chance. Don't ask me how did I spend that night in my bed as she was sleeping just a yards away from me in my mom's room.

Next day, the Sunday my wife told me that she wants to go for some shopping she asked Saroj to come along with her but she convinced her that she has to do some homework first. I told the driver to take my wife to the shopping centre. There was no one else except my wife at home. My heart was pumping with such a great speed that one could easily see it. As soon my wife left, I immediately took Saroj into my bedroom, turned on the AC and inserted a xxx movie into my VCR. I offer my sweet sister-in-law to sit beside me on the bed. I turned off all the lights and the climate of the bedroom turned romantic. As the movie started, I have seen the impression on the fact of Saroj were changing. For the first time I saw her so closer and my horny and nasty dick was rock hard on its full length. I was wearing a boxer short and a T-shirt. I had no patience left in me but thought to act wise. During the movie I started talking to her. She told me that she is still a virgin but had seen and read about sex. I told her not to worry I'll be very careful. She also told me that she was really impressed with my decent personality and is feeling embarrassed to be with me in this condition. I told her that don't think on that was just presumed that we are good friends. I praised her and said that if you were not my sister-in-law, I would have married her (it was the peak of my Bastard plan). I slowly put my arm around her shoulder and pressed her towards me. She was talking to me but her eyes were still on the TV screen where a hunk was eating a pink and wet pussy. She started shaking as I pressed her tightly into my broad chest. I asked her whether she wanted me to lick she didn't say anything but closed her eyes and moaned like a kitten. I asked her to remove her clothes as I was losing my control.

She helped me in removing off her clothes and knowledgeably she had not worn any panties or bra. Oh my, my here she was naked in front of me, she was marvellous, not a single spot on her whole body, she was burning like a heater. She was pink, soft, hot, neat and clean. Her pink pussy was neat and clean, her pussy lips were squeezing into each other. Her pink breasts were like small rocks and the nipples were erected. I could not resist any more and started sucking hungrily on her tits without even undressing. Saroj moaned a bit as she felt the first mouth on her tit. I kept on shifting her tits in my mouth. All the while my hands were playing with her tight pussy and I could feel the heat in my groins. My dick was straining against my short and would have made a hole if not Saroj had asked me to remove my short. I very impatiently tore open my short and T-shirt. My cock swung majestically in the air. Saroj could not take her eyes of the first dick of her life. Seeing it she must have thought that how was she going to take such a monster in her virgin hole. She held my cock in her hands. I told her to suck it but she hesitated. I showed her the woman in the movie hungrily sucking the cock of the hunk. After coaxing for a long time, she became ready to suck on my cock. She removed her tongue out and licked the tip of my mushroom. She later took her tongue back. Then after taking a deep breath, she put my dick into her mouth, first an inch then other and finally almost the whole of it. She removed my dick out of her mouth slowly and put it in back. Then she gave me the greatest blow job of my life. As I was about to cum, I told her to remove her mouth off my dick and as soon she removed her mouth, I cummed all over her face and breasts.

She went to the toilet to wash herself. When she came back, she looked even sexier as she had wet her beautiful curly hairs. I grabbed her by the hair and our lips met. She was kissing for the first time so she seemed a little inexperienced. But I touch my tongue through her lips and our tongues met. I pushed her on the bed, and jumped myself. Then I spread her legs as far as I could and put my cock slowly into her cunt. She let a scream as the head of my cock entered her. Slowly and steadily, I put the whole of my cock into her. She was very tight as she was a virgin and this made my dick ache but that increased the pressure more. Saroj kept on screaming for some time but later thought of enjoying the feeling of being fucked and coordinated with every thrust of mine. Slowly I could feel the pressure on my groin. But I didn't want to make her pregnant and like, seeing no other alternative left I told her to suck my dick. When I took my dick out of her pussy, I could easily see the something red coming out of her pussy's lips, she was so involved that she didn't notice. She obliged like a pet dog and started sucking me. I came in her mouth and thought that she would spit the cum away but to my surprise she drank every drop of it. Happy with what she had done to me I licked her into her orgasm and believe me her juice tasted just like nectar.

Whilst licking her pink, neat and clean pussy I again got a hard on (I really have a nasty dick). Now, it was the time to fuck my favourite hole, yes, ass hole. But I knew that she is just 18 and quiet young to be fucked in the ass hole but I couldn't help doing that.

It was good that she was not aware of what is wrong with an ass hole fucking. I applied lot of oil on my dick and asked her to turn over. At first, I showed her an ass hole fucking shot in the movie and made her curious. As she bent over and brought her ass hole just in front of my jumping dick I put it on her tight ass hole, at first, I rubbed it gently on her ass hole. Then slowly I pushed it inside her ass, she screamed with a pain and tried to get rid of it but now that time had passed as I was going to be crazy to dig into her ass hole. I thrusted my dick with a great power and it went deep down into her ass hole. She started shouting, I stopped a little while to make her to recover from that severe pain, then slowly and gradually I started pushing my dick in and out.

After a couple of jerks, she stopped shouting and started moaning and that was the time to increase my speed. I became wild and fucked her ass hole with my full speed. It was so tight and hot that I couldn't stay for a long time and burst my think deep down into her virgin ass hole. I could see the something red pooling around my dick. But it was not a time to concentrate on that. I knew that, this is only for the first time I could see red that is a real pleasure for a horny and ass hole crazy man like me. After that both of us took showers and I asked her to bring her books and sit in the drawing room just to pretend to my wife that she was studying. Only I knew that what she learnt today. She stayed for a week and during that we fucked several times, whenever we got a chance.

10. Taking a married woman on her marital bed

It took me some time to track Saroj down. Finally, I got the name of a village where she is supposedly staying now. Looking it up on the map, I realized it was about half a day's bus journey away and there was only one bus that went near that village. I would have to take the afternoon bus from Kolkata which would reach a nearby city in the evening. From the bus station there, I would have to be lucky to find a rickshaw to her village – and hopefully her house. And if I was unlucky that she wasn't there anymore, well, then I would have to find some way back.

One day, after tying up some business in Kolkata, I took the afternoon bus. It was a long and tiring ride, but finally we reached the city that was closest to Saroj's village. All along I wondered how Saroj would look like now. I was now thirty, so she would now be thirty-five. Would she still be chubby and attractive and have a fantastic rack that I had loved to lick? Would she remember me, how she had caught me peeking at her in the shower one afternoon, and had proceeded to slap me, before letting me lick and kiss her feet? Would she recall how one day she made me sit on the couch, and then plonked her butt on my face, and pushed me to lick her asshole? Would Saroj recall how, one day, pleased at my obedience to her, she finally allowed me to suck and fondle her huge set of jugs, before giving me a blowjob that I had dreamed of ever since I started to ogle and stalk her? My cock tingled slightly at my thoughts, and I hastily decided to sleep on the ride.

It was evening when I reached the city. I didn't have anything on me except an overnight bag with a change of clothes and my laptop, and also a bag containing some gifts for Saroj. Immediately I descended and started to look for a rickshaw. There were a couple of empty ones; one driver saw me and approached.

"Sir, where do you want to go?"

I looked at him; he was an old man, probably fifty or fifty-five. He was short, and thin, with a scraggly white beard; but he looked fit enough to pull the rickshaw. I gave him the name of Saroj's village and a smile appeared on his face.

"Sir! That's my village! I live there. It's only 25 minutes away. Let me take you there. My name is Pankaj."

We negotiated on a price and were off. As he cycled, my thoughts turned to one evening when I was nineteen. Saroj had just baked some cookies for guests we were to have later that night, and I had come home early and tried to sneak one out. She had come into the kitchen and caught me, hand in the cookie jar.

"Now, now, darling, what do we have here?" Saroj smiled as I froze. She then caught hold of me by the ear and led me away to my room, and closed the door.

Saroj quickly stripped off her sari and petticoat and rolled down her panties, so she was naked waist down. She then grabbed my ears and twisted hard.

"So dear," She said mockingly, "You want cookies, eh? Now you can kiss my big ass and beg for your cookie."

I crawled around her back and planted several wet kisses on her butt cheeks and asking, "Oh Saroj! Can I have a cookie please?"

"Not on my bum, you idiot! Kiss my asshole." Saroj yelled.

I immediately started pecking at Saroj's asshole with my lips as she fingered herself.

"Alright, enough!" Saroj commanded. She then pushed me away and sat down on my bed, and parted her legs.

"Lick me, love."

I meekly obeyed her. My cock was sticking straight out and swaying sideways. Saroj knew I was so horny; I would do anything she ordered – which was the usual state of affairs anyway. My only reward was that at the end of it, Saroj would allow me to suck her boobs and give me a blowjob. Throughout my two-year affair with Saroj, she never allowed me to cum inside her - she had always said she was saving herself for her husband.

Suddenly there was a bump on the road, and my thoughts of my past as the fuck toy of my beautiful maid was broken. Immediately I was brought back to the present.

"Careful!" I ordered the rickshaw driver Pankaj. "Go slowly!"

After some time, I asked Pankaj, "I am looking for a woman named Saroj from your village, do you know where she lives?"

I could see Pankaj freeze. "Sir, what do you need with Saroj?"

"Oh, he knows her, perhaps." I thought.

Aloud, I replied, "She used to be a maid in the employment of my father, a long time ago. I have come to see how she is."

"Oh!" Pankaj resumed pedalling, coughing a sick cough as the road became uphill. "Sir, Saroj is my begum (wife), I am her husband."

A pang of regret immediately flooded me. If Saroj was now married, she would hardly agree to return with me to Kolkata to be my maid, and she would surely want to forget her past. I could see my fantasies of Saroj and me, alone in a mansion in Kolkata for days, go up in smoke. I didn't say anything, as Pankaj cycled on and on until we were standing in front of a hut. He was tired and wheezing when he stopped in front of his residence.

It was a small hut, poorly constructed, made of mud and had a thatched straw roof. Inside were probably just two rooms – a main room to receive guests and a bedroom for the couple. A small kitchen was adjacent to the hut. Like all village houses, the bathroom was a little bit of walk away, in a stall by itself.

"Salman!" Suddenly a shout of delight rang through the air as Saroj opened the door and spotted me. She straight away ran past her husband and enveloped me in a bear hug. My face was crushed against her boobs as she held my head in her hands and sloppily kissed my cheeks.

"Oh, Salman, darling! Smooch! Smooch! It's really you. Smooch! Smooch! Oh, my goodness, I never thought I would see you again. Smooch! Smooch!" She covered my face with wet kisses and pressed my lips to her chest. I drunk in her smell and sweat in ecstasy as I too hugged her back, wrapping my hands around her waist and giving her butts a squeeze.

Mmm! Her boobs smelled lovely. I drew my head back, giving her a big smile, and then kissed her a big sloppy kiss on each of her cheeks, before giving her ass a pinch. She squealed in delight. I noticed that her husband remained standing on the door steps, silently watching and saying nothing as I now openly groped his wife.

Saroj was the same. Her hair had greyed just a bit, but she retained her firm fat figure, her big butts and her ample bosom. With age, her face seemed to have become even more beautiful, though Saroj still retained the plump squeezable cheeks. Her breasts were still round, sharp and shapely – and of course – huge. Her buttocks seemed to have become even bigger, more fleshy, firmer and absolutely delightful.

She was dressed in a simple cotton sari, worn the way I remembered - loose, clasped to one side exposing her big belly and the navel, with her blouse one size too small, barely able to contain the big melons hiding beneath. Though the pallu of her sari covered her chest, due to their large size, I could see her jugs protruding and juggling beneath her pallu as she bounced about in greeting me.

"Come, come, Salman, come on inside!" She gave me a little bow and invited me into her house.

"Husband!" Her tone changed to a command one as she turned to her husband. "Get Salman's bag and bring it in. Don't just stand there!"

"Yes, dear." I noticed her husband meekly respond. Pankaj picked up my overnight bag and we followed Saroj into her abode. I kept my eyes on her shapely buns, and noticed to my delight that her sari had ridden up her ass crack, just like old times.

It was a very simple dwelling. It was clear that Pankaj did not make much as a rickshaw driver and I noticed several gifts from ours to Saroj – such as curtains and an old television set – adorning the hut. We sat down on some raised cushions, set on a mat on the floor in the living room. A small partition separated the bedroom from the living room.

"What are you doing here, darling? Are you staying nearby?" Saroj asked, as she plonked down next to me.

"I am here for two days," I replied. "I came to this village to see you actually. I haven't yet made any arrangements to stay, so I have to still go and do that…"

"Oh, Salman, stay here! Two days and you want to go to a hotel! Stay here!" Saroj pleaded, jumping forward and clasping my hand. "I don't have much, but I will treat you like a king. Oh, do please say yes, my fuck toy!"

I noticed that Saroj hadn't lost her potty mouth in the intervening years.

"Well, I...." I hesitated. I didn't really want to stay in this slum, but then I realized Saroj, while holding on to my hand, was gently stroking the underneath with a finger. I looked up to her chubby face and saw a smile. And then she winked at me.

"Oh, do stay, Salman! I promise you two very memorable days! It will be just like old times!"

That did it for me. I liked old times with Saroj.

"Oh, why not? Thank you Saroj. I will stay with you."

"Perfect." Saroj grinned.

I looked around the small place. "But where will I sleep?"

Saroj turned around to look at her husband. "Husband! Salman needs to sleep comfortably. So, he and I will sleep on the bed in the bedroom. You will get your stuff and sleep here on the floor in this room. So, take his overnight bag and put it in our bedroom and put your clothes out here."

Pankaj started to say something but one glare from Saroj shut him up. Instead, he timidly replied, "Of course dear."

Wow, I thought, I must be dreaming. Here was Saroj informing her husband that he would be sleeping on the floor of his own house, while his buxom wife would be sleeping with me, in his house, on his marital bed, right in the next room, and he was accepting it. And what did Saroj have in mind? I looked at the thin straw partition separating the bedroom from this room. The bedroom wasn't even a different room, just another space behind the partition. There was no door. You would be able to hear everything that went on inside the room.

I felt Saroj give my arm another squeeze, and she winked again, before standing up. So did my wiener.

"Husband, where are your manners? You have a guest; we have to give him food and drinks. Get up!" She nudged her husband with a foot, who immediately got up and obediently picked up my bag to place on their bed, before going to the kitchen.

"Darling," Saroj turned to me and beamed me a lascivious smile. "Would you like to change?"

"Yes, I would," I answered. "I have a set of clothes in this bag." I stood up too.

"Please go to our room and change your clothes, Salman. It's your house now, please feel free. And honey," Saroj slightly bent forward so I could stare down at her ample cleavage. "Feel free to use anything in this house, dear. Anything. All we have here is yours to use."

As she said "anything", I saw Saroj grab her left boob through her blouse and give her the nipple a slight tweak. She stuck out a tongue, winked at me and licked her lips seductively, before disappearing into the kitchen. Damn! Merely ten minutes after meeting Saroj, and I already had a huge hard on!

I walked into the bedroom. As I said, it wasn't really a room, just a bed behind a partition. There was a small wardrobe, an old dressing table whose colours were faded with age, on top of which was placed some simple jewellery. A mirror was taped to the wall on one side of the bed. If you sat down on the bed and looked into the mirror, you could see the partition reflected. I could even see into the kitchen if I looked hard enough into the mirror, where Saroj was busy running about.

My bag was on the bed. I opened it and changed into a T-shirt and a pair of soft, silky shorts. Tired from my trip, I sat down on the bed. It creaked! I looked at it in alarm, but it was OK. The noise was merely from old joints and a really old mattress with springs that were past their sell by age. Every move on the bed made the springs creak.

"Did you find everything alright?" I saw Saroj standing at the entrance to the room, a spatula in her hand. "I am making some kebabs for you."

"Yes," I replied. "Saroj, I need to pee. If you can tell me where the bathroom is …"

"I will show you. Give me a minute." She disappeared into the kitchen, probably to return the spatula to its proper place, and reappeared with a small torch in her hand. "Come," She grabbed my hand, "let's go to the bathroom."

We stepped out from the backdoor. It was now quite dark. It would be a full moon night, but the moon wasn't out yet. As in any village hut, the latrine was a few yards away from the house. It was just a commode surrounded by four walls, and open to the sky. Saroj lit the torch and led the way, my hands clasped in hers.

"Here," She opened the door and pointed at the toilet. "Salman, there is no light here, so I will have to stand here with the torch, with the door open. You don't mind peeing from your wee wee in front of old me, do you?" She grinned.

"Of course not, Saroj." I gave her a sudden hug, surprising her. Unable to control myself, I started to kiss her cheeks and paw at her breasts.

"Now, now, darling, control yourself." Saroj laughed. "Such a behaviour would have definitely NOT gotten you a blowjob in the old days."

"Oh, I love you, you sexy bitch, you!" I gushed out. "I love the old days …"

"Oh my, calling me a bitch!" Saroj raised her eyebrows, before bursting out laughing. "Clearly you need some control, darling!"

She pointed at the commode, and then commanded in a stern voice, "Salman, pee!"

I walked into to the toilet and got out of my shorts. Saroj moved the torch and shone a beam of my light on my penis, giggling. Holding my soldier in my hand, I aimed and started to pee. The urine came out in a long spurt, splashing against the hole on the ground. Saroj smiled as she saw what she had seen many a time before – me standing in front of her, naked, and peeing while she watched. When I was done, Saroj showed me where the water was so I cleaned myself and rubbed my hands on a rag that was hanging. I then put on my shorts again.

Saroj suddenly shut off the torch. Immediately it was very, very dark. I felt her press against me, pushing me against the wall. Her breasts were on either side on my face as she crushed me hard. Her hands rubbed against my bulge, going inside my shorts and caressing my manhood. She grabbed my balls and gave me a quick squeeze, making me draw my breath. And then she stepped back.

Smack!

She had slapped me!

It was just like old times. Smack! And then another Smack! I could feel my cheeks stinging, and I blushed deeply in the dark. Smack! Smack!

And just as suddenly, she stepped back and switched on the torch again.

"Come, lover boy, we are getting late for dinner."

A few minutes later we sat down again on the floor, on top of some mats, for dinner. It was evident that there was not much food in the house. I noticed Pankaj was "setting the table", placing the dishes on the ground on the mats and bringing out the spoons. Dinner was lentils, some bread and vegetables. For me, Saroj made some kebabs, the only meat on the menu.

"The kebabs are for you, Salman." She announced. I noticed Pankaj made no move for the meat. "I know you like these."

"Oh thank you, Saroj." I grabbed a couple of the kebabs. "Pankaj, why don't you have some as well?"

I noticed Pankaj glance at Saroj, who shook her head.

"No, Sir, they are for you." He smiled nervously and lied, "I don't eat meat at night."

"Here," Saroj poured me more lentils. I realized by now that Saroj, while commanding her husband around, never took his name, like any respectful Indian wife, instead referring to him as "husband".

"I am sending Husband to the market tomorrow morning for foodstuff." Saroj told me. "Is there anything I should get especially for you?"

Pankaj turned to his wife. "But, dear," He started hesitantly. "I … I … I have to work tomorrow. You know with the debt and all…"

"Husband!" Saroj almost hissed at him. "Whether you go to work tomorrow is not for you to decide! My former master is here and as long as he is here, we have to take care of him completely! We have to make his stay completely satisfactory! You are to be at Sir's beck and call from now on."

"Yes, dear." Poor Pankaj's week just got harder.

"Enough food for you tonight." Saroj grabbed his plate which still had half a bread on it. "Go get me some pen and paper. I want to make a list."

"Yes dear." Pankaj stood up, washed his hands in the kitchen while Saroj ate his bread. I felt bad for him, as he came back with some pen and paper, while I was finishing off the kebabs.

"Good thing he studied till Grade 7." Saroj told me, while putting some more bread and lentils on my plate, as Pankaj stood to one side like a faithful dog. "At least he can read, and is good for something."

I hunted in my shorts and found some money. I gave it to Pankaj – "for tomorrow", I told him. His eyes bulged – this was more money than he made in a week. Immediately I noticed his attitude to the whole situation suddenly became less grumpy.

"What a lackey," I thought. "I am going spend the night with your wife on your bed, and the sight of my pocket change makes you happy."

Saroj made a list, and I added some more items to it and she gave it to Pankaj.

"Salman and I will probably not go to sleep until late at night," She informed Pankaj, making my dick rise in anticipation as to "what" we would be doing until we went to sleep. "So we may wake up late tomorrow. You are to wake up early, cut the vegetables and onions so we can make our breakfast when we wake up. And then you will go to the market to get this list. Go early so you get the best stuff."

"Yes dear." Pankaj promised her. "I would go very early."

"Good, now clear these dishes. Sir," Saroj giggled as she called me by what her husband called me, "Come this way and you can wash up."

Soon, I was ready for bed. I saw Pankaj in the bedroom and followed him there. He was picking up a blanket from the cupboard and then his pillow.

"How will I sleep without a pillow?" I told him. "There will only be one pillow left. Surely you don't want me to share the pillow with your wife?' I asked him with a grin.

"Of course not, Sir." He croaked, dropping the pillow back on the bed that I would soon be sharing with his wife. "I will find some clothes to pack into a pillow for me."

"Pankaj," I instructed him as he was about to leave. "Why don't you get my overnight bag. There's a packet there. I have some gifts for your wife. Be careful not to scratch the laptop."

Dutifully Pankaj took out a polythene packet from my bag.

"Why don't you take the items out and put it on the bed?" I told him. "It's a few items I picked up for your spouse."

"Yes of course, Sir." He was the ever-dutiful servant and host.

I continued to watch, silently laughing. Pankaj hesitated as he picked out a white brassiere from the bag and put it on the bed. Then he brought out satin lingerie and it too went on the bed. He continued to empty another couple of bras and then a few panties on the bed from the bag.

"What do you think?" I picked up one of the bras and held it out. "Do you think it will fit her?"

"I... I... I think so." Pankaj stammered, looking extremely uncomfortable.

I stretched out the bra, "Do you think it's too large, Pankaj? No ... I don't think so. Your wife does have large boobs, right?"

"I... I... yes, Sir."

I enjoyed his discomfort, and picked up a panty.

"What about this Pankaj? Do you think her butts will fit into these?"

"Y... yes, Sir." Pankaj was now sweating. I noticed he had developed a bulge in his lungi.

So, my guess was right – he was a pervert who enjoyed the thought of his wife with another man. Or at least another man talking about his wife's big boobs and butts.

"Hmm," I picked up another bra. "This should go well in contrast with her skin complexion, what do you think? She is a little dark around the nipple..."

What Pankaj thought I wouldn't know, as he was saved from answering by Saroj squealing in delight as she entered the room and saw the expensive under wears.

"Oh, Salman! These are for me, oh thank you! Smooch! Smooch!" Saroj hugged and kissed my cheeks. "These look great!" She dropped her pallu and her sari soon fell on the floor, so she was just dressed in a blouse and petticoat, her belly and navel exposed for all to see. Pankaj gulped as Saroj picked up the bra and held it on top of her blouse.

"Oh, it fits perfectly! Thank you darling!" She kissed me again, and then, with her arms around me, turned to chastise her husband.

"Learn from him, husband! He knows how to give proper gifts to a woman! When was the last time you bought me something nice like this?"

"I am sorry dear..." Pankaj started to say something, but Saroj would not hear it.

"Get out!" She ordered her husband out of their bedroom. "Your Sir and I want to sleep now. Go!"

Pankaj left the room to make his bed on the other side of the partition. Saroj turned to me. "Salman, do you want me to wear one of these?" She pointed at my gifts.

I bit my tongue. What was I to say? Let me explain.

For the longest time I wanted to fuck Saroj. She was a constant presence in my wet dreams and many a times I had jacked off to her. Yet, while she had been our maid, and we continued to have our sexual trysts, she clearly wore the pants in that affair. I was used strictly for her pleasure. What I got out of that relationship was seeing a beautiful goddess like her in the nude, and having the good fortune to suck on her tits and kiss her gigantic ass, and when she allowed me to paw her breasts. She always permitted me to cum and sometimes, when she was in a good mood, even gave me a blow job, but it was always after I had managed to satisfy her.

She would find the slightest excuse to call me names or ridicule me. Whenever my parents were out and we were alone in the house, I knew she would call me to her room. And slap me. Or command me to lick her cunt. Or kiss her feet. I was never, never, never to fuck her. And after she humiliated me and made me lick her or finger her to an orgasm, that's when she would show mercy on me. If I asked, she would stroke me and make me cum in a condom, or gift me a blowjob. But those were rare and it never got further.

A few times while we were in the house, I had gotten bold and had pawed her breasts and hugged and kissed her – like I did tonight at the bathroom – but all those times I got punished and slapped – just like today. So now, the situation seemed uncanny.

Here was Saroj, seemingly eager to please me, offering to put on some sexy lingerie. What would I say?

Seeing my silence, Saroj grinned. "Oh, don't worry lover boy. We have two nights together. I can wear these tomorrow."

Saying that, she gathered my gifts, walked over to the cupboard and placed them there. Then she turned off the light. The room was suddenly dark, but not completely. The moon had risen now, and cast a soft white glow inside the room. I could clearly see and make out objects close to me.

I jumped into the bed on one side and waited. Saroj plugged in a night lamp. It cast a small soft blue glow, enabling me to see Saroj's beautiful plump figure as she sashayed to the bed and climbed in. We both lay facing each other, smiling.

"You look beautiful," I told her, and moved forward and kissed her on her lips. I waited for a resounding slap, but it didn't come, so I kissed her again and stepped back.

"Thank you," Saroj beamed. "You look great too. You have grown tall, kept in shape, and are now a handsome young man!"

We kissed again, this time hugging each other tightly and I felt her tongue probe deep inside me.

"Saroj," I whispered, as we came up for air, "What about Pankaj?

He is right next door, and can hear everything!" I spoke softly so as not to be overheard.

"Oh, don't worry about him." Saroj informed me, as her hands gently stroked my cheek. "Pretend he is not here in this house. My husband will not dare set foot in this room now, Sir."

This was said quite loudly, and I am sure Pankaj heard it. I looked at Saroj's body, now bathed in the moonlight. Her hair was loose, and lying across her breasts. Her face was a little sweaty from the work she had done in the kitchen, and she hadn't taken a bath before lying down for the night. The pallu had gone to one side and her right breast was protruding from under her white blouse. I stared at her tits and her round figure. Her smell was intoxicating me.

"Oh my maid, my sexy goddess, I want to make love to you." I told her.

"Salman," She replied. "Don't make love to me. FUCK me."

That did it. I pulled away her pallu, un-hooked the blouse, and pushed her white bra up to expose her large round breasts, the big black areolas standing erect. I played with the right breast, squeezing and pinching it, rotating the nipple between my thumb and fingers, then sucked on it.

"Mmm...mmmm...." Saroj began to moan loudly.

I threw my arms around her and again kissed her deeply; she responded by hugging me around my neck and offering me her tongue to suck. Her unwashed body smelt sweaty and was highly intoxicating. I had to fight to control myself to not cum. I kissed and licked her face, eyes, lips, nose, nibbling her earlobes and biting her neck. I unclipped her bra completely and freed her heavy breasts, pinching, biting and sucking on them.

Saroj was now moaning loudly, completely lost in throes of passion. As I suckled her boob, a movement in the mirror caught my eye. I grinned. There was a small hole in the partition, and

I could see Pankaj hiding himself in the shadows, watching me enjoy his wife, with his pecker out. Wanker! I decided we should put on a show for his benefit.

"You," I decided to be bold, and took a chance. In a commanding voice, I ordered Saroj, "Stand up and lift up your petticoat and show me what colour panties you are wearing."

The bed creaked as Saroj got off and lifted her petticoat to her waist, revealing her smooth chubby dark brown thighs and black panty, which had a damp wet patch on the front. I asked her to turn around and kneel on the floor and lower the panty over her bottom, with the petticoat rucked up over her back.

I marvelled at Saroj's voluptuous buttocks, and told her to pull her cheeks apart and show me her black hairy cunt and anus. She looked back at me, smiling. My dreams were being realized, finally! Here was the object of my fantasy, the wife of another man, revealing her inner most secrets to me, ready to submit to me the ultimate submission, and completely enjoying herself while being so wanton. I told her to stand again as I stripped her, pulling off the petticoat, blouse, and black panty. Saroj now stood in front of me completely naked and vulnerable; I embraced her pushing my crotch against her naked vagina, caressing and squeezing her arse cheeks.

I undressed completely. Living in the US I had made it a habit to go to the gym regularly, and Saroj squealed as I revealed my muscular body to her. I was proud of my big dick, and I was now rock hard, with veins in protuberance and my massive balls waiting to hammer against her milky white thighs. Saroj's eyes followed my body down until she stopped at my crotch - and a big smile enveloped her lips.

My former maid laid down on the bed on her back as I began licking her hairy pussy, making her shiver and tremble as she experienced her cunt being expertly sucked for the first time in many, many years. Her eyes were closed and she was purring as

I squeezed her breasts. Saroj arched her back to allow me easier access to pull and twist her nipples, making her wince with pleasure.

I pulled her thighs apart and positioned the thick bulbous head of my cock over her labia. I put the tip of my penis into her, then slowly pressed in a few inches, pulled out then pushed back in a bit further, pulled out again before finally penetrating her fully in one push up to my balls, causing Saroj to gasp as the air was pumped out of her body, stretching her cunt fully.

Saroj was now mumbling, "Oh Sir! I am a married woman. You have now shamed me. You have taken a married woman on her marital bed. You have taken away my honour. My husband was not man enough to stop you."

I could see Pankaj in the shadows, stroking his small wiener faster and faster as his wife called him names while being pounded by my monster cock.

Saroj was now sweating profusely, screaming and grunting loudly in time to my pounding. We were now copulating strongly; my cock fully buried inside her. I was fucking a married woman, on her marital bed, that too in front of her husband. I slammed into Pankaj's wife, causing the old bed springs to squeak and groan noisily in rhythm to our hammering.

"Saroj, I am going to cum inside you." I told Saroj as I humped her.

"Oh, Salman, it will be an honour and pleasure." Saroj murmured. "I want your sperm in me. Fill me, Salman!"

I grunted as I ejaculated, filling up her vagina with my semen till it overflowed, staining the bed sheets. Saroj grasped my balls, squeezing out as much juice as possible. I bit her neck and kept ejaculating for quite some time before finally collapsing with my full weight on her. I remained inside her for almost ten minutes, making sure my seed-soaked in. We caressed and kissed before I finally rolled off her, my cock semi-erect and still dripping cum.

I looked at my freshly fucked former maid and the object of my wettest dreams, covered in sweat and love bites on her breasts, neck and thighs, my semen oozing out of her vagina down her arse, the room reeking with the aroma of sweat and sex.

"Wow, wow." Was what Saroj repeated loudly, several times. "Wow. Now that's what I call a fucking. My husband never fucks me like that, Sir. You know how to satisfy a woman. If I knew you fucked like that, I would have let you fuck me a long time ago."

I could only grin at the compliment. Saroj's legs were still spread out, and a full ten minutes later cum was still oozing out of her pussy. Saroj moved so that she now faced me again, the cum making slosh noises as it dribbled down her thighs.

"Salman, why did you really come here?" She asked. "Did you really just come to visit me?"

"Oh yes, Saroj." I took her face in my arms and kissed her cheeks. "Actually, I have a job offer for you."

"Oh?"

"Yes, Saroj. You see, I am now a very rich man. I have a business in the USA. I also do some import work from India, so I have a mansion in Kolkata. My family lives in the USA, but I come every month to Kolkata for ten to twelve days. I need a maid to work for me there, and rather than any maid, I thought of you."

There was a pause as Saroj digested this. Seeing a little hesitation, I kissed her gently on her eyes, took her hand and placed it on my now erect again cock.

"And I am always ready to be your bitch, Saroj."

Saroj mulled over something for some time, then told me softly so only I could hear, "We will discuss this later, darling. I have to talk with my husband. He is my husband you know."

"It's all right." I told her. "You can let me know later."

"Actually," Saroj continued, this time raising her voice so that Pankaj could hear. "My husband has a huge debt. He is a useless man, really. He gambled and lost and gambled again and lost. Now day and night we work hard to be a little less poor. He is really not a man. He lied to my parents by pretending to be well off when he was always borrowing money and always in debt, and he could never satisfy me in bed, darling."

This was said quite loudly and I could imagine Pankaj in the next room flushing in humiliation.

I responded by placing my hands between her legs, rubbing her clit.

"Salman," Saroj commanded. "Take me again. Fuck me. Enjoy me. Play with me."

"My pleasure, you sexy randi." I told her, ready to mount her again. "You are such a whore!"

It was a bad night for Pankaj. He had to sleep in the hall listening to the bed springs creaking all night and his Saroj's constant moans and groans. All night he felt helpless and tried to stop himself from watching at his vivacious wife.

What must have been surprising to him and he knew it, was that instead of feeling anger he got an erection. He must have known that's why Saroj never respected him; she always suspected he was not a complete man. Saroj rubbed it in, as she weeps out, again and again, "Thank you for the fuck, Salman. I will do whatever you ask of me to please you. Please fuck me again, Salman. I can never get enough of you."

I must have woken him up several times. In my wildest dreams I had never imagined Saroj to be so playful and so submissive and I took full advantage. Once, Pankaj peeked and saw me slapping his wife's butts, spanking them hard and watching her rump quiver in the moonlight. The spanks left bright red marks on Saroj's butts as I called her a bitch, a slut, a whore, and she purred in delight at the insults. Other times he would wake up to the sounds of her screaming my name so loudly that Pankaj felt the whole neighbourhood would hear it, as I drilled my manhood deep inside her.

Throughout the night, I could see Pankaj repeatedly jerking off to the sight of his wife completely nude in front of another man, eagerly taking my cock in. Much later on, Saroj told me that though Pankaj was always a submissive man, and Saroj enjoyed dominating him, as she enjoyed dominating anyone, she had never cuckolded him openly. They did talk in bed about another man violating Saroj, but that was always said to spice things up. Sometimes, during sex between Pankaj and Saroj, she would take another man's name, either one of Pankaj's friends or the guy who lent him money, and pretend she was submitting to him rather than Pankaj. It always made Pankaj shoot his load in a hurry.

When I had showed up, Saroj's long dormant passions rose up radically, and this time she knew she would give in to her desires and finally cuckold her wimp of a husband. When Saroj told Pankaj she was going to share the bed with me, and Pankaj was to sleep in the next room, she was testing the waters. Saroj must never have imagined that her having sex with another man would turn Pankaj on so much that he would agree to it so meekly.

"Oh YESSS!! Ahhh! AHHH!! OH Yes!" Saroj weep as the bed began hitting the wall. I was fucking her once again. The bedsprings began squeaking furiously as she received my thrusts.

"Oooohhh! slow ....sl..o w.....please! Mmmm. Ahhhhh. No!!" The bed began hitting the wall hard and the springs sounded as if they were going to break. Saroj was grunting in short bursts as I groped her breasts, calling her a whore and bitch. Her breasts were smacking back and forth as I pushed myself in and out, in and out, in and out, in and out, in and out.

Saroj let out a tremendous noise as she climaxed on my glistening, thrusting pole. For what was probably the fifth time of the night I was squirting a good quantity of semen into Pankaj's wife. Saroj let out a long sigh as her orgasm subsided.

Pankaj too let out his pole, hardest in life, but now it was only a few drops of semen that hit the hard wood floor. He listened as we fell silent. He knew though, it would not be long before we were at it again. With a groan, he realized Saroj had wanted him to wake up early. As the bed springs began to creak once again, Pankaj tried to shut out the noise and get some sleep. For me, the night would continue long into dawn as I enjoyed his lovely wife.

Pankaj woke up early the next morning. For a second, he wondered where he was and what he was doing on the floor. Then a warm feeling of shame crept over him as he remembered the events of last night and how his wife Saroj had cuckolded him with me. Pankaj got up, walked over to the partition and peeked in.

It was merely 6 in the morning, and both Saroj and I were fast asleep. I had been tired out after a night of repeatedly fucking Pankaj's gorgeous and buxom wife, while Saroj was spent after being continuously pounded on all of her holes. Her hair was plastered to her face and there were a few mottled red patches around her neck, throat and breasts. Saroj was asleep on her belly, her naked butt exposed for all to see. Pankaj stared at the big wide seam of her buttocks hanging over the edge of the bed in the early morning light. Her clothes were all crumpled and lay on the floor to one side of the bed. Even hours after her final fuck, Saroj's naked body was sweating and glowing. Her relaxed breathing made her plump derriere rise and fall. Pankaj's loins stirred, and he took out his cock and started to rub the tip of it.

He remembered how he hid and watched my strong pounding of his wife, of Saroj's fleshy buttocks quivering and wobbling as she was being continually mounted. The sounds of the rhythmic creaking of the bed frame as she was repeatedly penetrated rang in his ears, as did the humiliation of his wife's unfaithfulness and arousal for other man. What excited Pankaj more was that he himself had allowed her, by not stopping her. Both Saroj and I, her lover, knew he, her husband, was in the next room, and we didn't care. As Pankaj remembered the increasing squeaking of the bedsprings, he began to stroke his rigid tool furiously, until he came in his lungi.

Ashamed at his inadequacy, Pankaj cleaned the area and began to attend to his tasks. Mindful of Saroj's orders, Pankaj freshened up, went to the henhouse to collect the eggs, and then chopped up the vegetables and other materials that would be used later by his wife to make me breakfast. He made himself a simple meal of milk and bread, and was off to the market.

I woke up late – it was almost 10 in the morning. Bright white sunlight streamed into the window. I turned over and hugged Saroj, who began to stir awake as well. I took in her curvaceous figure, squeezed her big tits and gave her round arse a big smack, making it jiggle. Saroj giggled.

"Salman, we have one whole day. There will be time for my butts later." Saying this, she got up and went to freshen up in the washroom. I also stood up. My cock throbbed; I needed to pee and Saroj was in the bathroom. I stormed out of the house, down the back alleyway and to the latrine. The door was slightly ajar, and I pushed it open and entered.

Saroj was naked, squatting on the toilet, peeing. She looked up in surprise, but when she saw it was me, she relaxed and continued to urinate. I waited until she was done. Saroj got up and started to dress. I unzipped my shorts. Saroj watched as my hot salty piss gushed out, meeting her own urine at the bottom of the commode, two becoming one.

We both walked back to the house. Anyone watching from next door would have seen Saroj and another man who was clearly not her husband emerge from the lavatory together. Luckily, there was no one around.

As we entered the house, Saroj made a move to the kitchen, but I grabbed her round behind and started to grope and massage her tits and ass. She responded by inserting her hands into my shorts, and playing with my cock and balls. At that moment I noticed that Pankaj was coming up the pathway. He had of course heard his wife's wanton noises. Saroj moaned uninhibitedly and loudly as I pawed at her breasts. Pankaj crept to one window to the side of the house, where he could hide in the bushes and watch. I of course noticed his reflection in one of the mirrors and grinned.

I made Saroj kneel in front of me, grabbing her by her hair and pushing her down. As Pankaj watched, I lowered my shorts so that it fell to my ankles. I was now naked from the waist down, and rubbed the tip of my prick over his wife's eyes, nose and lips before placing it in her mouth. I bent down and whispered into her ears so only she could hear, "Your husband's watching us from a window, and wanking off."

Her eyes glistened, and she nodded.

"My whore," I asked her loudly. "Who has the bigger cock, Pankaj or me?"

"Mmmm.. mmmm" Saroj was in heaven as she licked my penis up and down. "Salman, my husband is at least 2 inches smaller than yours! You are a real man!"

I laughed. "My tool can reach parts of you that your husband's never been."

Knowing Pankaj was silently watching as I was pleasured by his wife, I ordered Saroj to give me an early morning blowjob.

"Baby," I told her affectionately, "how about you suck my cock and give me a blowjob before breakfast?"

"Thank you Salman, I will do as you say. I never give my husband a blowjob." Saroj confided to me loudly. "But for you, darling, I will do anything! You are welcome to all of me!"

Saroj's big eyes widened as I tried to push my snake down her throat, her dark lips stretching wide, cheeks bulging. Before last night, for the last ten years or so, she had never sucked a cock that large before. She held my manhood and kneaded my balls. Pulling her hair, I began fucking her face, "Baby, you make a very nice cum dump, now suck me off."

Saroj grabbed on to the base of my cock with one hand and she started to rub my balls with the other. She stroked me and felt my dick get even bigger as I pushed it into her mouth one more time. She started sucking on my penis as hard as she could while moving her head back and forth. With each thrust, my dick was able to get a little farther into her mouth and she soon felt it touching the back of her throat. Knowing Pankaj was watching, she kept sucking me harder and harder. I knew I would cum any time now.

"Mmmm... mmmmm ..." Saroj continued to moan as she sucked me.

She moved her other hand back toward my asshole and rubbed around the rim at first and then tried to push a finger inside. We could hear Pankaj's panting as he rubbed his little wiener and jacked off while watching his wife give her lover an expert blowjob. Saroj squeezed and jacked my prostrate in time with the movement of my prick into her mouth. Pankaj could not understand why, but his wife was giving her former employer the best blow job she ever gave to anyone one, and he seemed to be getting aroused as she continued with her efforts to perform this humiliating act.

In less than two minutes, I shot a big load of sperm into Saroj's inviting mouth. She knew that she had to swallow every drop of my spunk before she could expect me to take my dick out of her mouth. I continued my, in and out motion causing the last vestiges of my seed to dribble into her mouth. Her furious sucking cleaned out the last milky white drop and she let all of it go down her throat.

I pulled my dick out of Saroj's mouth and stopped when it was just in front of her face. I looked at her with an evil grin and said, "Clean it off, beautiful and don't leave a speck of anything on it."

Saroj quickly started to lick my dick to clean off any remaining traces of my orgasm. She pushed back the foreskin skin of my circumcised dick and used her tongue to clean the area under that protective skin. She deep throated me a couple of times and finally felt that she cleaned off every bit of the mess from my orgasm.

"Good!" I helped her up to her feet and whispered to her ears. "Now go outside and kiss your husband a nice, warm, salty welcome!"

Her mouth filled with my cum, Saroj wrapped the pallu around her shoulders and walked outside the house. Pankaj had just managed redo his lungi before she discovered him.

"Dear husband, you are back home!"

"Yes, dear.... I .... was...." Pankaj mumbled. Saroj threw her arms around him as if she was elated to see him, surprising Pankaj. He could see a bit of white cum between his wife's lips. Saroj kissed him deeply, pushing her sperm filled tongue into his mouth, in full view of all the neighbours. Pankaj could taste the residue of my cum and smell his own wife's cunt juices as they permeated through the air.

"My... dear... I" Pankaj gasped as Saroj let him go. She turned and walked back in without a word, and Pankaj followed her in, carrying the produce he had bought from the marketplace. Soon, we were sitting on the floor and enjoying a delicious breakfast of puris, idli, beef, omelette and tea.

"Pankaj," I spoke to Saroj's husband between mouthfuls. "I have been thinking of gifting your wife some furniture. What do you think?"

"Furniture?" His eyes went big. "Clearly you are very rich and generous, Sir."

"Yes. I have been thinking of getting you a dining table today, with some chairs, so we can sit and eat our meals. And also, a sofa set for your living room. What do you think?"

Clearly Pankaj was over the moon. Even if he didn't like the furniture, he knew he could always get rid of it for more money to pay off his debts. He clearly liked my proposal and thanked me profusely.

"Don't thank me, it's for my baby." I turned to Saroj who had just entered the room with my tea and had listened in on the conversation. "What do you think, randi(whore)?"

Here was I, in his house, eating his food and insulting his wife by calling her a randi (a prostitute), and all Pankaj could think of was his furniture.

Saroj mulled it over. "Is it needed Salman, you are already so generous with me, having given me so much happiness last night by just being here."

I noticed Pankaj almost choked on his food. I grinned.

"I like you, baby, and I want you to be in comfort." I patted and kneaded her behind in full view of her husband, and Pankaj hastily gulped down a glass of water.

"Salman is so kind hearted, is he not, husband?" Saroj turned and asked her husband, as I continued to grope and squeeze her buttocks.

"Yes, yes, dear." Poor Pankaj was almost in tears. I noticed he had a bulge in his lungi too. "Sir has indeed been very kind with us."

"Yes, husband. We must repay his kindness with our warmth. We may be poor but we have a lot of love to give him."

"Yes, dear, you are right. Sir is indeed very compassionate to us."

"A dining table and a sofa set." I decided aloud. "Saroj, what do you think about the bed? I think the bed is fine, it seemed strong last night, what do you think?"

Saroj burst into a snigger, and a very red Pankaj just stared at his shoes in shame.

As breakfast was being cleared away, I told Pankaj that I wanted him to first take me to the furniture store in the village. Then he could take me to a mall in the city, where I would buy some clothes. I was secretly planning to stay longer than the two nights I had originally planned, and I needed more sets of clothes. Then I told him he had to drop me downtown in the city, where I had some work, and pick me up later. I would have lunch in the city, and return home in time for dinner.

"Yes, Sir." Pankaj kept nodding obediently. He went out to pump air into the rickshaw tires.

As I dressed and got ready to go out, and Pankaj was away in the yard where he could not hear us, I pulled Saroj into the bedroom and asked her in a soft voice about Pankaj's loan. A plan was forming in my mind. When Saroj replied it was ₹2,00,000, I thanked my lucky stars. That amount of money was a mountain for a rickshaw driver, but pocket change for me. My wife bought saris on a single shopping trip, each worth twice that. Very briefly, I told Saroj about my plan, and she giggled like a college girl. She agreed to it immediately, as I knew she would. I gave her a kiss on each cheek for being such a sweetheart.

"Pankaj, get the rickshaw out." I yelled, appearing at the door. "Let's go."

"Yes, Sir." As Pankaj came back stood near the door, I grabbed Saroj by her caboose and kissed her as she eagerly opened her mouth for me. I squeezed her ass over the thin sari that she was wearing. Pankaj stood like a wimp watching me caress his wife.

I gave Saroj a parting smack on her trunk and she purred with pleasure.

"Let's go."

Our first stop was the furniture store. I picked out a nice dining table with four chairs. It was small enough to fit their hut, but of good material and expensive. Then I picked out a luxurious sofa set containing a three-seater and a love seat, with deep cushions that made you sink in, and dark colours to match Saroj's hut. Pankaj's eyes bulged at the cash that I casually handed to the cashier. I paid extra to have it delivered that afternoon. It would be there at her house when I returned for dinner. I told the cashier to deliver it to Saroj, and under "care of" I put my name, rubbing it in to Pankaj that he was not man enough to provide the necessities for his wife.

Then we went to the clothing store where I bought some lungi's, t-shirts and underwear for myself. If Pankaj wondered why I was buying quite a few change of clothes he kept his mouth shut.

And then we entered the ladies' section.

"Let's buy some more undergarments for your wife." I told him, much to his discomfort. "A beautiful woman like her always needs beautiful lingerie."

"Thank you, Sir," Was all he could muster in reply. "I could never afford to buy her these."

I bought some bras, all the time asking Pankaj whether his wife's breasts would fit them or if the bra was too large or too small. He stammered in his replies, once saying, "You know best Sir."

I laughed silently.

"I am making sure all the bras we buy are half a size small." I told him. "They would not be uncomfortable for her to wear, but would make your wife's perky breasts stand up and be noticed. She has big breasts, whore and she should be proud of them."

"Yes, Sir. You are right, Sir. I am also proud of her breasts, Sir."

"I like her nipples best." I told him. "They are quite round."

I made him drop me downtown at the city, and handed him all my purchases and ordered him to put them on the bed.

"And make sure to tell Saroj about her gifts." I told him. "She can examine the bras before I return in the evening." Pankaj nodded meekly. I gave him some money – much more than he would earn for the day – and told him to pick me up at 7 pm sharp and not to be late.

It was late afternoon when Pankaj reached home after working for a shift. The furniture had already been delivered and arranged in their places, and Saroj was busy cooking.

"Hungry?" She turned to her husband as he walked in.

"Yes, dear." Pankaj's stomach growled. Ever since I had entered his household, he had been a distinct second best at the table. Saroj gave him a good meal, and Pankaj ate everything. He burped, much to Saroj's annoyance.

"Husband, you have bad manners!" She told him. "Salman would never do that. He is a proper gentleman, you should learn from him!"

Pankaj wanted to tell her he knew how much of a gentleman I was when I was slapping Saroj's butt at night, but he bit his tongue. Instead, he said, "Oh, that reminds me dear, Sir has purchased some more gifts for you. I put them in the bedroom, on the bed."

"And you tell me now?" Saroj scolded him. "Husband, you should have told me this immediately! Now you go clear the table and clean the dishes, and make sure you don't scratch the wood! Look at this table! You could work for a thousand years and never afford this!"

"Yes, dear." Pankaj stood up. "Sir is indeed very liberal with his gifts to us."

Once Saroj saw the gifts, she called out her husband to the bedroom.

"Look at this bra, isn't it lovely! I am going to try this on right now!"

She dropped her pallu and popped open her blouse. Reaching around her back, she unclipped her bra and it dropped to the floor. Her boobs sprang out, free. Pankaj's cock stirred. Ordinarily he would have rushed to grab those udders but he knew that temporarily, Saroj was someone else's property, even though she was his wife. Saroj made it a point to try out all the bras.

"Look, husband! Salman is so clever! He bought it just small, so it smashes my boobs together."

"Yes, dear."

"Do you think he will like me in these?" Saroj modelled one black bra and swung her chest about, her boobs juggling beneath the bra.

"I am sure Sir will love it." Pankaj replied. "You look lovely in these bras."

"He also likes me without bras." Saroj giggled. Then she started to put away the bras, and Pankaj made a motion to leave; Saroj stopped him.

"Husband!" Saroj sat down on one side of the bed and beckoned her husband to come over to her. "Did you sleep well last night?"

Pankaj froze. "I … I .. of course, dear. I slept well."

"Hmm. Husband, you didn't hear any noises last night, or see anything?"

Pankaj started to get aroused, but he managed to control his voice.

"Not really, dear. I was very tired."

"Husband, you didn't stand near that spot, that hole in the partition," Saroj pointed to the spot, "and watch me and Salman in bed, did you?"

Pankaj remained silent. Saroj continued.

"Husband, when I was cleaning today, I saw cum stains on the floor there. Were you, or were you not, watching Salman ravage my body last night, and jerking off to the sight?"

Pankaj knew he was defeated. So far, no one had openly mentioned his cuckoldry to him. Even though I had groped and kissed his wife and enjoyed her body in front of him, he did not say anything about it to me. Saroj had not mentioned sex either, and everyone was carrying about as if it was normal to have your houseguest enjoy the hospitality of your wife in bed. Now, Saroj was confronting him.

"Yes, dear, I did stand there ... and ..." Pankaj began.

"What did you see, husband?"

"I saw... Sir and you ..." Pankaj's dick was quite hard now.

"Husband, did you hear Salman ask about you last night?"

"Yes, dear."

"Husband, did you hear me telling Salman not to worry that you were in the next room?"

"I.... Yes, dear."

"And you just stayed there and listened to it, husband? Even after Salman expressed his ardent desire to ... to .... to FUCK me?"

"I am so ashamed, dear."

"Salman made me his sex slave for the night, and you just let him?"

"I ... I ... I am so sorry, dear."

"How come you so weakly agreed when I said Salman and I were going to share our marital bed? Do you not have any honour? Your own wife wanted to spend the night with another man, and you let her do it, dear husband!"

"I ... I ... I ...." Pankaj was lost for words.

"Husband, did you see your own house guest penetrate and fuck your WIFE last night?"

"Yes, dear."

"Husband, did you not hear me scream his name as he repeatedly plunged his giant cock into my cunt?"

"Yes, I did, dear."

"Husband, did you notice that Salman had a much larger dick than you? And he could cum more than once in the night?"

"Yes, I did, dear."

"Husband, did you see last night how Salman put his penis into my mouth and I gave him a blow job?"

"Yes, dear."

"Husband, did you see Salman fuck me in the ass last night, 'doggy style' as he called it, and call me a 'kutti' and 'bitch' and a 'randi' while furiously slapping my ass?"

"Yes, dear."

"Darling husband, you saw a young man slap your wife's buttocks until she weep out in pain, and you did nothing. A visitor to your house called her a bitch and a prostitute, and you watched. Salman plunged his manhood into me and FUCKED me in the ass, and you just watched and jacked off to it? Why did you not rush to save me?"

"I ... I ... I didn't know what to do, dear!"

"And Husband, did you see Salman order me to give him a blow job this morning, while you so miserably hid in the bush over there and watched my humiliation?"

"I ... Yes, dear."

"Husband, did you feel Salman's cum in the kiss I gave you this morning?"

"I ... I ... Yes, dear."

"Husband, have I ever given you a blow job or let you fuck me in the ass?"

"Never, dear."

"Husband, then doesn't it bother you that I let him do what he wants with me, while I deny you, my husband, the same enjoyment?"

"I ... I don't know what to say, my dear. It should make me angry, but ...."

Saroj knew she had him.

"I am doing this for you, husband dear." Saroj answered him in her sweet, seductive voice. "Salman loves me a lot and he is very rich, dear husband. He can help you with all your debts."

"Really?" Pankaj's heart gave a sudden flutter. "Oh, yes, dear, and I remain so grateful to you for making such a sacrifice. I thank you for it."

"I am doing all this for you husband," Saroj's voice was dry. "I hope you will still want me after he has dishonoured me but it is my duty to pleasure him for you."

"I will always love you Saroj you are my wife", Pankaj could not control himself; he had now taken out his cock and was rubbing it. "But I don't understand why watching another man taking you sexually is giving me so much pleasure."

"It's understandable, dear husband." Saroj declared. "Salman is a real man, and you want to see your wife service a real man's cock."

"Yes, dear." Pankaj felt sperm rising up his shaft and quickly came, making a mess on the floor.

"Now, look at this!" Saroj was angry. "I have to clean this up! Salman wanted you to stay out of this room, and you made it dirty. You will be punished!"

Saroj put her hand on her surprised husband Pankaj's back to guide him over her lap, and she spread her thighs apart a little. Pankaj was positioned over her knees, face down, his cock between her thighs. To his surprise, he felt Saroj's fingers undoing the knot in his lungi, and then pulling it down to his knees. It fell on the floor. Now Pankaj's ass was completely naked and totally exposed to be spanked.

Smack! Smack!

Saroj started off slowly, cupping her hands and alternating on each cheek.

Smack! Smack!

She had a life time of experience in spanking and Pankaj felt his cock stiffening again. Here he was, being punished for watching his wife have sex with another man on her marital bed, and he was getting a woody!

Smack! Smack!

Saroj continued her spanking until she felt her old husband couldn't take it anymore.

Smack! Smack!

At the end of Pankaj's spanking, Saroj ordered, "Stand up, dear husband, and don't pull up your lungi, and walk over to the window."

As Pankaj stood in the corner, he felt his wife's hands rub his bottom.

"Your ass has turned a nice even red colour." She told him. "It will probably feel warm for a few days as you work the rickshaw." She laughed. "Now go and get dressed. You must soon leave for the city to pick up your wife's lover."

"Yes, dear." His ass still smarting, Pankaj picked up his clothes and withdrew before Saroj could change her mind. His mind was in a whirl. Though Saroj had always bossed her husband around, she had never gotten physically dominant with him. And today, she had spanked him!

Pankaj decided his life and his relation with Saroj was probably going to change forever.

What neither Saroj nor Pankaj saw at that point was that on the other window, Saroj's younger sister Savitri had been standing, watching in amazement as she saw her sister Saroj first admit to adultery, then see her brother-in-law Pankaj admit to voyeurism, and then getting a spanking from his wife after he had ejaculated at the thought of his wife's infidelity.

Pankaj picked me up at 7.20 pm from the main market (I had been late -- he had waited patiently). It was a hot evening, so I was sweating and was hungry. I noticed that Pankaj was squirming every time he had to sit on the driver's seat of the rickshaw, and I grinned. My plan was working! Saroj must have spanked him, and spanked him hard.

"I say, Pankaj," I asked him as he pedalled hard. "Tell me about this debt of yours. Saroj was telling me you owe some people a lot of money."

Pankaj told me he had a gambling problem some time ago, and owed a lot of people money. To get them off his back, he had borrowed ₹100,000 from a money lender who had a reputation for organized crime. He had paid off all his creditors, but now owed this one man ₹100,000 with interest, and he had only a year to pay it. The amount due now was nearly double at approximately ₹200,000. The more he delayed paying it, the greater the interest was.

"What happens if you cannot get the money in a year?" I asked him.

"Sir," Pankaj's voice was sad. "If he does not beat me up, I will lose my rickshaw and my house, and Saroj and I will be forced to be on the streets."

"Not only that," I continued, "I heard such men don't like losing money. They will make a lesson out of you for others. Either they will really beat you up, or they will kidnap and repeatedly rape your wife."

"Yes, Sir."

I did not say anything after that, but let him ponder on the consequences he knew he was facing, as he ferried me back to his residence. As far as he knew, I was staying for one more night, so Pankaj knew after tonight he would get back his wife. Little did he realize my plan! Once I had a taste of Saroj, how could I just enjoy her juicy delights for only one more night! Saroj was like an intoxicant -- once you had a taste of her unbridled passion, you didn't let go easily.

Saroj greeted me with a wet, sloppy, slurpy kiss on the lips, on the doorstep of the house within full view of the neighbours as Pankaj squirmed uncomfortably. I had Pankaj take my bags to the bedroom. Saroj had just taken a bath and smelt like fresh roses. I could see the faint outline of one of the new bras inside her blouse. Still at the door, I grabbed her boobs and pinched her nipple through her blouse, jiggling them for my pleasure, and she laughed. Wrapping my arms around her exposed waist, we walked in.

"My sister Savitri visited me today," she told me, when I asked her if anything was new. "And she forgot her cell phone here. I have to return that tomorrow."

"Hmm. Is Savitri as beautiful as you, or is she even sexier?" I playfully asked her.

"Oh, you!" She playfully swatted at me. I once again grabbed her, and kissed her forcefully on her lips as she melted in my arms. After probing her mouth deep with my tongue, I let her go as she caught her breath. All this time, Pankaj watched awkwardly as I enjoyed his wife's charms openly.

I took a bath, and soon, dinner was served. After we had eaten and washed up, I sat down on their new sofa and discussed Pankaj's loan with him. I told him his life was ruined and he would be out on the streets in a year. He could probably go to jail, and Saroj would then have to fend for herself, if the loan shark didn't kidnap her and ravish her every night. Pankaj agreed, and looked hopefully at me. I took my time, before I replied.

"Pankaj, you certainly have more than ₹200,000 in this house."

"I am sorry, Sir, I don't have any such money," Pankaj replied, looking at me as if I had gone crazy.

"Pankaj, I have already seen the wealth in this house, and if you wish you can clear your debts with the loan shark with that money," I said.

He asked me, "Sir, where have you seen such money, please tell me! I would be the most relieved person in the world!"

"Saroj!" I called out. Saroj came from the kitchen, wiping her hands on her *sari's pallu.* She walked and stood beside me obediently. I got up and walked around to her back. Pankaj was watching me keenly as Saroj let her hands loose on her side. The sexual tension in the air was palpable. Here was a man, Pankaj, who had just watched his wife cuckold him the previous night and then spank him, now hoping expectantly for debt relief from the very same man that had ravaged his wife. And that man, I, was circling the vivacious Saroj like a shark circles its prey.

I pressed my dick into Saroj's ass cheeks, reached around and cupped her breasts through her blouse.

"Here, Pankaj." I rubbed her left breast.

"₹100,000."

Then I massaged Saroj's right breast.

"₹100,000."

Saroj giggled, as Pankaj looked at me, puzzled, and helpless to stop me from groping his wife's mammary glands. "I am sorry, *Sir*, I don't understand."

"It's very simple." I continued to knead Saroj's boobs, getting no objections from her, or from her cowardly husband. "I am here for the night. You are to allow me to spend the night with your wife and she has to do what I order her to do. If she gives me her body absolutely, then I will loan you 200,000 rupees. You can pay off the money lender, and take your time in paying me back, with no interest."

Of course, I could have just gone to bed with Saroj, and she would have been my willing fuck toy, but I wanted to drive home the point to Pankaj that I would be sleeping with his wife, on his marital bed, with his explicit permission. My cock poked Saroj's butt crack.

"Think about it." I told him. "If you say no, your wife will have no recourse but to submit to me anyway, but then you will still owe that money. You may even go to prison! And then who knows who your wife will submit to!"

I pinched Saroj's left nipple. It was a signal to her that it was her line now.

"No, dear husband, I will not allow you to go to prison," Saroj declared bravely. "I am your wife and your welfare is my concern. You tell *Sir* that he can have my body for his pleasure, if that's what will satisfy him."

I could again see a bulge grow in Pankaj's lungi.

"It will be only for one night and no one will know your wife has slept with another man, and that you were helpless to prevent that," Saroj told her husband. "So dear, do what I say; let him enjoy my body and he will loan you ₹200,000."

"Your wife is very pretty." I told Pankaj. "I like her breasts and her ass and her lips and her cunt."

Once again, I grabbed Saroj's left tit, and held it up. "₹100,000."

Then I grabbed her right boob and kneaded it. "₹100,000."

I could see Pankaj's bulge growing bigger. It was time to close the sale.

"Pankaj," I told him in my most authoritative voice. "I want your wife, and no one will know except the three of us. Your honour will remain intact, but if you get arrested, your self-respect will be torn to shreds, and besides, I plan on enjoying her wet loins anyways."

I rubbed Saroj's crotch, through all the layers of clothes, and held my hand up.

"She's wet and dripping like a faucet, Pankaj. You wife is as it is turned on as me by our affair."

"Sir," Pankaj croaked. "You are very generous to offer me that money and my wife is so brave to help me by satisfying you. I agree to your demands for the night, Sir."

"Excellent." I pressed myself more firmly onto Saroj and she could feel my manhood now invade the space between the cheeks of her buttocks. I could feel the dampness of her through her clothes, and she seemed to encourage me by pushing back onto me. Pankaj felt defenceless and tried not to stare at me molesting and mauling his buxom wife, cupping her tits and fondling them to my heart's content.

"Let's watch some television." I ordered Pankaj to put a cricket match on. "We can sit on this new sofa that I got for you, all three of us."

"Yes, Sir."

"You know, Pankaj, you are not man enough to even afford a sofa. You should be glad I am giving you ₹200,000 for your wife."

"Yes, Sir."

We sat on the sofa and Pankaj handed me the remote. I put it to one side as the cricket match came on. Saroj came down and sat on my lap. I turned her around so that she was facing me.

"What do you think, Pankaj, who will win the match?" I asked him, as Saroj pressed her boobs to my face. She was a woman in heat.

"Sir, hard to say." Pankaj hummed and hawed, trying desperately to concentrate on the action on the screen, rather than on the sofa.

I pulled away Saroj's pallu, un-hooked the blouse, and pushed her new bra up to expose her large round breasts, the big black areolas standing erect. I put the left nipple into my mouth while I played with the right breast, squeezing and pinching it, rotating the nipple between my thumb and fingers.

"Saroj, you are a very attractive woman and I am going to fuck your beautiful firm body," I told her in a loud voice.

"Thank you, Salman!" Saroj replied with a smile. "I will do whatever you ask of me to please you, that's the agreement my husband made with you."

I turned to Pankaj. "What do you say Pankaj?"

"I ... I..." Pankaj was at a loss for words as I pinched Saroj's left areola. "Sir, you have the full right to enjoy her as you wish, tonight."

To demonstrate my power in his household, I mocked, "Who is going to fuck your wife, Pankaj?"

"You will, *Sir*." He replied. "And I remain your grateful slave for your generosity."

"Then you will watch me powerlessly as I violate your wife, Pankaj. You are the cause she will be penetrated by another man's penis," I pronounced.

"Yes *Sir* you such a considerate person and a dear friend that you are most welcome to fuck her anytime you want," Pankaj grovelled.

Saroj was now moaning loudly.

"Oh, husband!" She gasped. "I must satisfy Sir and we must do everything to please him."

"Yes, dear." Her husband feebly agreed.

"Pankaj," I instructed Saroj's husband. "Your wife is sacrificing her honour to another man just for your sake. She is going to lose her chastity and it's all due to you. Show her your appreciation by licking her feet."

"Yes, Sir."

Pankaj jumped to his feet and knelt down in front of us, lowering himself on his stomach at Saroj's feet. He started to lick and kiss her feet as I tweaked her nipples.

"That's it, Pankaj. Pay your respects to your brave wife." I demanded. "Lick her feet like the lowly dog you are. You are the dog and your wife will be my bitch."

"Dear husband," Saroj taunted him, "A man is in your house, he has your wife's breasts in his hands, and calls her a bitch, and you grovel at his feet. And look, you have a hard on!"

Poor Pankaj had no place to hide. There was a damp spot on his lungi now.

"Husband, stand up!" Saroj ordered, and he complied.

"Take off your lungi."

"I ... I ..." Pankaj turned to look at me for help, but I was having none of it.

"Do as your wife tells you to do!" I ordered him. "She's helping you out -- the least you can do is be an obedient slave to her!"

"Yes, Sir."

Saroj's husband undid the knot and his *lungi* fell to the floor. His small dick was now rigid hard.

"Husband, take off your shirt too." Saroj ordered, and he complied. Pankaj was now standing before us, completely naked.

"Look, Salman!" Saroj told me. "He is hard. My dear husband gets aroused when he sees you enjoy his wife's body."

"Really? How do you know, Saroj?"

Saroj was getting into her part. "Salman, I asked him today if he saw us together last night, when you ravaged my body. He said he did."

A visibly humiliated Pankaj was turning bright red, standing there, butt naked, his small dick erect.

"He said he saw us last night, and did nothing but jack off in that corner." Saroj told me. "Even when he was confessing this to me, he could not control himself and came in the bedroom. I had to punish him for that."

"Really, Saroj, how?"

"Salman, I spanked him. If you ask him to turn around, you will notice his ass has red marks!"

Pankaj was now trembling. I ordered him to turn around. His embarrassment complete, he faced the other way, and I could clearly see the results of Saroj's handiwork on his butts.

"Your wife will now punish you, Pankaj, when she wills." I told him. "No matter how humiliating it is for you, you deserve to be her whipping boy."

"Yes, *Sir*."

"Now turn around, and get on your knees."

Pankaj turned around, and knelt in front of us. We were still seated on the sofa.

"Apologize to her for putting her in this situation, and humbly beg her forgiveness." I ordered him.

Pankaj swallowed what was left of his ego and pride, and began to meekly plead for forgiveness from Saroj, who was having none of it.

"Husband," she told him. "I am going to slap you now."

"Yes, dear. I deserve it."

SLAP!

SLAP!

SLAP!

SLAP!

As if having your own wife violated in your own house wasn't bad enough, Pankaj was now a cuckold who was being humiliated by his own wife in front of the bull who was going to fuck her. As I watched Saroj slap her husband, I decided it was enough for the time being.

I tapped Saroj, and we both stood up. Saroj grabbed her clothes, putting on her bra, then blouse, and then moving her pallu in place. I walked up to Pankaj and ordered him to stand up. His cheeks were now bright red with the marks of Saroj's fingers on him. Whether he was red due to the slaps, or due to the embarrassment of his situation, I didn't know, and didn't care.

"Pankaj! We are going to bed now." I informed him. "I want you to remain completely naked through the whole night. If you put on your clothes, I will not give you the money. You are a lowly dog, and dogs don't wear clothes."

"Yes, *Sir.*"

"Also," I continued, "you will remain here in this room while I enjoy your wife on your marital bed. In case we decide to call you, you will come at once. Otherwise, you are to remain out of sight and quiet. You may watch us if you wish through the other side of this partition."

"Yes, Sir." Pankaj was relieved. He was afraid he would be sent away and not be allowed to watch.

"Come, Saroj." I put an arm around her waist, poking her navel with a finger, and led her to the bedroom. My hands made an unmistakable brush across her hips.

Once in the bedroom, I stripped completely, my cock now rock hard. I sat down on the bed, reached out and pulled Saroj down onto my lap and kissed her. She was still dressed, and returned my kisses loudly. My hands wandered over her body and stopped to pay homage at her breasts. If my intentions weren't plain enough, what Saroj felt through my shorts as she sat my lap made them abundantly clear.

"Thank you, Salman, for helping my husband with the loan." Saroj told me, as I unbuttoned blouse. "You are truly an angel." She rubbed her breasts in my face.

"Mmm... your breasts are lovely, Saroj. They just cost me ₹200,000."

I feel her tits jiggle and bounce in the palms of my hands.

"Ohhhh my goodness! Wonderful!" I sighed, "Ohhhhhhh my goodness. You are a sex goddess, Saroj!"

Saroj laughed, and allowed my tongue to enter her mouth and her tongue to enter mine. She shivered as my hands reached under her breasts and slowly lifted them up and then down. As we continued our long French kiss, I gently bounced her breasts and squeezed them playfully.

Through a reflection in the mirror, I could see her husband watch us through the partition, his pecker in his hand.

My fingers slowly slipped down inside the front of Saroj's brassiere. I softly caressed and then cupped one of her breasts, and tenderly lifted it out of the bra. It flopped out to hang free. Saroj's other breast was then similarly lifted gently and it too flopped out -- so now both of her enormous breasts hung naked for all to see. The soft flesh on her massive boobs jiggled in waves as she French kissed my mouth before coming up for air. Pankaj could see his wife heave a loud sigh as I stared at her with my mouth open, drooling at the sight of her incredible chest.

Lifting a breast in each of my hands, I leaned forward and asked her loudly, "Does your husband appreciate these nice big jugs of yours?"

"No, Salman, he just undresses my sari and cums quickly."

"Does he suck your tits?"

"No, Salman. It causes him to cum quickly, so he tries not to."

"Does he like to suck your nipples?"

Without giving her the chance to reply, I then started to suck at her udders.

Pankaj's face flushed a deep shade of red as he watched and heard his wife's reaction to me fondling and sucking her breasts. He stiffened and shook each time Saroj grunted and squealed as her nipples were bitten and flicked by my tongue.

Releasing one tit from my mouth, I moved to continue to suck and nibble the other one. Then I bounced them gently up and down, looked into the Saroj's eyes and asked, "Does Pankaj bounce your tits like this while he's sucking them, honey?"

Saroj squealed a little girl squeal and replied, "Nooooo."

"PANKAJ!" I yelled loudly. "Come here!"

Pankaj ran into the room, his hands holding his dick, and stood to one side of the bed.

I lifted his wife's breast with one hand, and with the other I grasped the nipple between my thumb and middle finger, rolled it around and asked him, "What do you call these breasts, Pankaj? What do you call your pretty wife's great big tits? Melons? Jugs? Boobs? She really has an amazing rack. Come on, what do you call them? Knockers?"

Pankaj didn't reply, puzzled at my taunts, as Saroj started to moan loudly. I felt a bit of dampness between her legs. Saroj's face was now beet red and she was wheezing hysterically as both her breasts were ravished again. She started to groan and buck.

"Look, I am giving your wife an orgasm by just playing with her tits." I told Pankaj.

"Yes, *Sir*. You are a much better man in bed than I can ever be. It's an honour for me that my wife is pleasuring you in bed, *Sir*."

Saroj continued to cum for some time. Both the men in the room, her husband and I, watched her face as she closed her eyes and grimaced. She was on my lap, and her body quivered and trembled uncontrollably in the throes of a passionate orgasm. I could now feel her wetness leak through her clothes and dampen my thigh. When she was done, I told her to stand up.

"Strip her." I ordered Pankaj, as Saroj stood up and wobbled. Pankaj caught her and steadied her. Then he obediently took off her blouse, her bra, and her sari, leaving her in her petticoat. One tug and the petticoat dropped to the floor. Saroj wasn't wearing any panties, so she was now completely naked.

"Here she is, *Sir*, ready for you."

"Step back." I told him. Then I stood up and turned to Saroj "Look, Saroj, your husband has undressed you and presented you to me. He has bartered your body, and his respect and manhood and honour, for a measly ₹200,000."

"Yes, *Sir*." Saroj moaned. "My husband is not a man like you are!"

Every word reminded Pankaj of his inglorious demotion in status in his own house.

I told Saroj to open her mouth. She opened big. I gathered my saliva and spit into it. She squealed in delight. I collected more of my hot spit in my mouth and commenced my perverted liquid assault on the Saroj's glistening big tits and her pretty face all over again. Laughing and hooting, Saroj tried to dodge, and it became a sick contest to see how I can land the biggest wad into her screaming, gurgling mouth.

Pankaj watched as his wife's cheeks and bosoms were filled with the slimy, grey saliva. Saroj tried desperately not to swallow but I suddenly pinched her nostrils shut and placed a big hand over her mouth, forcing her to swallow the bubbly swill. Pankaj watched as his dazed, naked wife was being hugged and given hot sloppy kisses as if her husband wasn't even there. But he was there. And Pankaj felt very defeated and useless. And aroused.

"Pankaj, I know what I'd like to do to her.........look at that big, round, beautiful ass." I told him. I then placed Saroj on the bed, on her back. She was now lying there, like a woman waiting for her man to mount her. I then climbed over onto the bed, and with one move, plunged into her.

Saroj's feverish passion was at a peak as she cried out, "Salman! Darling! Don't stop, oh please don't stop, fuck me harder, fuck me dear, fuck me now, I love you!"

I plunged into her, and out, and into her, and out. My cock rubbed against the wet damp skin of her clit, ploughing deep into her folds, going where her husband could never hope to go. With her eyes tightly shut Saroj hugged me tightly, screaming as she once again had a massive orgasm, cumming for almost a minute. I slowed down and fucked her with long slow deep strokes deep kissing her mouth. Then I looked over and saw that Pankaj was masturbating.

I shouted, "See Pankaj, that is how to fuck and satisfy your wife, now watch me plant my seed in her unprotected cunt, she is going to be sullied by my semen, her pussy belongs me now."

"Sir, it will be an honour and pleasure if you deposited your hot sticky sperm into my wife," Pankaj said.

Pankaj watched as my butt cheeks tightened to form a slit, my face contorted as I bellowed, "Bitch! Take my sperm into your fertile womb."

I squeezed Saroj's massive boobs. She was now blubbering incoherently.

"Yes, Salman fill me up with your seed, put your sperm in my belly, oh my dear come inside me," She screamed as she hugged and kissed me, wrapping her powerful chubby legs around my ass.

I grunted as I ejaculated, filling up her vagina with my semen till it overflowed, once again staining the bed sheets. Saroj grasped my balls squeezing out as much juice as possible. I bit her neck and kept ejaculating for quite some time. I then collapsed on top of her, lying there as my dick throbbed, the sperm slowing down to a trickle.

Then I decided I no longer wanted Pankaj there.

"Pankaj, turn off the lights and get out."

* * *

The next morning (which Pankaj thought would be my last day here), both he and I ogled his wife Saroj's gyrating fleshy ass and wildly swinging breasts as she happily carried out her duties around the house, humming a Bollywood tune, completely un-inhibited about being naked in front of us. Even Pankaj seemed to have come to peace with his own nakedness, standing there obediently carrying out mine or his wife's orders as needed. In fact, the only one dressed was now me.

When Saroj went in the small washroom outside to take a piss, I told her to wait.

"Pankaj", I took her husband with me to the washroom. Saroj stood there, naked, ready to pee.

"Yes, *Sir*?" Pankaj was trying desperately, like he had all morning, to hide his hardness.

"Your wife has saved you from being in debt, and perhaps from going to prison," I informed him, "You must show her your grati-tude by satisfying her."

"Yes, *Sir*."

I ordered Pankaj to lie down on the dirty wet washroom floor.

"Saroj," I turned to his wife. "Squat over to his face, and urinate there."

Saroj didn't hesitate at all, and quickly placed her ample thighs either side of Pankaj's head and with her cunt over his open mouth, gushed out a salty piss drenching Pankaj's face and hair.

"Now rub your ass over his filthy face."

She sat down with her full weight on his head, rubbing her wet pussy and the smelly unwashed anus back and forth over her husband's crestfallen but aroused face. He could almost hardly breathe as Saroj began to cum, squirting her pussy juices all over Pankaj's face and into his mouth.

I wasn't done humiliating Pankaj yet.

As Saroj got off Pankaj, he could see my zip undone, and my cock dangling over his piss and cum covered face, and his wife Saroj was then standing behind me, giggling like a schoolgirl while holding my cock.

I then started to pee. I poured out a hot stream all over Pankaj, drenching him from head to foot. Shaking the last drops of pee from my cock, I ordered Saroj to lick and clean my cock.

"You are fit to use as a toilet," I told Pankaj, "And your wife is my toilet paper, cleaning my dick of pee."

"Yes, *Sir*." Both husband and wife replied in unison. Their submission to me was now complete.

I smiled. The first of my slaves were now here.

Ever since Saroj had come willingly into my arms, leaving her hapless husband watching, I had hatched a plan. I am a rich man with a big business in the USA. I also do some import work from India, so I have a mansion in Kolkata. My family lives in the USA, but I come every month to Kolkata for ten to twelve days. And I usually hire maid servants from a temp agency. Now, I could see myself at the head of a harem. A harem headed by Saroj, my chief concubine, with her willing cuckold of a husband as a bonus servant. The first of many, I confidently thought. Seeing the husband and wife, naked, on their knees, submitting to me, was the first step in the realization of that plan. I had to make sure Pankaj was a willing slave. If he had the slightest hesitation in this affair, this wouldn't have happened. He enjoyed being a cuckold; he enjoyed the humiliation. I knew I had the slaves I wanted to start my household.

* * *

"Pankaj", I told him, once the couple were inside and cleaned up and dressed. "I have decided to stay a while longer."

"Oh." His crestfallen face betrayed his anxious disappointment. "Sir, were you not supposed to leave today?"

"Are you telling me to leave?" I thundered.

"Of course not, of course not, *Sir*!" Pankaj hastily tried to pacify me. "I was merely asking, Sir."

"I am going to stay here in your house for some time more, at least a week." I told him and Saroj. "While I am here, Saroj will be my wife and you will be our servant. Do you understand?"

"Yes, *Sir*."

"Saroj." I turned to her. "Come here."

"Yes, Salman." Obediently she stood in front of me, overshadowing her husband. "I am glad you are staying a bit longer, dear."

"How can I stop myself from enjoying your lovely body, Saroj."

"Thank you, Salman."

"Now, Saroj." I listed my orders for her. "While I am here, you will remain naked or dressed, as I tell you. I will fuck whenever I want and you are to pleasure me before, during and after our copulation, do you agree?"

"Yes, Salman."

"What about you Pankaj?" I turned to the husband. "What do you say?"

Pankaj turned to see his wife smiling and surrendered to his fate. "Yes *Sir*, I accept fully," he replied.

The next week was utter torture and humiliation for Pankaj.

When he was away working on his rickshaw, his mind was on what I was doing to his wife, and it kept him hard all day. He would often arrive home where he would find his wife naked, in bed, serving her master -- me. Sometimes I would make him watch as Saroj knelt in front of me and sucked me to hardness, before I had Pankaj put my cock inside his wife and watched us fuck. Saroj and I were like a freshly married couple on our honeymoon. We didn't care where Pankaj was. I loved to grope her all the time and play with her tits and her gyrating buttocks. Sometimes after our lovemaking we would call Pankaj and have him masturbate to the sight of us kissing, and laugh at his tiny manhood as he shot his sperm on the floor. Then we would have him clean up, of course.

After seven days were up, I gave Pankaj his ₹200,000 that he gave to his money lender, who was no doubt surprised that this pathetic man was able to cough up the money. What he didn't know, of course, was that Pankaj, and more importantly his wife, were now my property. I was heading to Kolkata, but before leaving I gave Saroj one quick good bye fuck, and told the couple that they would hear from me shortly. On my next trip to India, I would be the lord of a harem.

11. City Bitch.

Saroj was driving a little too fast on the highway, she realized, too eager to overtake a tractor in front of her. The tractor was pulling a trolley, which was cramped well over its capacity with labourers presumably, heading back to their village after a tiring day in the city. She swivelled in and out of her lane, gearing up impulsively and then breaking precariously, right in the face of oncoming traffic, trying to squeeze her way past. It was getting dark; she was getting restless and irritated, a bit angry at herself. She was going to see a doctor who posted at a small town outside the city where she lived with her husband and two children. She travelled up and down every day, a distance of forty kilometres each side, in order to go to work. She could have lived in the small town itself, in the campus of her hospital, but that would have meant staying away from her two adorable kids, aged three and five. She had decided to take this extra burden on herself in order to enjoy a peaceful family life. And usually, it was a driver who drove her up and down, but that day he was on leave.

She honked irritably at the tractor that was slowing her down, as she headed for her night shift. She preferred to be off the highway before darkness fell, but she had started late. She didn't want to be late for her night shift. She managed to overtake the tractor on her next attempt, just managing to slide back into her lane as she approached an oncoming vehicle. The labourers on board the tractor cheered and clapped at her overtaking success, shouting something which was incoherent to her. She thought she would be relieved. With a clear road ahead, she would manage to reach her destination within an acceptable amount of delay. But what she saw in front of her annoyed her further. There was another tractor, similar to the one she had just overtaken, pulling a trolley that, too, was overflowing with labourers. It was almost as if they had been heaped one over the other.

Again, she faced uphill the task of overtaking this second tractor. The labourers were watching her futile attempts with quite an interest. After all they had nothing else to do! After a couple of attempts, she gave up and began to gesture to the labourers at the extreme end of the trolley. Get out of the way, she mouthed, waving her hand to ask them to give way. They saw her and laughed. She was now overflowing with anger and irritability. In that moment, she, uncharacteristically, gestured aggressively. Get out of my way or I'll kick you to death, she shouted, her head hanging out of the window she had just rolled down. The labourers heard her threat. They laughed even harder. Most of them were humoured by this city Memsahib's meek efforts to gain way. Some of them were furious, how dare a woman shout at them like that? The dissent amongst the labourers was growing, what was this city bitch thinking? How dare she order them around? After a very brief discussion, it was decided that this city bitch needed to be taught a lesson.

She was in for a surprise. Her anger and irritability vanished in a moment, to be replaced by fear and helplessness. A couple of labourers, at the extreme edge of the trolley (near her), undid their lungi's (traditional garment worn around the waist), and began pointing their penises towards her. Looking at her, they started stoking their penises, shouting out obstinacies. Why you are in such a hurry, bitch? Are you eager to get back to your brothel, whore? Want some quick cock in your sophisticated pussy, you city slut? You drive fast and I'll cum fast! Do you want this dick in your mouth? Shout one more time and I'll make sure it is there! She was petrified. She hadn't expected things to take such a turn.

Shocked, she braked, but the tractor behind her got into the act. It pushed her car forwards in a jerk, and she had no choice but to accelerate, to avoid being hit again. Her car was now sandwiched between the two tractors, as she was in between these low-class men. The two tractors slowed down, almost as if only inching forwards; slowing her car down along with them.

Although she couldn't see the labourers in the trolley behind her, she was sure of what they were up to, as she heard the choicest insults been thrown at her from behind. Let's fuck this bitch here! I want to fuck her asshole! I wonder what this bitch looks like naked…let us strip her! It was completely dark by then. All she could see was the back of the trolley, illuminated by her car's headlights. She felt her mouth go dry. She was actually scared to death. Her mind had absolutely stopped working. She was blank. She absent-mindedly stared at the action taking place in front of her. The labourers, making smacking noises with their tongues and blowing obscene kisses at her, were still stroking their penises, which had become erect.

She saw a silvery semi-solid blob heading towards her car, when it was inches off her windscreen, and splattering on impact. Her mouth opened in horror and her eyes dilated with disgust, as she realized what that blob was. Those filthy labourers were actually masturbating at her! She recoiled in horror as one after the other, the labourers shot their semen at her windscreen. With many more joining in the act, they were taking turns at aiming now. As one group finished masturbating, it was replaced by another group, who by now had erect penises, presumably stoking them since the action had started. In no time, her side of the windscreen had been splattered with a huge amount of semen. After splattering on impact, the blobs were now beginning to slowly slide down the windscreen.

It was almost as if she felt those blobs striking her face, her tongue, her eyes, her hair, and slide down her pink soft cheeks. Along with these unique cum-shots, she was also being bathed with vulgar comments by the labourers. She felt her fear and disgust increase thousand folds with each ejaculate of semen that splattered on her windscreen. She was sweating excessively due to fear; she could feel it dampening her smooth shaved armpits under her kurta (a traditional loose over-shirt worn by woman). Beads of sweat rolled down her face copiously, in tandem with the semen of the labourers which was making its way down the windscreen. She lost count of how many men had ejaculated on 'her', thirty, or fifty?

After a brief respite, when she thought that her humiliating ordeal was over, she was hit by a wave of nausea. The labourers, having emptied their balls, were now on to another thing to further humiliate the city bitch! She retched with nausea as she saw a bunch of them, lined at the edge of the trolley, aiming their now limp penises at her, and urinating on her windscreen. She was certain she was going to vomit, as she saw (and heard) their strong streams striking the glass in front of her, and ricocheting in all possible directions. It was as if she was being urinated upon by this group of filthy labourers. Hurriedly, she rolled the window back up, something she realized she should have done before itself.

She watched in horror as man after man took an aim at her face and let go of his sphincters. Laughing amongst themselves and cheering each other, the labourers made merry at the humiliation they were bestowing on the city bitch. Hoping for her ordeal to end, she waited desperately for each labourer to urinate on her windscreen.

After what seemed like eons to her, the labourers finally emptied their balls and bladders. They had humiliated the city bitch to the core. She had felt the humiliation to the core. Figuratively, she had been masturbated and urinated upon by almost fifty labourers, low class men who were way below her in the social scenario. In her mind, fifty filthy sweaty men from villages had ejaculated on her face, making her a cum bucket. Then almost all of them had urinated on her, degrading her to the lowest level possible. Then the tractors stopped completely, bringing her car to an abrupt stop. She wriggled in her seat as she saw the labourers jump off the trolley, on to the bonnet of her car and make their way towards her. Those from the tractor behind were making getting down too. She panicked. What would these lust-filled men do to her, their city bitch, out here on the highway in the dark? She knew the answer perfectly, as a handful of them started pounding on the glass windows on either side. A couple of them were licking the side window glasses shamelessly. In total, there were about a hundred of them, all hungry for the delicious city bitch they wanted to devour.

Listening to their vulgar comments, she knew she would be minced meat if they got their hands on her. She felt dampness at her thighs and on her buttocks and a wave of eerie coldness radiating from her waist to her knees. The fear had driven her to pee all over herself. She was now sitting in a puddle of her own urine. Absent-mindedly, she put the car in reverse gear, fully aware that the tractor behind her was too close; as if hoping that her life would actually go in reverse! She heard an annoying sound, which cars made when put in reverse gear, fill up her brain; it was weird as her car did not have such a device.

At that moment, she woke up to what was the annoying sound of her alarm clock. She sat up in her bed, next to her husband, who was snoring loudly, unaffected by the alarm clock as he had always been. It was not long before after waking up that she realized that she was actually wet, not just with the copious amounts of sweat but also with her womanly juices. Smiling coyly, she headed to the bathroom to have a few moments with herself, before her husband and children woke up.

12. Booklet

I am 45 years and live in Delhi. It happened when my distant cousin came to our house 4 years back. I was living with my parents as I was separated from my wife. The cousin's wife Saroj was very attractive and they were married for one year. Cousin came to Delhi for a job and we told him till he collects good amount of money, he can stay with us so that it is easier to find a good house for a rent.

Saroj always helped my mom in household works and was very helpful. Within 15 days I got attracted to her and started thinking of getting her on bed. She never talked to me much as I was elder to her husband and in our culture, they are not supposed to talk much with them.

Anyway, few days later I got an idea. I had a one porn booklet of hardly 20 pages with great exciting pictures of fucking. One day I put that booklet in open on my bed so that she can see it while she comes to my room for cleaning and setting. I prayed God that my mom does not come that day.

I went to the bath room as soon as I got an idea that she is coming. I just concentrated the room activities and when I was sure that she has left, I came out from toilet. And I was looking for that booklet. It was nowhere, I searched my room completely but all in vain. I wanted this and next day when I was in my room and Saroj came to set-up my room, I took a courage and asked her that did she see a booklet.

She denied, but then I requested her, that it was not mine and I have to return it to my friend, if she like that I can give her another one but not that one. She did not say anything and went. Next day in the evening she came to my room and told me that "Brother, I have kept the book were it was)"

I was happy that she has seen that book and now I had more courage and waited for next day when she comes to my room. Next morning when I got to know that she is coming to my room, I went to toilet and did not close the door and was sitting on my western toilet. She opened the door and started managing the items in the toilet.

She did everything without seeing me. I knew that she knows I am there. I did my stuff and got out of the toilet, and then she again went to toilet to clean the huge mirror in the toilet. This time I gathered my full courage and hugged her from behind. She was little shocked and said, "Brother don't do this someone will come to know" With her reply I was now sure that she was only scared and not that she does not want to be touched.

I took her on my bed and started pressing her boobs. She had small one but they were very firm. I took out her salwar and panty. She had a cute pussy; it was small and had very few hairs on it like a gal of 16 years. This excited me too much. I started sucking her pussy and the juices were flowing like anything.

I could not control myself and took my pants off and put my dick straight in. Ooooooh my God, it went in so smoothly because it was wet or else my 7" dick would not have been easy for her. While fucking I kissed her and she was enjoying it too. She said, "Brother you are very bad" But I did my fullest exploration and we fucked for 20 minutes and then I came.

And then I saw her fully, her waist was so sexy, slim and slender. We did few sessions whenever we got time and later, they moved. But since than we never had chance. I still remember her marvellous body.

13. *Prey*

I am a 35-year-old housewife living in Bengaluru. I would like confess how I was prey to my husband's boss Rakesh.

My husband works for a well-known appliances company. Rakesh, his boss, is around 43 years of age, fairly good looking but a hard boss to work for. He was also well known for his roving eye and we had heard stories about his escapades. I had also seen him on one or two occasions at parties. In fact, many a time I have had a laugh about these stories little realising that I too would one day fall prey to his lust.

A little over 3 years ago my husband was due for his promotion which he very badly wanted. Rakesh Sir, as we call him, however was delaying this one pretext or another. About this time my husband was sent abroad for a fortnight.

One evening a couple of days after he left, I was surprised to get a telephone call from my husband's boss saying that a very important document was inadvertently kept by my husband in his briefcase and could I search for it and if possible, bring it over right away since his car was in the workshop. I managed to find the document and took an auto to the office. It was close to 7 PM and on reaching the office I found that everyone had left and only Rakesh Sir was in his room. I knocked and went in. Rakesh Sir thanked me profusely for taking the trouble and apologised for the trouble. He said that he had to make up for the inconvenience caused by taking me out for dinner. I was rather taken aback and as I was stammering excuses and that I was not even dressed for the occasion he said, "Saroj, I insist and will not take no for an answer. In any case you look absolutely attractive dressed as you are."

I could not refuse without offending him and therefore reluctantly agreed. He called a cab and we went out to a cosy little place and had a very good dinner. Right through the meal he kept a lively conversation going with his pleasant experiences during his various overseas trips. I gradually felt more relaxed and was in fact a little sorry the evening was drawing to an end. He then took me back home in an auto and as we reached my place asked, "Saroj, aren't you going to invite me for some coffee?" I started feeling very nervous but again had to call him for fear of offending him.

We went in and I asked him to wait in the sitting room while I made coffee. I went to the kitchen and while making the coffee he came in apparently to help out. Once or twice his hands brushed against my hands and I pretended not to notice. We went back to the sitting room to have the coffee and he came and sat close to me on the settee. He started saying how nice I looked, how he was dying to meet me when he saw me at a party and so on. He then caught hold of my hands and said "May I just kiss these lovely fingers to show my admiration at their beauty?" While I tried to pull back, he started kissing them. I stuttered "Rakesh Sir please, this is not right." He moved closer and said I must kiss you at least once otherwise I will go mad." Ignoring my protests, he pulled me to him put his lips on mine and kissed me. I tried to pull back but he caught me in a tight embrace and started to pry open my lips with his tongue. Slowly he managed to open my lips and put his tongue inside my mouth. My heart started hammering and with an effort I managed to tear my mouth away protesting feebly. He passionately again kissed me and said, " Saroj darling! I am going to fuck you nice and proper tonight and you are going to willingly submit because when your husband gets back, he will get his promotion which he longs for." Saying that he put his mouth on mine again and roughly opened my lips with his tongue and rolled his tongue over mine and started sucking my saliva. I knew I had to yield to his desire, and while one part of my mind was recoiling at what was in store the other side was excited by the prospect of forbidden sex with this attractive man.

After what seemed an eternity of passionate kissing, he asked me to lead us to the bedroom all the time his hands roaming over my body. We entered the bedroom and he asked me to undress fully doing so himself at the same time. He said, "Darling I am going to really fuck you properly throughout the night so let us enjoy our bodies properly."

After both of us disrobed completely he again hugged me and started caressing my heavy breasts. He bent down and put his mouth to my right nipple and started licking it. I began to get turned on and moaned slowly. He licked the other nipple also and then slowly started taking turns in sucking them, gently at first, then harder and biting them with increasing passion. All the time I was moaning and putting my hands on his head to encourage him to suck and bite harder. He slowly started kneeling down kissing my abdomen, navel and then to my lower lips. He started rubbing his face on my pubic hair and slowly parted my cunt with his nose exclaiming, " Saroj sweetheart you smell heavenly." His tongue shot into my vagina and started licking and sucking frenetically. I started writhing about and said "Dearest let us go to bed." He lifted me and put me on the bed and lay down next to me slowly and steadily licking every inch of my body. My pink nipples had become an angry red by the frequent and rough attentions of his mouth. My nipples felt as if they were bursting and my cunt was moist and literally thirsting to be taken by my lover's organ. I started begging,

"Please take me now", hugging him tightly and scratching his back with my fingers. He slowly wrapped my fingers around his pulsating organ to make me guide him. Momentarily the logical part of my mind had a pang of regret that I was cheating my husband and that madness that we were about to indulge in sexual intercourse without precautions. However, I was past caring and eagerly guided his throbbing sex organ into my thirsting vagina. He opened my mouth with his chewing on my lips as he entered me. Ooh! I was fairly tight and the feeling was incredible as he penetrated me slowly and with a jerk pushed in completely. He lay still for a moment locking his eyes into mine and then put his mouth to my nipples one by one and as he sucked them hard, he fucked me. I began to move to his rhythm and as his thrusts became harder his sucking of my breasts and kissing of my mouth became wilder. His steel like organ was going berserk inside my cunt and I was on cloud 9. Slowly his thrusts became violent and I was feeling that I would be torn and would melt into him by his furious assault on my body. I started pleading, "Please sweetheart, please cum hard inside me. I want every drop of you." I starting climaxing as the world spun crazily and then he went still deep inside me. I could hear myself screaming as his love organ started shooting his copious discharge deep into my womb. Shuddering and almost weeping with pleasure my legs wrapped around him and my vaginal muscles tightened involuntarily milking his organ to the last drop. Slowly he relaxed and said "That my love was the most pleasurable experience of my lifetime."

We coupled twice more that night and the next day I was drained with my nipples slightly cut and my cunt aching with the intense lovemaking. Rakesh Sir came home to fuck me every night till my husband returned and as a result of the most intense and frequent lovemaking, I became pregnant. Initially I was shocked but my lover persuaded me to have the baby since there was no risk and my husband was completely in the dark about our affair. I now have a girl and Rakesh Sir and I still continue our illicit affair secretly and as often as we get a chance since I am literally an addict to the most pleasurable sex sessions I can imagine with this fantastic lover. He now wants to father another baby by me saying this time we will hope for a son. My plight is both pitiable and pleasurable.

14. Unquenchable

Saroj is my beautiful wife and her mother Lata is beautiful too. This story is about how my mother-in-law seduced me to have sex with her. We were visiting her house shortly after our marriage. Saroj was busy with her female friends once she got there. I was getting bored until my mother-in-law Lata entered the room. She was a gorgeous lady with decent boobs and a very luring ass. I have always fantasised about her from the day I have seen her. Her age is 44 but still looks like 35. She was wearing a black saree, which was almost transparent to see her navel. She was also wearing a low-cut blouse, which I was amazed to see. How could she wear such sort of things in front of her son in law!! The golden sleek chain on her neck gave her a sensuous appeal.

"Pankaj, you must be feeling bored!" (She likes to call me by my name), she asked me with a charming smile. Forcefully removing my eyes from the impression of cleavage that was created by the sexy blouse,

I said, "Yup, a little. But don't you worry, it's OK."

"No! NO! How can it be OK! You are in my house, it's my duty to attend to your pleasure."

"Saroj has not seen her friends for a while, so I thought of giving you company for a while. Would you feel disturbed in presence of an old woman?" she asked me laughingly.

"What are you saying!! Don't dare you call yourself old, you are so beautiful!!", I said to Lata touching her hand.

"Thank you, Pankaj, but am I as beautiful as my daughter Saroj, your loving wife? ", Lata asked this pressing my hand.

"Off course, in fact...", I stopped saying anything."

"In fact, what Pankaj, please don't hide anything from me baby", Lata continued pressing my hand. I was shocked by the use of the word "baby" but I could not stop my flowing at that moment and I blurted out " To me, you are more beautiful than Saroj ".

Hearing these words Lata became more emotional and embraced me tightly saying "Oh, my baby! No one has praised me, since a long time. Thank you very much baby", she kept hugging me. I was out of control, my feelings started gushing out from my mouth.

"You know Lata," (Please note, Lata persuaded me to call her by name, her explanation, it makes her feel young), I continued "I have many feelings for you, I have dreamt of you , in my fantasies you are my queen , and ...", I stopped for a moment.

"Don't stop baby, please don't hide anything", she pleaded, pressing herself more tightly against me.

I gasped and finally said, "In my dreams, we make love all day, we caress each other all the time."

"Oh, my sweetheart, my baby", Lata was rubbing her hands against my back.

"Why did you hide your feelings from me, baby!". I could feel Lata was kissing my cheeks deeply, and then, she kissed my lips. I responded also, in emotion, pressing deeply my lips against hers. Soon our tongues were exploring the insides of one another's mouth, tasting each other, teasing each other. I broke the kiss almost strongly when Lata pressed her one hand on top of my trousers, feeling my cock.

"Lata, "I said, "We shouldn't do this, I have a wife and she is your daughter."

Lata pleaded, "Please baby, just for one time, I can't control myself. I need to release my sexual tension. Please satisfy my thirst with your manhood," she was constantly pressing my penis from above my trousers. Seeing me hesitating, she started kissing my body saying, "Saroj will never find out, what has happened between us. I promise you; she will never know; I just want you to satisfy the lust your mother-in-law's vagina with your rod."

Saying this, she started removing my shirt and then my trousers. I was completely naked in front of a heavenly beauty. Lata made me lie on the bed and then stood up and undressed completely. There she was, a lusty mature babe standing by the edge of my bed, assuring to fulfil all my fantasies. She sat beside me and said, "Pankaj, before we engage into this sinful act, you should first drink from your mother-in-law's bosom. This should give you the strength and lust to continue the sin of sexual pleasure, the sin of cheating. She lowered her luscious tits to my mouth and her hands started caressing my dick. I was already hard from her words, without saying anything I gladly took her tits in my mouth and started sucking them. Caressing my manhood with one hand and holding me with another hand, she was saying, "Saroj can never satisfy your lust which I will, I am your sex-goddess and you must satisfy my carnal desires. You must satisfy the hunger of my body."

I felt like my whole body was just a single organ, created with only a single purpose, to satisfy this woman completely. I touched her vaginal lips, a "AHH!!" of pleasure came out from her mouth, she was already hot there, she straddled me and said "Pankaj, there goes your manhood in my sex cave", saying this, she pushed her vaginal opening against my cock, and my penis slid inside, rubbing with her cave walls. What an intoxicating pleasure, her walls were pressing and making love to my cock,

I was amazed to see she was still tight at such an age. She embraced me tightly and began the magic of her waist and butts, they were assisting her vagina to completely devour my cock. She was kissing me deeply, her tongue mixing mine with her saliva. I was in heaven. Her every thrust of her hips, was sending me to gates of immense penile pleasure, which was drenching my body with a lustful pleasure. She was moaning all the time, like her body was having immense pleasure in devouring my sexual urges. Her moans intensified with her thrusts; she was trembling with sexual fervour. I could feel her intense climaxing, her grip hardened as if she wants to put my entire body in her vagina and with one last violent shake, she orgasmed with me following her, her vaginal walls pumping my man juice and drinking it in immense hunger. I could feel her womanhood not releasing my cock, until it has given its every last drop.

We were so exhausted both mentally and physically that we lied there in the same position of our mating, for minutes. After sometime she moved and laid down beside me, dragged me to her bosoms, and pressed my head over her red areola. I slowly started kissing it, and then moved my head and deeply kissed her lips. She was like an angel. A post orgasm glow was emanating from all over her body. We fell asleep in each other's arms, only one thing I could make out before delving deep into the world of sleep.

"Sleep tight my baby, No one will know of our sin. We will commit it every day when you are here. We will commit it whenever you come to visit me, or I come to visit you. The thirst of this sin is unquenchable."

15. Perverted night

I got a mail from Pankaj who asked me whether I would like to fuck his wife. I agreed. He asked if I am really kinky. I said yes again. So, he invited me to his house to have a nice fuck session with his wife.

We talked over phone and fixed an appointment. I went to their house on a Saturday evening. I was greeted by Pankaj at the door. Pankaj was a medium built man of 45. He ushered me to the drawing room and I was asked to sit on a sofa. He then called his wife Mrs. Saroj Sharma. Saroj was a very plump lady of 40. She was 5' with a figure of 42-44-52. Her cup was at least an FF or something as she later said that no bra fits her. She was wearing a saree clad in a typical Indian style. She wished me with a namaskar. Pankaj introduced me to her saying "here is your adultery partner from tonight."

She blushed.

Pankaj laughed and said, "Hey, if you blush like a newlywed bride, how are you going to get your legs spread and fucked by him?"

She said, "OK, that will be later, first let him change and relax. Let him eat something".

Saying this she indicated us to move in. They took me to a room and gave me one "dhoti", a traditional Bengali dress and told me "Wear this only. No under wears please". I wore it and came out of the room she took me to the bathroom and washed my feet with water and wiped it with her hairs.

I knew this was an age-old Bengali custom, which was performed by newlywed brides to their grooms and kings etc to show extreme respect. She then bowed to me. I just started drooling seeing her enormous ass clearly visible from within her saree. She was wearing a very thin white cotton saree with red border. It was clear that she was not wearing any under garments. I took her by her arms and helped her stand. Pankaj came in and ushered her out and requested me to follow her. Her very big swaying ass was almost tantalizing me. We went to a room where Pankaj gave the two of us two flower garlands. On his indication we wore them and then Pankaj told us to exchange the garlands. It is actually the marriage rituals of Bengal. We exchanged it three times. Then Pankaj gave me a small box of vermilion. I put it on her. She then bowed again and touched my feet. When she stood up Pankaj took her hand and put it into mine and told me, "From today she is your kept woman. You can use her in any way you like. Within our family she will be your wife and if you want you can make her pregnant too. I completely surrender her to you. This woman is sexy and I request you to touch and feel all her intimate parts so that you can know that you get a good woman." I put my hands within her saree and just fondle her enormous breast, her ass and her hairy pussy and then took her in my embrace and kiss her passionately in the lips.

Saroj now said. "Now you two please have some food, then only we will start the Nuptial Night."

Pankaj said, "Bring some drinks also." We went to another room and sat side by side on a sofa. Soon Saroj came with some snacks and a bottle of Vodka. She mixed vodka and water in two glasses and gave us and sat on another sofa. We said cheers and started sipping it. I then thought I should be bolder now. I told her, "Darling, come here and sit with me." She sat beside me. I put my hand on her shoulder and surrounded her neck to put it on her left tit. I went on drinking with an occasional squeeze of her tit. After half glass I put the glass to her lips and told her "Drink it darling".

She hesitated saying, "Please, no, a Bengali housewife should not drink wine."

I said, "it is OK darling, when you drink from your husband's glass, it is nectar to you."

Reluctantly she gave a sip.

I grabbed her head and poured the entire glass. She drank it. I poured another and made it really stiff. I took a sip and gave it to her and said, "drink it as if it is nectar."

She said, "I will be drunk."

I said, "It is ok., I want an extremely drunk wife."

She drank it like water and made a face worth seeing. Soon she became half drunk. Now Pankaj suddenly took out my cock and said, "Saroj, see, your husband has a good cock for you." All the three of us giggled.

I grabbed Pankaj's cock and said, "you also have a good one."

Pankaj said, "No, I don't like to fuck anymore."

By then Saroj was caressing my pecker. She said, "Pankaj, make it harder for me." Pankaj knelt down and took my cock in his mouth and started sucking it slowly.

I poured more drinks and started the routine, a sip for me and the rest for Saroj. Soon she was fully drunk and asked to be excused for a minute. Knowing the cause well, still I asked her where she wanted to go? she blushed heavily. I insisted, "tell me, or you won't get to go."

She said almost whispering, "To the bathroom" and blushed again.

I said, "you tell me exactly loud and clear, what you are going to do there?"

She blushed again and said, "No, please, I cannot say that"

I said, "ok, then just sit as you are and see how he is licking your husband's cock."

She blushed and said, "I have to pee."

I poured another glass and said, drink two more glasses and you will be allowed to pee. She swallowed two glasses in a breath. Pankaj was seeing some pure bliss. I told him to stop sucking. I winked at him and asked, "Pankaj, should I allow her to pee now?"

Pankaj said, "no, three more glasses should be drunk slowly."

I looked at Saroj and said, "So be it." It was too much for her. A very beautiful woman in the first place has less control on her bladder moreover she was drunk and had so much liquid. So, when the second glass was half empty, she was almost whimpering.

She was saying "I cannot hold it any longer, please let me pee." I took out her saree and stripped her completely. I rolled it in a bundle, put it on the floor and told her to squat on it and finish the three glasses. Her face was red by now and the squatting position was making it excruciating to hold the urine. She gulped the second and third one.

I got a good chance. I said, "you wicked wife, you were ordered to sip not to gulp, you have to start again from number one and this time no gulping. She was almost weeping and finished the three glasses somehow. When she started to get up, I pushed her to the squat position again and said, "I said you can pee. I never said you can go to the bathroom." Saying this I just gave her sexy ass a small kick. She could not hold it any longer and started peeing on her saree with a hissing sound. I and Pankaj was looking closely. When she stopped the saree was all wet in her urine. I told her "Now you will be your husband's moving toilet." I then stripped and pissed on her face, her hairs, tits and cunt. Her saree became wetter. I then told her to wear the saree again. It was a real sight to see her saree all wet in her as well as my urine. Pee is dripping from her whole body and hairs. I just kicked her again on the ass and placed my leg on her head and pressed it to touch the floor. She was placed on all fours with her ass in the air. I folded her saree to get her buttocks and cunt exposed. I grabbed her ass and inserted my cock in her cunt in a single thrust. She was moaning in pleasure and ecstasy. I grabbed her tits from behind. Her urine-soaked wet body was trembling in my thrusts. Within a few seconds she came. I went on fucking her for almost half an hour and then ejaculated in her cunt. Pankaj came and started licking the semen from her cunt. Then the two of them licked my cock clean. We stood up and hugged. It is going to be a very long perverted night.

16. Close friend.

When I reached my friend's home I was welcomed by his wife. Her name was Saroj. I was just shocked at her beauty She was just looking very beautiful. Her figure was very sexy with 34-29-36.

She asked me, "Who are you."

I did not reply her at first because I was not in this world as I was lost in her. Once I was back, I replied I was Rahul her hubby's close friend.

Then she said, "Oh please come in. I am sorry. I haven't met you is that right"

"Yes, that's alright."

She was in a blue saree. It was so transparent that her navel was clearly visible through her saree. I had a problem of looking at beautiful navels. I was just starring at her navel. That thing she didn't notice and that saved me. She asked me to get fresh and showed me the way to the bathroom. My friend also had a son who was six years old. I asked Saroj where their son was. She then replied that he has gone to school and would return by evening.

From that time I was staring at her sexy navel. As she was walking her buttocks were moving up and down. As she showed me the bathroom, I thanked her. That bathroom was attached to their bed room. I scanned their house but their house had only one bedroom. When I enquired it from Saroj she said "Me, Rohit (their son's name) and Pankaj would sleep in the same bedroom".

After that she happened to lift her both hands and at that time, I was made unmoved. I saw her beautiful navel which was very deep and very much round which we usually see in cinemas. I was shocked at that. After taking bath I told Saroj that I was going to the Company and would return in the evening. But all the way through the day I wasn't able to concentrate on my work because I was only thinking of Saroj's sexy navel. I wished to suck her navel and eat honey in her navel and decided to have her before going to Hyderabad.

After finishing my work I came back home. This time I was welcome by Rohit. He asked me who I was. I lifted him and said that I was his father's friend. I asked him where his mom was. He said that she was taking bath. I became mad with lust. I gave him a chocolate and told that his friends were playing outside and that they were calling him to play. As he went out to play, I rushed to the bedroom. I peeped through the key hole and I saw that Saroj had worn blouse and petticoat and was about to wear her saree. As she was rolling her saree around her waist, I was watching the beautiful scene. Her navel was very deep and very much round. I wished I would open the door and caress her navel and boobs which were even sexier. She was looking very beautiful in her half-worn saree condition. As she was coming out, I quickly went to drawing room and sat on the sofa and pre-tending that nothing has happened. She asked when I came and enquired about my first day at work. She asked me where Rohit had gone and I said that he has gone to play with his friends. As she was little bit wet, she was drying her hairs. While she was drying her hairs, she lifted her hands. And again, I was tempted at the look of her navel. But I kept myself quiet and decided to taste her navel one day.

At 7:45 in the evening Rohit came back after playing with his friends. Till then I was watching T.V. As he came inside Saroj told him to take bath and have his dinner. After Rohit came back, I took him close and talked to him. Very soon he became close to me. As I was talking to him, I came to know that there was a problem between Saroj and Pankaj. Pankaj used to insult Saroj after coming home late night in drunken condition. This made me sad. But my lust for Saroj made me very happy and the thought that I had a chance to get closer to Saroj. After having dinner Rohit played with me for a while and soon, he went to sleep. By then Saroj was preparing the bed. She asked me to pass Rohit to her. As I was passing Rohit to her, I touched her boobs and her waist. This caused a current of lust flow through me. But she did not show any reaction to it. I enjoyed the touch of her silky body.

Throughout the day I was observing Saroj, she seemed a little bit inactive and she didn't talk to me very frankly. As she was placing Rohit on the bed her pallu slipped and her cleavage was visible. But she did not notice I was watching. As she was setting Rohit on the bed her boobs were shaking and that made me horny. My cock got erected to work on. But I had to control my feelings. As Saroj noticed her pallu she set it right. The bedroom contained two single beds attached to each other. She asked me to sleep on the bed and was making a move to sleep in the drawing hall. I stopped her and told that I would sleep in the drawing hall.

She said no to it. But I warned her what if Rohit wakes up in the night. My plan was to convince her to sleep along with her son Rohit on the bed. She agreed to it.

I felt very happy that my first plan was a success. She slept on the other side of the bed and I slept on the second side of the bed. Rohit was between us. Soon I was fast asleep. I woke up some time around 2:00am. I was feeling a little bit thirsty. There was water in the jug next to me. I had water and as there was nightlamp glowing I looked toward Saroj. My god her pallu got off from her body and she was facing towards me. I became mad with lust and at least wanted to touch her boobs lightly and insert my little finger in her navel. I was very curious to know its depth. I slowly pushed Rohit to my side and i came in to middle. Meanwhile Saroj moved and now she was sleeping on her back. I was very close to her; I was so close that I could hear her breathing. I slowly touched her boobs and moved my hands over her body. Slowly I brought my face near her belly to see her sexy navel very close. I slowly inserted my little finger in her navel. My hands were shivering. Wow it was almost an inch deep. I wanted to taste her navel. Slowly I inserted my tongue in navel. Suddenly Saroj made moment and I got back to my position back.

Next day I went to office and came back in the evening. It was raining out so Rohit didn't go out to play. Saroj gave me a towel and I came back after getting fresh. Rohit was getting bored of staying at home, so I offered to play carrom with him. He agreed but he said that he was just a boy and how could he win with me. This gave me an idea to get closer with Saroj. I asked Rohit to convince her mom to play with him. He did and Saroj also got ready to play. Saroj and Rohit were on one side and I alone was on one side. As Saroj was sitting beside me I could smell her perfume. As the game was going on when ever Saroj and Rohit put the coins in the hole they were shouting loudly in happiness. For the first time I could see joy and real happiness on her face.

Meanwhile she too became close to me Whenever I cracked a joke she tapped me on my thigh, that would make me still. Soon we were very close. This gave me an opportunity to move around and close to her.

Next day I came back home a bit early. By then Saroj was cooking something in the kitchen. I went in the kitchen and asked her what she was preparing. She told she was preparing kheer. I said wow and I told her I love kheer. I asked her to show me how to prepare it even though I knew how to prepare it. But even then, just to get closer to her. I sat beside the stove, where there was space. Saroj wrapped her pallu around her waist and her navel was exposed. I was making her laugh with some jokes and she too added a few in those jokes. Meanwhile suddenly I put my hand on her waist saying her that there was something on her belly with an intention to touch her navel.

She shouted, "Ahh" and suddenly removed my hand from over her belly. She gave me small smile and this gave me a confidence. I told her that she was very beautiful and she smiled again. I continued praising her figure was very sexy for that comment I was really afraid but instead she told me that I too was very handsome and strong too. That increased my confidence. From that moment I was moving still closer to her and sometime I would even press her buttocks with my cock by standing behind her in the kitchen room.

She didn't object for that action meanwhile Rohit came back from school and we both played till dinner time. As we were on the table Rohit wanted me to make paper flights and we were playing till Saroj brought the dishes. While she was bringing the dishes her navel was exposed. I tried to hit her navel with the paper flight and suddenly by luck it hit her navel. She moaned slowly in sexy way "A-aaye."

I apologised for that and with a smile she said, "it's OK."

By this time, she was looking at me and knew what I wanted for which she too was ready. After having dinner, we went to bed but Rohit was in no mood to sleep. As he was kid, he didn't know what was going on between his mom and me. I told him that I brought a top (toy) for him and he was very happy to have it. I showed him how to play with it. As Saroj entered I told Rohit to play a game with her mother too. I told him it would be very fascinating if you make top revolve in hole.

To this Rohit asked, "there was no hole on the floor in the bedroom."

I said, "we have got a hole."

He asked, "where".

I said, "your mom's navel was a beautiful hole."

After hearing this words Saroj was shocked and said no no at first but I went to her and said that all these days I was fascinated about her navel. She agreed for that. I made her lay on her back and slowly removed the saree from her navel. After all, the day came for which I was curiously waiting for but I couldn't kiss her navel due to presence of Rohit. I rotated the top and placed it in Saroj's navel and she was moaning sexily. "Ahhhhhhhhhhh-h....Ooooohhhhhhhhhhhh hhhhhhh".

She was pleading to remove the top from her navel. "pppppppp-pleaseeeeeeeeeeee remove it "ahhhhhhhhhhhhhha ooooohhhhh-hhhhhhhhhhhhhhaaa" That night we slept late.

Next day I came late from the office around 10:30pm. As Saroj opened the door all my tiredness was gone. She was wearing a black saree and a black blouse which was little bit transparent. I could see her navel and boobs through it. She took my bag and asked me to get fresh. She was acting differently that day. She had also put white fragrant flowers in her hair.

I could easily understand her intention. After taking bath I was sitting on the dining table. As she was bringing the dishes her waist was swinging with her navel at the centre. It was sexy scene. I got aroused. My cock got hard. I started eating. I asked what Rohit was doing. She said he has gone to his mama's house for holidays. And said he would be back after a month. That still aroused me. I couldn't stop myself now. I quickly finished my dinner.

Then Saroj came closer to me. I was sitting on the chair. She was looking like an angel. She too was in a mood a have sex. Suddenly I caught hold of her waist and started kissing her navel. She was moaning, "Ahhhhhhhhhhhhha.. ....ooooohhhhhhhhhhhh-hhhhhhhhhhhhhh."

I was sucking it like a ripe mango. She caught my head with her two hands and pressed me into her belly. I was pressing her buttocks and pressing her towards me.

I lifted her in my arms and took her to the bedroom and made her lay on her back. I removed her saree and again started sucking her navel with my tongue. While moaning she said that she liked it when I first inserted my tongue in her navel. This made my cock hard. I removed away my tongue from her navel and poured some honey in her navel and started licking. While I was tasting honey from her navel, I was pressing her boobs. I removed the hooks of her black blouse and her petticoat. Now she was only in her bra and panty. I was caressing her navel and pressing her boobs. She was shouting to press her boobs tightly. "Oh, Rahul squeeze my breast the way u squeeze a ripe mango Ahhhhhhhhhh ooooooooooohhhhhhhhhhh".

Then I removed her bra. Now she was only in her panty. Her boobs were very big with brownish nipples which were a centimetre long. I made her to sit with her thighs folded. I was eating honey by pouring it on her nipples. While eating honey with tongue I sometimes bit her nipples lightly with my teeth for with she moaned "aaaaaaaaaaaaahhhhhhhhhhhaaaa ooooooooooohhhhhhhhhhhhhaaaaa". She said, "come on Rahul eat away my breasts and press them as you like it and Aaaaaaaaaaaaaaaaaaaaahhhhhhhhhhhhhhhaaaaaa Ooooooohhhhhooooooooooooooaaaaaaaaaaaaaaaa." She then removed my shirt and pant. I too was in my underwear now. This sucking of her navel and breasts went for almost an half an hour. I removed her panty. I was excited at the look of her pussy. I started sucking the juice of pussy. Saroj removed my underwear and was playing with my cock. She was shocked at its look. She said it was larger than her husband and started sucking it like an ice-cream. We continued in 69 position for a while and Saroj told me that she can't wait anymore as she didn't had sex for a long time.

My dick was ready to drill a hole. I just put my cock on her pussy and just moved it up and down. Saroj moaned, "emmmmmmmmmm Rahul come on I can't wait anymore."

So I put my cock in her pussy and gave a jerk. She shouted "Aaaaaaaaaahhha."

It was tight as she didn't had sex for long time. I moved my cock back and forth. Saroj was moaning sexily. Again, I slept on my back and Saroj started sucking my cock. I inserted my cock in pussy and started banging her.

She said, "Rahul come on bang it, drill it, come on Rahul." I drilled her for a long time and I cummed the white juice in her navel and slept on her. That night we had sex five times.

17. Hesitant.

I am Saroj and I'm a 35-year-old housewife. I am married to Pankaj couple of years ago and I'm enjoying my life quite well in the metro. The incident I am going to narrate is my sexperience with my brother-in-law, Pranav. Even though I am not very adventurous desi wife my situation has taken control of to have sex with Pranav.

He is a great flirt even though he's just 19 when he fucked me. May be its my voluptuous structure that's making him even a bigger flirt. He would never miss a chance to steal a glimpse of my milky globes which are more than a fistful for him. There were numerous incidents where he tried to rub his limbs to my arse or boobs.

Actually Me and Pankaj were staying in an apartment alone and having a great life until Pranav came in to have some coaching in the city. Now we are having a hell of a great life. Pankaj as he is doing job in an emerging software company, he will always have to put that extra effort in the company which means extra pleasure for both of us.

All this seducing episode from Pranav has started very recently. In fact, he was a virgin until he lost it to my pussy where his very own brother lost it. It was Monday morning, me and Pankaj woke up early. As he is to go to the office by 8, I had to hurry with all the early household work. Pranav's coaching starts at 10 so he can wake up late so he is still sleeping in his room.

I was wearing a red cotton sari and a matching blouse and there is nothing inside my faintly transparent blouse which if observed keenly can make my dark nipples visible over my white tanned boobs. I rushed through most of the work and sent Pankaj to office. The I started to mop the floor.

I was carrying a bucket of water a cloth with my sari below my belly button exposing navel and with tight blouse which gives a very clear out line of my breasts and loose pallu. I went on to mop the floor of our bedroom and went next to Pranav. Pranav was still sleeping there on the bed. He was just wearing a boxer and was exposing his sensuous body.

He had an athletic and strong body. I never had any bad intentions until then but just for a second felt that itching between my legs. I then started to mop the floor by sitting on my knees and bending forward and most of my cleavage was clearly visible from the front with my pallu loose.

Even though I was busy mopping the floor I constantly kept looking at him, the boxer has not covered more than his thighs and I had a great view of his tight buttocks. He wore no shirt and his body was great to watch. I finished moping on one side and went to other where I was facing him. He was lying side on.

It was almost time and had to wake him up but I thought otherwise to just enjoy looking at him and continued mopping while feeding my eyes. And at one moment when I looked up, he was feeding his eyes on my cleavage while I was bending to mop. I know what he must be thinking, he would love to have my nipples on his tongue and my globes squeezed under his palms.

But when I saw straight at him, he just pretended to sleep. So, I thought to play it naughty. By calling his name and waking him up I kept my cold palm on his naked thigh and pushed him he didn't wake up. I knew he was acting. He simply changed his angle as if sleeping upright. There was a huge tent under his short where he wore nothing underneath.

My next thought is to reach the top of his tent and hold his bulb. By calling his name again and waking him up from sleep I raised my hand and just when I was about to reach his manhood the clock has struck 8. I came back to conscious and I was taken aback. What am I doing? The situation is quite hot in the room I just took the bucket and came out of the room.

I continued with other works and called out Pranav to wake up. He woke up and came into the hall, he still wore nothing on top and could see the tent is still on. He was daring me now I can feel it but I kept my cool. I gave him tea and told him I am going to take a bath and took the towel and went into the attached bathroom.

The handle lock of the door is broken and it left back a small hole to the bathroom door, as much as a 25paise coin. But I least expected him to take advantage of it. I slowly started to undress. Took the sari off and placed it on the hanger and the unhooked my blouse and my boobs have sprung to life like birds released from a cage.

Then I pulled the string of my undergarment below as it dropped to the floor. I placed them all on the hanger. The next thing I did was I reached to my hairy pussy with my right hand and was not surprised its wet. I know it needs some nice trashing. I smelled the hand and them I cupped my boobs with my hand felt proud of my sexy structure. My nipples were hard. I pinched them playfully.

I still had this naughty feeling to have my pussy filled by Pranav but was unable find courage. Out of excitement I slowly bent down sticking my arse in the air and peeped through the hole of the door wanting to watch Pranav. I never expected it but the sexual urge in me wanted to watch him and I got it.

He slowly walked into the room and opened the wardrobe and searched and pulled out my bra from it. He buried his face into it and smelled it like a dog. He then reached for his pole inside the boxer and brought it out with his right hand and placed my white bra over his dick and rubbed it.

At that moment I felt like he is gently stroking his penis in between my boobs while I was holding them together. I was seriously getting wet in my puss y.I kept my middle finger deep inside and started to stroke it while watching him play with his penis in front of the dressing mirror. Then he walked forward and started coming towards the bathroom door.

I know what he is going to do next. I immediately moved under the shower and took my position. Opened the shower fully and got hold of the knob with one hand for grip and bent forward slightly and reached my pussy with another hand. I closed my eyes tightly and was imagining being banged from behind like fucking dog by my Pranav. There was intense urge for sex.

I increased my speed of stroking and was gently touching my clitoris regularly and finally came to climax after sometime. I stayed like a rock for a minute catching my breath. I turned around and peeped through the hole but didn't find him. Guess he has spilled his seed. The I finished my bath and came out in towel, it was just about covering my nipples but revealing my cleavage and hardly covering my knees.

I was really excited with the course of things, I walked to the bed room door as I would generally dress up with the door closed. As I was about reaching the door, I saw Pranav sitting straight to door in the hall. The door is half closed and if it is fully open then he would be sitting straight to the dressing table in the bed room. I thought I to give him a nice show, so I opened the door ever so slowly.

Now he can directly see the dressing mirror. I started to dress up behind the door so he can clearly watch my juicy body through the mirror. I dropped the towel to the floor making myself completely nude. I know he will be watching me. I was expecting him to take a chance but he never did. I then dressed up.

I wore the white bra which he rubbed against his dick a few minutes ago and wore a skin colour blowse to arouse him and wore a matching sari. I made sure I did wear it below my belly button. The blouse was tight and my boobs were pressed up revealing my cleavage. Now I am mentally fixed to have taste of his cock. But I should tempt him to make the move.

I know he is burning with desire to taste my pussy juices. I went out very normally and asked him to get ready, then he replied that he will not go out today. Now I know he too is planning something naughty. I served him the breakfast after he has brushed and I finished all the work. Finally, I came and settled in front of the TV. We both sat in the individual chairs.

He still was wearing the short and his cock is throbbing from the side of his boxer I could the bulge quite clearly. He kept some channel and placed the remote on his thigh. I reached for the remote and by the back of the hand touched his cock. There was slight moment in him but still he not getting courage.

I have changed the channel and placed the remote on my lap and kept my hand behind the head giving him a nice view of my boobs side on. There were rabbits in the room beside the tv which we used to pet. Sudden they started to fuck madly and there was that funny sound. He then asked me innocently what are they doing?

I smiled and said they got the age and doing what they have to. Then he reached for the remote in my lap and pressed it against my pussy gently and touched my thigh. I was getting very excited. Then I asked him to go and bathe. He went and removed his clothes and tied the towel. I called him to get something from the top shelf in the kitchen.

He climbed up on the chair while I was holding it. I could have clear view of his manhood from under. He knew why I asked him to climb the attic now, he saw the excitement in me and the way I was watching his dick. He then let the towel to fall to the floor and stood naked on the chair with his dick standing like a beacon.

Ohh he said and before he could get down, I caught his penis with my hand and gave a gentle stroke.

"What is this Pranav"

"Sorry Bhabhi".

"It's not time to sorry."

"You need punishment, give me a massage right now."

As I stood there he hesitantly has removed my sari and the with both hands started to unhook my bra and with my hand I reached his standing dick and pulled him closer and started to stroke it gently and could see on his face he was enjoying it, as he unhooked me, my erect nipples came out and my boobs sprung to life.

He took them both in his hands like a hungry cat and he started to suck my nipples. I held his face and took him off my boobs and kissed him on his lips. He never kissed anyone like this I knew it the way he is doing it to me. I then made myself nude in front of him completely.

Pushed him on to the bed and spread his legs. Took his dick deep into my mouth and started to suck it.

He just gave a shiver. He didn't know what to do, He held the bed spread with his hand and the other was place on my head and he was pushing me on to his cock. I took his balls into my mouth and was playing his penis with my hand and as I was about to increase the speed he just exploded and the cum was sprayed over my face. He innocently said sorry.

Then I said no problem and I sat on the bed and asked him to lick my pussy. He hesitantly went down and brought out his tongue and placed it over my clitoris. I was just over the cloud nine. And as he went on to work out with my hairy pussy, I was rubbing my nipple and was swearing out loud. He is really a good licker though he was hesitant in the starting.

He was licking me so much but I never was at climax but he got back his erection, he was gasping for breath. Then I made him lay down and mounted on cock to ride it as I sat heavily on it the dick just deep into my pussy. I gently started to ride his cock. As was increasing speed he loved every bit of it and finally we came together.

18. My Husband hadn't a Clue

About ten years ago when my husband Pankaj had started the Garment Trade. Soon he met a man named Salman who was also in the same business, and he was senior in the field so and my husband became friends. Salman really helped my husband's Company. Being the same age as myself, Pankaj and Salman had the same ideas about life and shared ambitions. They both loved the fast pace of commerce and wanted their pots of gold to be plentiful.

Then one day, my husband told me that he wants to invite Salman to our house to share a meal together. He told me that he would not sit in drawing room but in lounge. It was so strange for me as my husband never invited any male guest in the house and he keeps me in vial. I don't know how he dared to bring a male at home. That day was the turning point of my life and the reason I have to write this story. I am bursting to tell you! To tell the whole world in fact!

Maybe at this point I should tell you something about me. I had grown up in a very small town in a very conservative family so I'm a little religious woman, and like me my husband also interested in religion activities. I don't like to meet any male other than our close relatives and I never allowed people to enter my house other than my relatives.

My body is thin although at the age of 35 and after birth of three babies. But have got meat on right places woman should have. My breasts are full and for the most part still as perky as they had been when I was twenty-five. I'm fair skin rather than other Indian women who are dark, with a long nose and regular features though I dressed conservative simply, like most Indian women normally wore shalwar (traditional baggy trousers) Kameez (long traditional shirt) suit. I wore baggy clothes and used Dupatta (head and neck scarf), draped around neck and chest to covered myself well. Yet my boobs and bottoms were so generous that they could not be completely hidden from view.

I dressed in my finest but a very simple way. A black traditionally kameez (long shirt) with white shalwar (baggy trouser) and a large white Dupatta (head and neck scarf), draped around my neck and chest to cover my chest in the most decent fashion

Salman was also dressed in a very simple way. White traditionally kameez (long shirt) with white shalwar (baggy trouser).

My husband formally introduced me to him, as I had never met him. Salman was tall, slim and in excellent shape with wavy black hair, fair skin, light facial hair and hypnotic black deep, large captivated and powerful eyes, Authoritative personality. He was one of the most incredible men I had ever seen in my entire life.

Over the course of the meal Salman was sitting just opposite me at the table. Salman made polite conversation with. He lived alone, because sadly his wife died few years back leaving him with two children who are away from him in boarding institute. As he told us that many noble ladies hoped to catch his eye for first two years. But from the time of his wife's death until this day, the day that he met us he had not looked at another woman. He told us that he had buried himself within his work.

Time seemed to pass more quickly now. My husband and I did not take a lot of time be convinced about Salman that he was not a wife seducer, a trouble-monger of ill repute, but a fine upstanding gentleman with extremely honest, loyal, good and jolly decent manners.

He got closer and closer to our family, I felt something for him from when I first saw him, I couldn't tell what? I didn't know what was that sort of fondness, as I never attracted to him or other man sexually as I was always one-man woman not only in my entire life but also in my dreams. No one male impressed me in any way in my life.

So I gave it name of sibling and started call him bhai (brother) and he called me Bhabhi (sister-in-law). The baby liked him very much. During our meetings, he carefully avoided looking at me. When he spoke to me it was with kindness, respecting my place as his friend's wife.

During one meeting, I was watching him, I noted that Salman didn't wear underwear, as a long, noticeable contour in the inside leg of his shalwar revealed what had to be an eight-inch cock at rest. I was getting a turn on thinking of Salman's masculinity and the enormous size of his manhood. My heart began thumping as I considered what he must be like with a full erection and that was because my husbands near five inch and thin cock. Above all these he never gives me the real pleasure of sex, he always left me dry and unsatisfied in bed but I never give at much attention because of my natural shyness and conservative mind. For most of our sixteen-year's married life we had treated sex with a reservation. Other than that, he was a caring man and a great husband. I had never once regretted marrying.

I don't want but from that day I was found myself always thinking about Salman and It was when I was in my bed at night; there wasn't a night when I didn't think about him. How I stepped into this New World. I was typical conservative Indian housewife with our set of values. I spent a lot of time thinking about him while he probably had no idea that I wanted him so badly. I love him. I had always loved him but I've done it in silence. I had been feeling guilty because I dream about best friend of my husband.

At that time my frustrations were so painful when I met Salman, I could not look at him because I was frightened of him, frightened of myself, my feelings for him. He never bothered to pester us with uninvited intrusions to our house, although I wanted to meet him every time, every day, but not meet him. I was like a tormented baby. I had no explanation what this man did to me; all I knew was that I was dying to make this man mine and there was no way in the world it could be possible. I could not foresee any way of achieving that.

Pankaj got a huge loss in his business because of over investing when the market was dead. Before he could control, it was too late his business was beyond irretrievability. Pankaj had fought his business with everything he had. Then, just as surprising he decided to go to America to seek his fortune. In many respects, it was the best of times and, naturally, the worst of times. But the problem was that he needed to leave us behind all alone during his stay in the states.

My husband Pankaj had lost his parents. Although my' parents were available for our care. But in Indian custom, the parents or relatives of the female would not stay with their daughter and son-in-law. My husband turned to Salman, his very good friend and adopted brother for help. I was a little uncomfortable about this situation because I was not sure how I'd keep distance from Salman, but agreed with my husband after a little argument. My husband was fully convinced that Salman was a thorough gentleman and not a scoundrel or opportunist at all. Thus, he asked him to take care of us in his absence. Needless to say, he willingly stepped into the breech to be a good caretaker and helper towards us in case of our need during my husband absence.

He assured us that he would do his utmost to make sure that all our needs, and attention. My husband thanked him profusely for being such a good friend and benefactor and told me and the baby to look to Salman for love and guardianship until he came back for us, that Salman had promised to take care of our needs.

Pankaj went to the USA but didn't t inform us of his arrival to the states. It was so strange not to hear from him. We feared the worst. We tried to get information but couldn't and after a month he himself informed us by telephone that he had been caught by the US immigration and has gone to be imprisoned for seven years.

The incidence was a big shock for us. We had to face lot of problems, and it had paralyzed me. I sobbed in the nights, mourning for my husband and my misfortune. I moped around the house, hardly doing anything, hardly going anywhere. For the next few months, Salman helped me with all the things that I had to do while at the same time comforting me. All I wanted that time was to have someone to hold, and Salman was the only one who done just that.

All my desire in life was brushed to one side momentarily as I took over my new role. I was more concerned about the uncertainty and insecurity of my small family. Although it was a big shock for us at the time, but time heals everything. Now Salman was a more frequent visitor. Salman held regular meetings with me and discussed the problems as well as worked out solutions in the smooth running of our home; Salman had gained quite a reputation as a member of our family. We gradually became friends and got to know more about each other. Salman now became my hero when he came to our aid like this. Weeks and months went by as Salman and I got to know each other better.

I would sometimes invite Salman over for an evening meal. I was also calling him more frequently for different kinds of help like the baby's institute matters and financial support for my family in our day-to-day activities. Several times we travelled from one place to another together for different reasons in his car. When we were traveling together in his car, so many time he touched my belly, breasts, and bottom accidentally. Every accidental touch of any part shook me and sent series of shivers down my body. I was expecting his response after each touch but he was amazingly unresponsive. Once Salman and I went to my baby institute and there was a cool brisk breeze blowing. It caught the bottom edge of my kameez and lifted it. I felt that for a split second, Salman saw the usually secret top of my shalwar, my shalwar covered hips.

It was no problem for both for us to stay alone in kitchen. As So many times he came and stood close by my side, not too close but close enough whenever I was making coffee or tea for him. So many times, he has brushed passed me or I have brushed passed him, and I was expecting his response after each touch but he was amazingly unresponsive.

Self- praise is not recommendation but let me do it that my body was really made for a sin and even a saint would lose his self-control in close proximity to me.

I meaningfully stared passionately into his lovely eyes, he also kept his eyes on me, and sometimes he smiled while looking at me but nothing more than that. Days passed us by.

On different occasions Salman approached me with small gifts for the baby, and me these I accepted with thanks. Each time he came to us he made up some business reason. He brought special gifts like chocolates for my baby and so on. For me he got perfume, body lotion. I started to hug him lightly whenever he returned from a long visit away. I have to admit, that I wished so many times to let my hands linger a little to feel his body, but I never did try.

Now Salman was like a member of our family and he used to have dinner at our place often. We talked for hours and I felt so comfortable in his company. We discussed a lot of things, my family, my family problems, and my baby. We would sometimes sit in my house late at night alone, and talk but never anything personal. I never saw him in a romantic mood. Once on a rainy night when we were sitting in our drawing room after dinner and were raining like a hell outside, I asked him, "When will you be remarrying, bhai (brother)? Tell me what kind of girl should I look for you?" (This is common in India that sisters search bride for their brothers)

Without any hesitation he answered, "Like you." he smiled nonchalantly at smiled nonchalantly at me, I froze for a moment. So, that night I'd seen Salman eyeing my full breasts for the first time.

"Like Me? What do you mean?" I moistened my lips and asked with a nonspecific smile.

He answered, "I mean pretty, attractive and beautiful like you." I looked stunned at me for a moment, clearly embarrassed. I did not know what to say and stared at me for a few seconds. Then a whimsical smile crinkled my lips as I answered quietly, "Salman, you make fun of me, Dear. I am not beautiful."

"You are the most beautiful lady in my eyes, you look great to me always!" he said to me passionately.

"Thank you, Salman!" I uttered quietly. I was blushing from head to toe.

"Only thank is not sufficient, do something for me."

"Salman, you're doing much for us and I owe you? I don't know how can I repay you?" I walked up and reached for a glass of water from the table beside his.

"No, Bhabhi don't say like this, I did nothing for you."

"I admit Salman, I could do nothing because I'm a woman and know I would have face lot of troubles, if you didn't help me,"

"This is my duty,"

"Anyway but you should tell me, how can I repay you?" I asked again.

"Search a lady for me like you," he replied.

"You'll put me in trouble, my sister has been married and I don't know where I should go for search woman like me, is there not any other way to repay you?" I replied him jokingly. I walked up and reached for a glass of water from the table beside him. Salman touched my arm very lightly and just from his light touch on my arm my heart was pounding and my legs felt weak.

"Ok! Bhabhi if you insist so, then I'll tell you at some other time," he replied.

"I may go now it's too late now" he said.

"It's ok, as you wish" I sighed with frustration, when drunk. Salman gave me a surprised look and then completely ignored me and walked to the main door of the house left me alone. I wanted to ask him to stop but I didn't want him to think of me as a whore. I knew already that I didn't want this to be totally from my side, I wanted him to respect me as he did all the time. I wanted to talk to him. No, that wasn't it. Not really. I wanted to touch him. And, I wanted him to touch me. But he didn't respond and I was thoroughly disappointed and realised that maybe I've lost my beauty and I couldn't attract him. So that night when I went to bath room for changing and wanted to use washroom.

"No, I'm still beautiful"

As I watched my nudity in the mirror. I was glad to see that my fair body was still much attractive at the age of thirty-six. Though I was 5' 6" tall, my weight never crossed fifty-four. The very least sag of my breasts added ripeness to it. My light pink nipples on my milky white were most prominent. I was really proud of my narrow waist that measured 32 inches. I had almost no tyre like layers of fat like most Indian women of my age have, a very little fat around my waist and that only smoothened the curve from the waist to hips. My belly has nearly flat. Skin on my belly was silky smooth and the only blemish it had was the stretch marks from baby birth. But those had become very faint and were barely visible. My thighs were a bit heavy but looked nice. My butts were really heavy, about 38 inches. Though this was a bit too much, as they curved out on the sides and to the back the look was nice. I knew it added sexiness to my body. I felt very proud that my body was undoubtedly the best.

I was wonder that how he had ignored a sexy body like mine. Is he blind? Doesn't he see? Doesn't he like woman? Can't he do? If he doesn't turn near this body, then he is a saint or impotent.

I was sure that he knew I was interested in him, and he had been interested right back. He was toying with me, flirting and playing it cool while I sweated it out. I was debating whether or not to just go over there and rush him. I decided to wait, and make him come to me. I was not going to fold so easily, and the game was becoming too much fun for me.

I changed and slipped into bed. My mind was in turmoil. I wished Salman were there by my side. I tried but for me, sleep wouldn't come I could not sleep for long that night. My sex was on fire, quivering inside and I was radiating heat and desire. Thinking about Salman, I explored myself lightly sifting with one hand, while the other squeezed and pinched my tits. My hand reached further down between my legs, which I spread and braced against the door of my tiny hiding place to touch myself.

With one finger I lightly traced the contours of my nether lips, and the gushing wetness from my pussy aided the process. As my fingers brushed against the small fold of skin at the top of my lips, I gasped as a delicious shudder of sensation speared me from my pussy, straight to my tingling nipples and waves of pleasure washed over my body. Squeezing my tits and pinching my nipples harder, I pressed the nub of my clit harder, stroked and circled it with my fingers, plucked at it and flicked it till the nub became hard and firm, and pussy juice streamed out of my cunt.

The torment didn't ease and my fingers slipped further and

dipped into my pussy.

I began thrusting a finger slowly in and out of my throbbing cunt, adding another finger to the first one I rubbed my clit with the heel of my palm while my fingers fucked in and out of my sweet, well-used pussy.

A sudden rush of sensation overcame and I had to bite down on my lip to keep from screaming as I climaxed and cummed with surprising vim.

"What the hell am I doing," I muttered to myself that night after masturbating three times. I tried every effort a conservative woman like me can do to convey my need for him but unfortunately, he didn't see me as anything other than his friend's wife. But it didn't stop me dreaming about him.

I am very fond of watching movies. We used to watch movies, but from the time my husband has left for USA so there was no one to accompany me to movie halls. Salman knew my fondness watching movies so once on Saturday afternoon he offered me to watch movie. I thought that company of Salman would be a great for watching movie and on one Sunday afternoon Salman, all kids and I went to a movie. I'd dressed so sexy in red shalwar, black kameez, and red dupatta around my shoulder. I thought I was mistaken at first. No, it couldn't be – nor could it? Was he staring at me? It was at first time that I noticed, as I caught him staring and glancing my cleavage hips, and other parts of the body. As we got down in front of the movie hall. I felt very proud walked side by side with him. I never used dress like this but that day I was wearing a red silk shalwar and black kameez, with red dupatta, which I had specially tailored for me so it hugged my figure and showed off my small waist and curvy ass to perfection, without being too revealing. As we got down in front of the movie hall, I felt very proud walked side by side with him. I felt thrilled like a woman going out with her husband. Few men and couple looked at us and I knew what they thought, really a nice family.

We were seated in the last row in the upper floor. The floor was almost deserted. When the hero kissed heroine for the first time, he couldn't help touching my hand. I was totally enchanted as he touched the tips of my fingers with his fingers but I thought that was an accident and looked at him. I felt wonderful as he softly touched my hand. Salman took my hand in his and held it tightly. This was an unexpected turn of events the baby was too curious and busy watching the movie, to care about Salman and me.

A little later, I touched his hand softly to let him know that I loved what he did. I wasn't sure how much of my emotions could be shown and gradually disengaged my hand.

As the romantic scenes continued one after the other, he held my hand and massaged it gently in his hand. I felt so very secured at his strong hand. After a while I realised, I was completely moist with love, so much so that juices of my love were dripping down my thighs. Once he clutched my thigh with his nails dipping in my skin thorough my shalwar. As the scene was over, both of us realised that we were emotionally and physically carried away too much and withdrew our hands.

As the movie was over, we both rushed to the exit. As we were heading back home, I was getting a turn on thinking of Salman's masculinity and the enormous size of his manhood. Then I decided to end up all this tonight. We went to home and it was almost 10 pm. I said to him, "Salman! You're not going home as we have to have dinner together."

"Is this a request or an order?" he enquired jokingly.

"This is an order from your Bhabhi." I said naughtily and then said, "After half an hour the baby went to sleep. Then I went into the kitchen and made us each a nice cup of tea. We sat and talked while we sipped our tea, and asked him, "Salman, you didn't tell me, how can I repay you?"

He looked at my eyes and said, "Shall I tell you, Bhabhi, how can you repay?"

"Yes, I'm waiting eagerly," I said.

He gave an amazed look at my breasts and adoringly touched them with his hands. He took his time to observe every square inch of my tits and very lovingly moved his fingers over them. He very lightly licked the silky-smooth skin of my breasts and that sent shiver down my spine. He looked fascinated with my long nipples and started sucking it. This ignited fire in me and I pressed his head hard on my tit and fiercely pulled at his hair. He alternated his licking and pressing between the two boobs and I deeply moaned. His skill of licking my nipples with his tongue, made me wild and I urged him to bite hard and tear the nipples off. He did bite me hard and I screamed in pleasure.

He demanded that I take off my shalwar to let him see me completely naked. I unknotted my shalwar string allowing it drop at my feet. Now I was naked before him, totally as naked as the day I was born. I want to correct that this is a country where still arranged marriage are still the rule. The couple doesn't even see each other until the wedding night, majority of the couples even don't see each other naked when they fuck, may be thousands young people are starting to find their own matches and experiment with sex but this country of more the one billon peoples.

Now he laid me on my bed on my back and sat between in my spread legs as I was expecting him to fuck me now but he bent on my belly and his mouth moved down kissing and licking all over my belly. He spent a lot of time licking inside my deep navel. I was moaning breathlessly. He tightly pressed and squeezed the fleshy waves and curves around my hips.

He went down to my thighs and hid his face between my thighs and rubbed his face all over it. I was wishing and dying for his mouth to reach my pussy.

He touched my pussy with his lips. It was like he gave me an electric shock! I bounced up off the bed shaking the bed violently. I asked wildly, "Salman, what are you going to do? Are you going to kiss between my thighs?" My heart nearly stopped that I have never touched there by tongue.

He said to me excitedly, "yes, Bhabhi You will love it," he assured me looking up, "I'm going to lick and suck your pussy my sweet Bhabhi, I have found the treasure, for which I was dying for, for so many years, Lay back and let me have a feast, for what I see here it's going to be a scrumptious meal!"

I giggled excitedly and said, "This is dirty Salman, don't do this," but in my heart I was praying for him not to stop, in my heart I was saying to him, "that is Bhabhi's cunt, it is yours and your mouth feels so good on it. Eat it! Lick it! Taste it and suck it well! Drink all my juices they are yours too. For years too, I have been longing for this kind of loving attention from you."

He dived again into my pussy and pressed his lips very hard onto the middle of my pussy in a very hot, deep kiss. Then he went on kissing all over my love triangle. I think he must have planted at least one hundred kisses all over it. Then, from the bottom of my pussy he ran his tongue licking deeply and strongly upward. My whole-body jerks and quiver. I was yelling in utmost ecstasy. He continued his licking and wiping my entire vulva with his tongue several times. I went into a state of trance and I could feel my cunt muscles get tensed and relaxed.

I said, "Salman, my husband never did this to me before and I can't tell you how good that feels. You know all erotic spots in the body of a woman to arouse her. Don't stop it is so exquisite. You are strumming all my nerve ends. It is excitement I am experiencing new way of life." I was about to cum in his mouth; I thought the time was right to get fucked. I moaned "Oohhh Please, Salman" I pleaded "Don't tease me any more do it. Do it now" I started pumping his butt with my feet and almost sobbed in frustration.

"Don't worry, I'll fuck you till you scream, Bhabhi, you can be sure of that."

He quickly moved over me, on top of me between my widespread thighs, and rested the head of his cock at my entrance. I spread my thighs wide as could as I do for him. He started rubbing his hard cock into my slimy slit, teasing me.

"Do it now" I said in a half whisper.

But he didn't hear me and was rubbing his hard cock into my slimy slit, teasing me. "Stop teasing me and put it in me" and once again I reached down feverishly to grip his hard erect cock, placing his cock head in my pussy hole.

I felt his knob and bucked my pussy up to meet it. My hands reached over his hips as he slowly started enter into me. He finally he gave a bit more pressure and pushed really hard and the huge thing penetrated me. It pained a lot and as he pushed the whole gigantic thing fully in. I felt that as if my passage would tear open. At the same time, it gave a maddening pleasure to me, I shrieked and a strong Aaaahhhh sound came out of my mouth. Oh, what a strong thrust it was.

"Oh yeah. That was good. I needed that." I said, breathless. I hooked my leg and my heel dug into his back.

He slowly thrust in and out, in and out. I moved my legs a little more widely for him. So, he could get all the way in he grabbed my leg and bent my knee and brought it by his side. He pumped back and forth with a slow pace several times, very slowly all the way out and all the way back in. I was sighing and gripping me tightly, my legs striking the air at each gentle inward thrust. I felt his knob knocking on the door of my womb, which made me grunt. He was getting now pace. I felt that my cunt sucked his cock like a baby sucking a feeder nipple.

He kept moving within me, in a steadily increasing pace. I felt like he was getting harder and harder inside of me. I loved the feeling of his cock sliding into me; I felt extreme sexual pleasure the way he was sliding.

"Bhabhi, your pussy is so fucking tight, I could stay in you forever," gasped Salman as he continued to flick his cock like bit of flesh at the entrance to my pussy.

"Yes and I 'm proud of it but you've also a thing to be proud, Salman."

"I think your husband left you sleep too much for many nights," he again teased me.

"And what you have in mind?"

"Yes! Bhabhi, I wanted your little pussy from the day I saw you first. And would try my best to show you how I want you," He told me how he had been watching me and wanting me from the day he had first set eyes on me. Salman grabbed my legs and pushed them so that my knees were bent against my tits. I was wide open now for him. He thrust me deep. My hips lifted off the bed and my leg tensed on his shoulder.

I couldn't stop myself to confess, "You don't know, Salman, that all that time, you were the one I wanted. You have always made me feel horny. I have always wanted you since you first sat opposite me at our dinner table. Even with Pankaj there in the room my knickers were getting wet thinking what you could do to me."

I was wondering why he stopped and pulled his cock from my pussy so I shouted, "what are you doing?"

"Be patient" he replied.

"Turn around, Bhabhi, Get on your knees, I want to fuck you from behind."

I turned over and bent on my knees upping my ass like doggy. "Like this?" I asked.

He quickly knelt behind me and aimed his cock at my pussy and I felt the head of his cock touched my wet pussy hole. He teased my pussy with his swollen cock. He thrust forward and his entire cock entered in my pussy. I moaned loudly and, in a few seconds, I was pushing back against him.

I began to push back in just as his tip slid out of my pussy hole. He fucked me in long, slow, steady strokes. With every stroke I raised and pushed my ass to meet him.

My tits were hanging as pendulum, so he reached in front to pull and pinch my nipples, while fingering my clit and cunt, my moans were so loud from the pleasures he steals from me and he began to fuck me deeply in my ass. I felt so full and my juices flowed freely for me to ride him, me and him not to stop,

I was asking his to fuck me hard, deeper, rub my clit, fuck me hard, fast and deep. This was incredible fuck I've ever received.

Salman fucked my pussy like this for many long minutes before he rolled over on his back while holding on to me. With his cock still in me he asked me to ride his cock. He lay on his back and I climbed up on his lap, rubbing my wet pussy lips against his hard cock, moving up and down but not putting it in. I was teasing him and myself with his cock, playing with it, pressing my cunt against it and moaning as I moved up and down against it. "Oh Salman this feels so good," I said. He grabbed both of my tits in his hands.

I then got up, grabbed his cock, placed it at the entrance of my cunt and slammed down on it so hard. I screamed, "Ohhhh, Salman you're so huge." His cock was hard and hot. I lifted myself up and came down hard. I was out of control and yelled, "Do me! Do me!" I was sitting straight up as I rode his cock. He had his hand on my waist as I went up and down, my tits bouncing and my long hair flying all over the place. I then leaned forward, so that my clit rubbed against his cock. "Oh, Salman! That's it! Oh Salman! I love you." He I then put his finger in my ass hole, moving it deeper and I shuddered and shivered. An orgasm was sweeping through me and I rode him even harder. "Fuck me, do me, Fuck me Ohhh Salman. Here it comes, I'm coming." I collapsed against him. His cock was still in me still hard as he entered me first time.

"Lay back," he said again firmly. He then lifted me up and lay me down on the bed on my back. He grabbed my legs and pushed them so that my knees were bent against my tits. I was wide open. He put his swollen cock at my entrance and then thrust into me with a loud grunt and then started ramming my hot wet cunt.

"Ufff I feel so tired. Now it's hurting me, Salman."

"Do you want me to stop?" he said.

"Oh no! Please don't stop, I love you, Salman, I love the way you make love. Please never stop. Oh, Salman, it's so good." I begged him, and I grabbed his hands, and laid them on my, throbbing breasts I wanted him to fondle them. And my both hands reached around his ass grabbing his hips.

"That feels so good," I said. "Play with my tits," He filled his palms with my breasts, the large mounds overflowing their captors, and plumping them together brought them to his lips.

Looking down at me with a fiery look in his eyes, he kept his eyes on my face as he bent to take one of my milky breasts into his warm mouth. He lightly flicked my breasts with his tongue; licking everywhere but my nipples.

I squirmed in agony, while he continued to feather my tits with love bites while my nipples burned to be suckled. His tongue flicked over my nipples like a tiny whip, and constantly teased and tormented my nipples till I shouted out for his mouth to please suck on them. He sucked the nipple first slowly and gently, still flicking it with his tongue and then increased the power of his suction, till the pleasure bordered on pain, and I screamed from the sensations.

He continued to rock his cock into me in a slow, unhurried fashion while ministering to my tits, but I had had enough and tightened my pussy walls around his thrusting member, slowly but strongly, which made him groan and thrust into me a little faster.

"Please, now finish it Salman. You want to fuck me more but I can't go with that cock of yours anymore" I begged.

He rode me toward the sky, hard, gentle, rough, and till my bearing ran out and with one last, sharp thrust upward I impaled myself on him and swirled into the oblivion of my orgasm. Laying there immobile, I watched his beautiful face, as he thrust almost violently into me as his climax raced through him...making him stiffen and roar in ecstasy, "I'm want to come Bhabhi, where should I come?"

"Don't care, I had tied my tubes, Cum on, cum inside me, I want to feel you do It." I murmured between subbing.

A Moments later he ejaculated deep inside me. He pumped me long, before shooting his load into me. I shuddered and came just as the first molten shots of spunk blasted from his balls deep into my already flooded hole. He squirted inside. He was pulling my hair, it was perfect, and he was riding me like a mare.

I waited patiently until he collapsed onto me, and I locked my legs around his hips, holding him to me - in me, and then kissed him deeply. We lay exhausted in each other's arms, drenched in each other's juices, breathing heavily. His cock was still stiff inside of me, and seemed reluctant to return to softness. I could feel his cum leaking out and running down my ass. We both lay panting and catching our breath on the bed as we recovered from our first round.

"Oh! What have I done, I've never thought, I've never heard about sex like this, who would believe?" he said.

"Are you going to tell someone about this?" I asked

"No, but that was incredible."

He was an expert He made slow, gentle love to me, pleasuring me in every way than a man can pleasure a woman, and I in turn did the same to him. We made love for hours, and I don't know how many times I cummed, but it was a lot.

We made love for almost till 3 am. He woke me again nearly at five in morning and fucked me to his last drop.

I got to know after making love with Salman, it became obvious that my husband hadn't a clue about how to treat women properly, while Salman knows all how to treat and please a woman in bed and out of the bed.

Life was great after that night. We started having sex few days in a week. We've spent several evenings playing out fantasies.